A Song of
Death

C.M. Quinn

To Kyona, my love and greatest champion.

CONTENT WARNING

This is a new adult sapphic fantasy, intended for audiences 18+. Below is a list of content warnings for the following story. Please proceed at your own discretion.

- Violence, containing blood and some minor scenes with gore (there is no sexual violence in this story)

- Torture

- Fantasy-based genocide (off-page)

- Explicit language

- Explicit sexual content

- Mentions of prolonged imprisonment

- Death

PROLOGUE

*Deep beneath the earth, she slumbers and dreams of a goddess with eyes
of death.*
She hungers for what she has lost.
And for the revenge she seeks.

CHAPTER 1

I'M NOT GOING TO make it, Elaine thought as she sprinted through the ancient forest, barefoot and bloodied, the bushes tearing at her clothes. Her cloak had long since been abandoned, exposing the remnants of her dress, and her hand pressed against her side, trying—and failing—to stem the flow of blood.

Bands of moonlight lanced through the dense canopy, with the glowing witchlight flying ahead of her, leading the way. Behind her came the distant howls of hounds closing in rapidly. She forced herself to keep moving, pushing back the waves of pain that shot down her side, and burning agony in her legs. If she could make it to the border of Purgatory, she'd be safe.

Shouts erupted in the dark, giving her a sudden burst of energy. She sucked in desperate gulps of air, and powbut ered on, leaping over fallen logs and sliding down steep banks. Leaves and twigs scratched her skin, and thorns slashed her arms as she ran past, but Elaine would not let herself slow.

At the bottom of yet another bank, the witchlight vanished. She stopped, heart-thumping as she scanned the woods. Raising a trembling hand, she closed her eyes, hunting through the night for a trace of its magic.

There!

With a gasp, she sprinted through a small clearing and across a moonlit brook. The icy water and sharp rocks stabbed at her feet, bringing a string of curses from her lips. She staggered onto the grass and took off running again. Back in the ancient woods, muggy air wrapped around her, causing rivulets of sweat to run down her face.

The light faded, the shadows closing in until she was running blind with only the witchlight to guide her as it darted among the trees.

Her muscles screamed at her to stop, and tears pricked the edge of her vision. She wiped them away and scrambled up yet another embankment. At the top, she clambered over a fallen log and onto a narrow path almost obscured under the forest debris.

A prickle of awareness brushed the fringes of her mind. Ancient magic whispered through the woods, flooding her veins and spurring her on. Purgatory was calling her, as it was rumored to call all those who sought sanctuary. After years of being hunted, finally, she'd be safe.

The path widened and the trees thinned to show a small moonlit clearing. In the distance, a faint shimmer came from the darkness of the forest. For a moment, she paused as her magic sparked in her chest and the fire within strained for release.

I can feel it. Purgatory.

With renewed energy, Elaine started running, but halfway across the field, the drum of hoofbeats and howling of wolves reached her ears.

No, she would not let them take her. Not when she was so close.

She spun and raised her hands, fire erupting along her skin as she shot flames at her pursuers. A pained yelp cleaved the air. She must've hit one, but didn't dare stop. All her focus was on reaching the trees ahead.

As she drew nearer, the shimmer hovering in front of the tree line became clearer.

The shield. It has to be. I'm going to make it—

A shadow darted in the corner of her eye. Before she could turn, something crashed into her back, sending her flying face-first into the dirt. A wave of pain smashed through her. In panic, she rolled onto her back as a force leaped and pinned her to the ground. Her hands flew up, grabbing matted fur. The empty eyes of a wolf stared down while she dug her fingers deep into its neck in a desperate attempt to hold it back. Over its massive shoulders, she glimpsed riders galloping across the meadow, a dozen more beasts in tow. In a few moments, they'd be on her, and all her efforts to escape would be for naught.

Fire erupted from her hands.

Flames swirled around her, a protective shield of fury turning the wolf to ash. Elaine rose shakily to her feet. She threw her hands wide, creating a wall of fire, and thrusting her palms forward, she threw it with all her might at the riders. The instant it left her control, she pivoted and shot forward. She had little interest in watching men burn.

A wave of magic washed over her as she hurled herself into the forest, sailing through the shield and falling to the ground. As she lay gasping and trying to still the rapid thumping of her heart, a shadow fell over her. A ghostly woman kneeled, clad in a flowing white gown, studying Elaine.

Through the woman, Elaine spied a man jumping from his horse, shadows flowing from his fingers. Panic tore through her. She looked at the woman, who stared with a curious expression. In those fathomless depths resonated ancient magic, calling out to the power burning within her own soul. For a moment, time seemed to slow to a crawl. Even the man advancing toward her appeared to slow. Elaine wrenched her gaze back to the woman, her mouth filled with ash.

"Are you going to kill me?" she whispered.

"No, my child. I offer you sanctuary, of course—"

"I accept!" Anything had to be better than the hell she'd been running from.

The woman smiled. "Know that if you do, you can never return to the land you came from. Do you still accept?"

Elaine looked to the man hunting her and knew the fate awaiting her if she said no. With a deep breath, she nodded. "I do."

"Then take my hand and receive the mark of Purgatory," said the woman, stretching out a thin, shimmering hand.

The moment Elaine lifted her hand, the woman grabbed her wrist. A fiery burn exploded along her skin and she threw her head back with a scream. Darkness surged across her vision, devouring her whole. As she tumbled into oblivion, a voice whispered through her mind.

You should have taken your chances with the soldiers you stupid girl.

....

Something cold and wet dripped onto her face, every droplet an icy dagger. Elaine jolted awake with a gasp, scrambling to her feet. The world tilted and she collided headfirst into a tree. Her forehead throbbed as she stepped back, rubbing the tender skin.

Night had fallen and thick shadows surrounded her, broken only by bands of moonlight cutting through the leaves. A steady rain fell, and the churning clouds spoke of a heavier storm on its way.

A rumbling from her stomach reminded her she hadn't eaten in days. Thankfully, her side had stopped bleeding. A quick inspection showed her clothes were stuck to her skin with caked blood. Her arm throbbed from whatever the woman had done. Turning her wrist over, a small mark was emblazoned on her skin. It wasn't like the ones covering the rest of her body. No, those bound her to the gods whose *gifts* left her hunted and alone.

This mark felt different; old, like their magic, but something she hadn't sensed before.

Whatever it meant, she didn't want to think about it. First, she needed to find shelter and food. Then she would figure out her next move.

Her stomach grumbled again, the pangs echoing through her body as she started to move forward. No sooner had she taken two steps than the wind whipped up, lashing icy daggers against her skin, pinching it red. A shiver rippled down her body, leaving her bones aching and joints throbbing. The dull ache in her side deepened, forcing her to move slowly. She wrapped her arms around her waist, calling on her fire to heat her blood.

The chill ebbed away as she stumbled onwards.

A growl came from the darkness, ricocheting among the ancient trees and tangled undergrowth. She stilled, biting back a shiver, as she scanned the gloom. She snapped her fingers to summon fire, but nothing but the tiniest of embers sparked before sputtering out in the heavy rain.

Fuck.

The sound rumbled from the shadows again. A pair of molten eyes pierced the dark, like the raging fires of Arcan's fury—the god whose fiery gifts she both hated and loved. The tattoos on her back heated. Whatever the beast was, it hummed with the same magic that flowed through her veins. Like calling to like.

The creature stepped into a band of moonlight. The silvery glow spilled over its glossy black scales and lean form. It had four legs, each with a set of claws that sunk deep into the soft earth. A row of horns ran from the tip of its swishing tail to the top of its head where a pair of tall ears flicked restlessly. The creature's forked tongue slid from the depths of its mouth, *scenting* her. It prowled forward, head dipped low. She snapped her fingers again, trying to summon a flame, but to no avail. A string of curses tumbled out as she patted herself down, trying to find something she could use. The empty pouch that once held coins, the dried waterskin—

The creature exploded forward, launching itself at her, claws drawn, mouth open to sink into her throat. Fear paralyzed her. A scream tore from her throat and death flashed before her eyes.

With a soft thunk, an arrow slammed into the side of the beast's head, the force of the impact crashing it onto the ground beside her—dead. Embedded deep within its eye was an arrow with glossy red feathers.

Leaf litter crunched, ripping her attention from the beast. A ripple of fear caught in her chest. A cloaked figure crept from the shadows, the hood pushed back. It was a woman, around her age, if she had to hazard a guess. Shoulder-length dark curly hair framed a hard face with tawny-brown skin. Amber eyes locked on her, examining her from head to toe, just as one might consider prey.

Tension was poised in every inch of that tall, muscled build, contained in a black tunic and pants. A shiver ran down Elaine's spine.

After a beat, the woman lowered her bow and slipped it onto her back. A flicker of irritation crossed her face. "You've got to be kidding me."

Elaine stared back, lost for words.

"The amulet in your pocket. Show me."

What amulet? She patted her side, frowning as she felt something cold and hard in her pocket. Lifting it out, she saw a silver pendant, round like a coin, with a scythe stamped on one side. How it had gotten in her pocket, she had no idea, for she certainly had not put it there.

A shadow fell over her. The woman snatched the pendant from her hands and inspected it with a hiss. Without answering, she pivoted sharply, the edge of the cloak flicking up behind her. Elaine could only stare at her retreating figure, which stopped at the tree line, where she turned back to her, calling out, "Come with me."

Elaine stood but made no move to follow. "I'm not going anywhere until I know who you are. And how the hell did that amulet get in my pocket?"

"By the spirit who gave you that mark on your wrist." The stranger paused for a moment, glancing back over her shoulder. "Are you coming or not?"

"I..."

A heavy sigh filled the air as the stranger cast a quiet, lingering look upon her. One that whispered of dark and terrible things, like the very monster that nearly devoured her. "You can stay here but I wouldn't advise it. Wicked things live in these woods."

Before she could speak, the stranger set off again, not waiting to see if Elaine followed. She cast a furtive look around but the deep shadows and chilled air offered only the promise of danger. A curse broke from her lips and she took off in pursuit.

"Why was there an amulet in my pocket? Why did you recognize it? And who—"

The stranger slowed their pace, allowing Elaine time to catch up. "You ask too many questions."

"Is your name to be a mystery as well, then?"

There was a pause in which she wondered if she'd truly lost her senses; following a woman she didn't know, rather than running in the opposite direction.

"Aya Sinclair."

Elaine was rendered silent.

CHAPTER 2

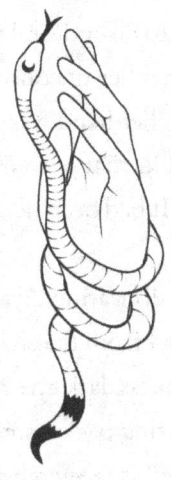

D OUBLE FUCK.

A witch? Why did the newcomer have to be a gods'
damned witch? And one bearing *that* bloody amulet? As the footfalls of the witch trailed softly behind, Aya pondered precisely what
in her long list of sins had resulted in this punishment. She doubted
the girl had any idea how close Aya was to leaving her for the monsters.

She certainly would not explain it, either. Having been rudely
woken by Sabra an hour ago, informing her that something had

intruded on their wards, she was in dire need of sleep. Their home wasn't exactly close to the edge of Purgatory, and even if the girl *had* been the one to trigger an alarm when she crossed the ward, there was no way she could've made it as deep into Aya's territory in that span of time.

Meaning a spirit had dumped her there, then triggered the alarm.

An act that rankled Aya to no end, and left her nearly abandoning the girl when she discovered her unconscious in the woods. When that damn beast appeared, her hand was forced, and she wondered if the spirits had meddled in that too. Why had they called in the debt she owed them now? It had been nearly ten years with not even a whisper.

As she stepped into a small clearing, Aya released a low whistle and a glossy black mare emerged from the shadows, ambling over in no particular hurry. Its fathomless dark eyes found hers as if to say, *why were you taking so long?* Biting back a smile, she grabbed the reins. The lightness inside dimmed as the witch appeared, resembling little more than a walking corpse.

It was the first time she let herself examine the girl; gray eyes framed by russet hair that tumbled in thick curls around a fine-boned face. She was pretty... for a witch.

"Are you going to explain the amulet now or what the hell this mark on my wrist means?" the girl asked.

"Right at this moment?" Aya would much rather be curled up in her bed, warm and a little drunk, than in the woods with a witch.

"I—" The girl's eyes rolled back, and she swayed, crumpling like a broken doll.

Aya stared for a moment, frowning. "Fuck."

She released the reins and dropped beside the girl, rolling her over. Something warm and wet touched her fingers. She jerked back, staring at her hands, slick with blood. Her gaze snapped to the source. A dark patch stained the witch's side, revealing a deep cut. Blood trickled from the wound.

Aya cursed. Why hadn't the idiot said anything? Scowling, she glanced around and, satisfied no one was close, scooped the girl up. It was startling to realize how little she weighed, almost nothing more than bones. She'd seen hunters return from monster hunts in better condition. As she awkwardly hauled the girl onto the horse, Aya tried not to think about what she must've gone through to reach this place.

No one ever came to Purgatory for a *happy* reason. Once you were in, you could never leave.

She swung up and settled into the saddle. Her horse snorted softly, and she imagined it saying, *This is a bad idea.*

With a flick of her heel and wrist, the mare lumbered forward into the dark.

"I know. We can always kill her later, though."

· · · • • • • • · · ·

The path descended into the valley floor where the whispers of the dead brushed her ears. Their cold presence brushed her skin, as comforting as a mother's touch. Haunting, black eyes stared from the darkness, curious about the stranger in her arms. Strangely, none hissed or snarled as they did when someone unwelcome intruded upon the woods she called home. It was as if they accepted the witch without question.

She didn't like that at all.

When the ground flattened and her dwelling emerged from the misty gloom, the tension inside of her eased.

It was a modest two-story abode, once belonging to a reclusive warlock, hidden among the ancient trees with their gnarled limbs and dense foliage. One side was consumed by a heavy beard of ivy, and the other was adorned with hanging plants in brightly painted pots. From the first-floor deck came the tinkling of wind chimes and the soft rustling of bundles of dried herbs and talismans.

She wondered if Sabra and Tobias, the other residents, were present.

Hopefully, she thought, eyeing the frail creature in her arms.

She stopped and slid down. The horse whinnied softly and ambled off to the woods. Aya tightened her grip on the unconscious stranger and stalked to the front door as it swung open. Two figures staggered out as if they'd been arguing over who went through first. Sabra pushed out in front, her clawed blue hands thrown up in warning to Tobias. Her long black locks tumbled freely over her bare shoulders, and she wore little more than a shift.

Tobias was dressed in a rumpled white shirt and fitting leather breeches. The towering alpha werewolf raised one brow but didn't fight. Wounds from demon claws tended to not heal, and he already had a scar running over one eyebrow.

His smile slipped when it alighted on the witch in her arms.

But it was Sabra, the demon with pale blue skin, who spoke first in a low, skeptical drawl. "*That's* who disturbed the barrier?"

"A charming gift from the spirits," Aya muttered as she carried the girl to Tobias. "She's injured badly. Fix her."

His brow lifted, but he brooked no argument as he took the witch into his arms.

As soon as the weight was gone from her arms, a hand shot out, seizing her by the wrist. Sparks jolted up her arm. She yanked her arm free, rubbing the spot where the skin prickled.

"What happened?" Tobias asked.

She rubbed her wrist for a moment, frowning deeply at the bare skin. There was no wound, no trace of whatever happened, only a lingering echo deep in her chest. Her gaze lifted to the witch, tiny and frail in his arms, and a shiver rippled across her skin.

As uncertainty crowded her mind, she squared her shoulders. "She's bleeding everywhere. It's making a mess."

Tobias snorted, saying nothing more as he took the witch inside, leaving Aya to Sabra's turbulent gaze.

Aya pinched the bridge of her nose, groaning softly. "The spirits certainly have a sense of humor."

"This isn't funny," muttered Sabra and slanted a hard look at the front door. "Why now? And what does this mean? Do we have to look after her now?"

"Your guess is as good as mine, but we should proceed carefully." Aya slanted a lingering look at the mark of Purgatory etched on Sabra's shoulder. "We owe them for giving you a mark. Remember that."

"I do, but doesn't mean I have to like this," said Sabra. A little of the tension bled from her shoulders. "Well, we better go inside. Can't have Tobias in there without backup." Sabra pulled open the door, glancing back with a furrowed brow. "Are you coming?"

Aya stared at her wrist where the witch had touched her. No, the girl was not to be trusted, and the sooner they got rid of her, the better. She shook her head and followed Sabra inside.

Tobias's workspace was a small room that had been converted into a makeshift infirmary a year ago. He had insisted on it after Sabra and Aya repeatedly returned bloodied and bruised from jobs, saying it was beneath him to stitch them up on the dining table. Apparently, it was *unclean*.

Sabra held off at the door, peering in with a shuttered expression. Aya could feel the storm of emotions warring through her friend through the thread connecting them. She touched Sabra's upper arm.

"Are you okay?" she whispered.

Sabra flinched. "I have to go."

In the next instant, she swept away, vanishing up the stairs. Aya stared at the retreating demon, wanting to follow but knowing that it was best to give Sabra space. She pulled her gaze away and headed into the room.

Tobias lit a lantern and set it on the table where the witch lay. He began carefully cutting away the cloth where the wound was.

Aya lingered in the doorway, her magic stirring beneath the surface. Her jaw tightened, wondering just when the spirits would reveal their plan.

"You don't have to stay." Tobias wiped away the blood, revealing a gash that ran far deeper than Aya expected.

"And if she wakes up?" she challenged.

Tobias rolled his eyes. "I'll give my best damsel in distress scream."

Her lips tightened. The girl *was* out cold. There was a good chance she would not wake for some time. It wasn't like Aya didn't think Tobias couldn't handle himself. She'd seen him rip apart monsters to save her life more than once, and even stand up against his old pack for her.

"Tobias..."

A heavy sigh filled the room, and he straightened up from the table. "Aya, go to bed. You haven't slept in nearly two days."

"I've slept," she defended.

He shot her a withering look. "There's a tonic by your bed."

She opened her mouth to argue, but a yawn escaped. Heat crept up her cheeks. Surrendering, she held up her hands.

"Fine. But if she even looks at you funny, wake me."

"Go. To. Bed."

She started out of the room when Tobias gasped. Pivoting around sharply, the room darkening around her in an instant, her gaze locked on him. In his hand was a folded paper with a red wax seal. The symbol of Purgatory, the very same mark emblazoned on the skin of every resident.

"It was in her pocket,"

"Open it," she whispered.

He glanced at her, then nodded. Her breath caught in her throat as he tore it open, read the contents, and handed it over to her. As she reached for it, her hand trembled, and it took her a moment to look upon the words.

The message stared back at her.

Protect her.

"Sabra is going to be pissed," remarked Tobias grimly.

Aya sighed and scrunched up the letter. "I'll handle it in the morning. Are you okay in here?"

Tobias inclined his head. "Go, Aya. I have it here."

Rolling her eyes, she stumbled from the room and stifled another yawn as she dragged herself upstairs. Her bedroom door gaped open, moonlight streaming into the hall. Inside, a cool breeze spilled in from the open window bringing with it floral notes from the garden. An assortment of furniture was placed haphazardly around the room, and on a small dresser, a myriad of trinkets tumbled from colorful boxes. As usual, her bed was unmade, the quilts scrunched across it, with a dozen pillows scattered on the floor.

It was just how she liked it. Her own little haven.

Except for the witch right beneath it.

A frown deepened her brow as she shed her clothes, abandoning them in the basket by the door, and crawled into bed. She swallowed the bitter tonic, wrinkling her nose as the taste lingered on her lips. Mercifully, Tobias had left her a glass of mulled wine, which she downed in a single go, before allowing dreamless sleep to claim her.

· · · · · · · · · ·

Morning came and the witch hadn't murdered them all in their sleep.

Aya discovered Sabra in the kitchen devouring an apple and scowling at Tobias's office door. She shuffled over, leaning against the bench beside her friend.

"The spirit left a letter with the witch."

Sabra stiffened. "I'm not going to like it, am I?" Aya relayed the message, and Sabra spun to her. "So, we're taking her to the witch temple in town, right?"

Aya glanced beyond Sabra to the door. "If they wanted that, then the message would have said that. I will look into a way around it, though; that is once I know your mark is safe."

"They can't take my mark away," muttered Sabra.

"We don't know that."

Truthfully, neither of them knew. There were no others like Sabra in Purgatory, no historical records to examine or stories whispered in shadowy taverns. Demons weren't of this realm, and to even exist in it, they required an anchor... and to live in Purgatory? A mark was required.

Aya didn't hesitate to become Sabra's anchor, or to strike the deal for her friend's mark—but the price she needed to pay hung over her head like a prison sentence. Witches in her experience seldom led to anything good, and she had little interest in being burned by one again. Both literally and figuratively.

When the door finally opened, Tobias swept out. Shadows darkened his eyes and he was still wearing the same clothes from last night, rumpled and stained with blood. She'd hoped he would've tried to get some sleep, but it was clear he had as much luck as she had of late.

"Dare I hope our guest didn't make it through the night?" Sabra asked, tossing the core into a bucket of scraps.

"*Sabra*," Aya warned.

Blue hands went up defensively. "What?"

She might've had an intense dislike of witches—hatred on her crappier days—but she tried to be mindful, for Tobias's sake. He got... attached to his patients, even if they were witches. He gave a little smile as if he read her mind, and she returned it. He slumped down on one of the comfortable armchairs by the cold fireplace.

"She's alive. Hasn't woken, though."

"Wounds?"

Tobias rubbed the back of his neck with a quiet groan, his eyes shutting for a moment. "Looked like the girl had been through hell to get here."

"Will she live?" She didn't want an angry spirit coming knocking if the witch died. The sooner the debt was paid, the faster it wouldn't be hanging over her head anymore.

It was a mark on her ledger she really hated.

Tobias shrugged. "If she keeps the wounds clean and infection doesn't set in, probably."

"Are we sure the temple isn't an option?" Sabra mused. "It would certainly 'protect her' from—"

The door flung open, and the witch stood staring at them with her cheeks flushed. The room fell silent.

Aya studied the girl; thin and frail, with a tiny spark of life in those pale gray eyes. She reminded her of a deer about to bolt.

Tobias rose and walked toward her, but a pale hand rose, stopping him. Her gaze slid to Aya, sending a prickle of awareness that lifted the hairs on the back of her neck. The witch straightened up, squaring her shoulders.

"I am not going to any temple."

"Is that so?" Aya retorted. "Witches belong at temples and in Purgatory—"

"I said *no*," snapped the girl, and she took a step forward. Her lips parted again, but as she opened her mouth to speak, her legs gave out.

Tobias caught her before she hit the ground. "Well, that went well."

CHAPTER 3

AFTER ELAINE'S UNGRACEFUL MOMENT where she blacked out, she woke in a different room. Although it was sparsely furnished, it at least had a proper bed. The morning light trickled in from the window above her and cast her surroundings in a buttery glow. She inhaled, savoring the floral scent hanging in the air, even as her ribs protested the movement. With a wince, she pushed back the blanket and swung her legs over the side. A shiver rippled through her when her bare feet collided with the cold wooden floor.

A memory flashed. A cell with an icy stone floor reeking of piss and shit and the stench of something dead. After her first attempt to escape, she'd woken up, confused and in pain. A collar had been fastened around her neck, and both her ankles secured to a long chain tethering her to the wall. They'd starved her until she passed out, and afterward beaten her until she was black and blue.

The Grand Matron of her old temple had loomed over her after, shaking her head. "All those who have walked your path before you embraced their destiny—why can't you?"

Because I want to live! She'd wanted to shout, but her jaw had been broken, her cheek too, and in the end, all she'd managed was a pitiful sob.

Elaine blinked the memories away. She'd escaped the temple, had run further and longer than anyone had ever thought possible. It had taken her years, but at last, she'd found the mysterious Purgatory. Protected by a barrier, it was a haven for those hunted and abused. The one place she might have a chance at being free of those who pursued her. Even if she couldn't exactly leave, it was better than what she'd escaped.

She shook her head and, determined to talk to the people who wished to send her away, she hauled herself up. The world lurched again and her stomach clenched, bile pushing up her throat. Swallowing it back down with a groan, she waited for her head to clear before shuffling to the door. The sound of muffled voices rising and falling in heated bursts reached her ears. As she crept down the hallway, a door slammed shut down below, and the voices cut off abruptly. She found the stairs and headed down.

The wood creaked underfoot, announcing her arrival by the time she reached the last step. Without bothering to knock, Elaine pushed the door open. The blue girl was gone, leaving only the other two.

To her relief, the man approached first. His warm brown eyes and open face eased her fragile nerves.

"You should rest," he said.

She started to reply, but the words died in her mouth as her gaze drifted to the woman who'd saved her in the woods—*Aya Sinclair.* A woman with haunting eyes that promised only death and carnage if crossed, and a swaggering air that appeared to mask something rather lethal and vicious beneath. A feeling of dread prickled her skin.

Aya stood by the cold fireplace, glaring at her. Shadows danced over her skin, and it was as if her mere presence snuffed out the light from the lamps hanging on the wall. Tension hung heavy in the air as if she were a predator coiled, ready to strike, and Elaine was the prey.

"Miss?" The man's voice broke her thoughts.

"Elaine." She clutched at the folds of her loose dress, feeling uneasy beneath Aya's piercing stare, and tried to focus on him. "Elaine Tormelin."

"A pleasure to meet you. You may call me Tobias. No family name. Did my surly friend here introduce herself when she picked you up?" he asked, grinning.

They're friends? It was hard to imagine someone so ill-tempered having such an amiable companion. Or perhaps they were lovers?

Aya snorted. "You make me sound beastly."

"You're not exactly the picture of charm," said Tobias.

"Well, I *did* introduce myself."

"Being polite? Now the world is definitely falling apart," he replied.

As the exchange continued, Elaine examined the chaotic interior. The cluttered shelves adorning most of the walls and the rugs spread across the floor made it feel homely. A mixture of fragrant spices and floral notes lingered in the air. She took her time to study it all. Aware that both of them were watching her until at last, she forced her gaze back to Tobias. "What happens to me now?"

Something flickered in Aya's eyes before she pushed herself away from the fireplace. "There's a witch temple of Dianera in town. You'd be safe there."

"No."

Aya cocked her head. *"No?"*

Elaine's body stiffened in an instant. Heat flared through her chest, rushing to her fingers, and fire filled her veins, pushing for release. It took some effort, but she forced it back down. It probably wasn't a great idea to burn down her rescuer's home.

"I ran from one. I have little interest in returning to another." She pressed her palms into her thighs, trying to stem the fire raging within. "Is there somewhere else I can go?"

Again, an unreadable look flashed in Aya's eyes.

"What skills do you have?" Tobias asked gently.

"What are you doing, Tobias?" Aya's voice was a winter's storm, icy and lethal as they squared off, facing each other.

Darkness flared in Aya's eyes, and it seemed as if the light in the room dimmed. Icy whispers brushed the nape of Elaine's neck, lifting the hairs, and a cloud of white spilled from her mouth. Her eyes widened. With an impatient sigh, Aya stepped back and the room brightened again, the chill vanishing in an instant.

"We'll talk about this later."

Tobias stared back, unflinching. "The letter."

"I'll *handle* it," she snapped back.

"She deserves to know—"

"Know what?" Elaine interrupted.

Aya narrowed her eyes. "Nothing you need to concern yourself with."

The air crackled with tension, but Elaine refused to look away.

"What have I done to offend you?" she snapped. The previous day had shredded her control to ribbons, and her temper was begging to be released.

Aya glared at her. "I don't owe you any explanation. You belong at the temple."

"And I said *no*."

Aya's nostrils flared.

Silence consumed the room. The pair shared a silent exchange until with an exasperated sigh, Tobias threw up his hands and stalked to the edge of the room. Elaine's heart slammed hard against her ribs as Aya stepped closer, leaving scarcely any space between them. Their height difference forced her to look up, and she stifled a gasp at the furious expression on Aya's face.

"No place in Purgatory will take you without coin. The temple is the only safe place—"

"Temples are not *safe* for me." She lifted her chin defiantly, refusing to cower at the darkness brimming in those fathomless depths.

Those once jeweled golden eyes were now near-black, piercing her like daggers.

Something flickered in Aya's eyes and she moved away. With a shrug, she said, "It seems you're staying here."

Elaine's mouth opened in shock. After being sold out or almost murdered by those she thought she could trust, so many times, her expectations of people had grown low. This was something she never would have expected from someone who seemed to despise her.

"Why? No one wants me here. Tell me how to get to the nearest town and I'll be out of your hair."

Aya's smile was mocking. "You'd be dead within a day."

Elaine stared back in defiance. "I can handle myself. I've survived this long." After all, she was well accustomed to being alone, even if she ached for that little comfort of a home in the distant crevices of her mind.

Tobias gave a gentle cough. "Until we figure out the next move, she could stay here."

To her surprise, Aya appeared to hesitate. Elaine knew uncertainty when she saw it. Tobias had given her an opening and she took it.

"I'm not useless. I'm good with tracking spells, knowing when people lie, cooking, mending clothes, horse care..." She was wary of divulging the depths of her magic, especially to strangers.

Tobias approached her side. "Aya, the letter..."

Again, the mention of this letter had her ears prick up. Whatever it meant, the fight bled from Aya's shoulders.

Aya rubbed the back of her neck, cursing softly. "Sabra is going to slit my throat for this."

"I think you mean she's going to murder us both."

Elaine stared, wondering if she might be safer in the town after all.

Aya gave another of those shrugs. "You can stay. For now, at least."

Until I figure out a way to get rid of you, she seemed to add on.

Elaine released a shaky breath and held out her hand. "You have a deal."

Aya stared at the hand for a moment, before shaking it. "One more thing. Steer clear of Sabra. I can control my temper much better than she can."

• • • • • • • • • •

The room she'd awoken in seemed the safest place for Elaine to retreat to, which really wasn't saying much. As she paced the small space, her mind churned with everything she'd heard and seen, and wondered just what strange place she'd found herself in.

When a knock rattled the door, starting her from her thoughts, she turned as it creaked open. Tobias walked in, carefully shutting it behind him. She watched him warily from the corner of the room, pressing back into the wall.

He offered her a warm smile. "It's okay. I'm just here to see how you're healing."

She shifted on the balls of her feet. "My chest hurts, but apart from that, I feel better. My head isn't pounding anymore."

He remained where he was. "Good. May I check your wounds?"

Wary, but sensing he meant no harm, she sat on the edge of the bed and let him approach. She stiffened as he carefully lifted the edge of her shirt, taking care to inspect the side of her wound.

"You heal fast for a witch." The faint lines around his rich brown eyes crinkled as he smiled at her.

She stared back at him; her guard up. "And you're as sharp as any wolf I've met."

"Indeed I am." He flashed a bright grin at her and a little of her uncertainty trickled away. "The two surly ones you met are my pack."

"Pack? But they're not... I mean, Sabra—"

"Neither are wolves, but that is how it is here. We might not be blood to each other, but we're family all the same." A shadow passed over his face. "Purgatory takes from you in unexpected ways, so it is best to find people you can trust."

"And I can trust you?"

The corner of his mouth twitched. "Trust is earned. Even for me."

Elaine fell silent, pensive in her own thoughts as Tobias continued his checks. When he finished, he stepped back.

"You should be strong enough to work in another two days I'd say. In the meantime, I'll see if we can get a proper bath drawn up for you. How does that sound?"

It had been a long time since anyone had shown her any hint of kindness, and it left her shifting restlessly. "Why are you so nice to me?"

His brow lifted. "Common decency?"

"There's *always* an angle." She crossed her arms. "So, what's yours?"

At that, a hearty laugh rumbled from Tobias, filling the room. She stared at him until silence claimed the room once more.

"You sound like Aya." At her frown, Tobias explained, "She always believes the worst in people."

"People or witches?"

The smile dimmed and shadows crept into his eyes. "Both."

CHAPTER 4

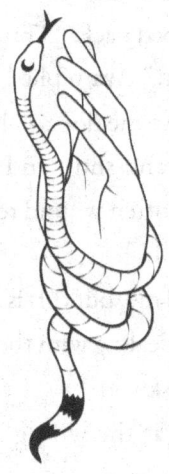

AYA PASSED THROUGH A stone archway into a small clearing filled with dozens of wooden statues, half of which had arrows embedded into them. Shadows stretched out from the ancient woods over the low hedge wall encircling the space. Dark clouds blanketed the sky, permitting only intermittent bursts of moonlight to peer through.

She inhaled and allowed her second sight to slide over her eyes, brushing the world in a pale blue glow. When she reached the middle, she halted. A cold breeze whispered among the statues before spreading its tendrils across her skin. Gooseflesh prickled her bare arms.

A soft tread came from behind and she turned as the point of a sword appeared at her throat. Trailing her gaze along the blade to the blue hand holding it, she met a pair of dark eyes staring back.

"She's going to stay for a while."

Sabra hissed as she stepped back. "This is foolish."

"I hardly welcomed her," Aya replied curtly. "The spirits... the *letter*. What would you have me do? Kill her?"

Sabra's mouth opened and shut, and all the pain that festered beneath the surface like a rotten wound tore at Aya. It was an agony she knew all too well herself.

"I knew the spirits hated me, but this is a new low," snarled Sabra.

Aya sighed, weary from dealing with the witch and the letter from the spirits. "And I won't risk you."

But that, apparently, was the wrong answer. Sabra swung her sword with a savage roar.

Aya ripped her own blade free, yanking it up just in time. Metal clashed with a ringing cry. Her arms jolted with a force so strong that her boots slid along the grass.

Sabra leaned in close. "Do you remember what you swore to me on the day we met?"

"Of course, I do." That day was burned in her mind. She couldn't forget the stench of blood or the sight that greeted her in that basement. The stains splattering the walls and floor were permanent fixtures in her nightmares. She blinked away the vision and dropped low, sweeping her leg. As her friend hit the ground, Aya scowled. "Do you think I was glad to find her in the woods?"

"You couldn't stop staring at her." Sabra scrambled to her feet and circled Aya, sword in hand.

Heat flooded Aya's cheeks. The insinuation twisted like a knife. "Because she's a witch!!"

The wind gusted hard, whipping up flurries of dirt around their feet. How could she explain to Sabra the witch meant nothing and that this was about clearing a debt, and nothing more? Once that was paid, they could pretend it had all been a bad dream and drink until they passed out.

"Call it a demon's intuition." Sabra sprinted at her, swinging hard once more. Their swords collided, throwing sparks into the air. "This witch will get us killed."

"Now, who's being the dramatic one? I thought that was my title." She tried to sound teasing, but the smile quickly fell, as Sabra came at her again, angrier than before.

Curses spilled from her lips. This wasn't the usual sparring. She parried off the dizzying rush of blows. Even with her heightened speed, she barely blocked the attacks. When Sabra launched at her, she dodged, narrowly missing the arc of the blade, and rolled out of the way. She surged up to her feet; and yanked up her blade as Sabra's descended. Heat burned through her arms and sweat gathered along her brow as she gasped for air.

She pushed a burst of magic into her arms and swung to the side, sending Sabra careening to the left. As her friend staggered and attempted to turn, she descended upon her with a flurry of strikes.

This time she had the offensive, driving Sabra to the edge of the clearing.

A rock caught Sabra's foot, sending her stumbling backward. Aya saw her chance, rushed forward, and slammed her foot into her friend's side, making her hit the ground hard. Sabra's sword slid across the grass. Not trusting her friend to make a grab for it, she kicked it out of reach and strode back to where the demon lay panting. Aya thrust out a hand, but Sabra stared up at her, sweaty and flushed, the anger still burning in those coal-black depths.

"Truce?"

Sabra batted her hand away and stood. Before Aya could react, Sabra stepped forward and threw a punch to the side of her face. Pain bloomed as she staggered back, a metallic taste pooling in her mouth. She spat the blood onto the grass and straightened up with a hiss. The side of her face throbbed and it felt as if her cheekbone was broken. It would heal in a day or so, but that wasn't the point.

"Cheap fucking shot, Sab." She stayed where she was, reluctant to be on the receiving end of another punch.

Sabra rubbed her hand, seemingly unrepentant. "I wish you were that witch."

"We both know if she were here, you'd be liable to kill her, but until that debt is repaid to the spirit, we don't do shit. Got it?" Aya dared to close the space between them, gently cupping Sabra's cheek. "We didn't go through all that hell to get your mark, only for you to lose it because of a witch. If you remember, one of them was the reason you were in chains. Don't let this one be the reason you lose your freedom."

CHAPTER 5

E LAINE WASN'T SURPRISED WHEN she awoke on the floor with
the blanket twisted around her sweat-soaked body. Her heart
thumped viciously against her ribs, trying desperately to pry its way
out and run from the darkness eddying around her mind. The cold
nightmare still whispering, its icy claws sunk deep into her skin.

She pressed her hands into her face. *I'm free of the temple. I'm not
going back. I am alive.*

As her heart slowed and her thoughts cleared from their muddied
chaos, she lowered her hands. Untangling the blanket from her legs,
she scrambled up, striding to the door. Rivulets of sweat still ran
down her face. She wiped them away before heading outside.

The hall was full of soft noises; the house groaning with creaking wood, a quiet whistle of wind through unseen shutters and cracks, and gentle snores from a room two doors down. She padded toward the stairs, where she paused with one hand gripping the banister. The polished wood was smooth to the touch, recently oiled and shining. A band of moonlight cut in from a narrow window behind her, throwing her shadowy form down the stairs like some outstretched monster.

She didn't know what to make of this home among the woods.

It was cozier than she expected; quaint touches of art on the wall, detailed cornices, and a carved banister. Most of the places she'd hidden in for the past few years had been dingy and cold, offering only the barest comforts. It was strange to walk among something so *gentle,* even as the eyes of Aya Sinclair resurfaced in her mind. A chill of awareness slid down her spine.

For a moment, she felt like an intruder, frozen in the dark, unsure of her next movements. Going back to her room where the rumpled blankets and empty bed served as a reminder of her nightmares wasn't appealing.

In silence, she crept downstairs and crossed the floor to the armchairs. She toyed with lighting a fire but banished the thought away. All she wanted to do was sit in the dark and try to clear her head.

As she reached for the chair, a creaking sound came from the direction of the stairs. A soft sigh rendered her still as a statue. She wasn't alone. The cold press of magic slid over her skin, lifting the hairs along her arms. Her heart gave a skittering thump before she turned slowly, her mouth filling with dust.

Aya stood at the base of the stairs, clad in a loose shirt and pants, watching her with dark, unreadable eyes. Her wild black hair hung unbound around her shoulders, the silvery light from the window dancing among the strands like ribbons. For a moment, she reminded Elaine of a spectral creature. Something entirely inhuman and utterly dangerous.

No word passed from her lips, her mind whirring rapidly, turning over what she might say. Only when Aya's mouth moved to speak did she find her voice.

"I had a nightmare," she blurted.

"I see."

Do you also have nightmares? she wanted to ask.

She said nothing, of course, and remained still as a statue. Aya swept forward, heading straight for the kitchen. Every step seemed poised, her body angled so that Elaine remained in view. Even when Aya poured a pitcher of water into a glass, she had a distinct feeling that Aya was still watching her.

"Tomorrow we'll head into town to see a friend of mine about some work," Aya said, turning to face her. "You should try to sleep."

The nightmare flashed in her mind, causing Elaine to doubt whether any sleep would occur. "I'll try."

Aya cocked her head to the side. What she was looking for, Elaine didn't know. A shiver flared across her skin, anyway. Aya thrust the cup aside and strode toward her.

Elaine froze. The temptation to run burned through her veins. A shadow fell over her, forcing her attention from the door to the gaze boring holes into her. Mere inches separated them. An earthy scent filled her lungs. She squared her shoulders as Aya leaned in.

"Interesting," Aya crooned.

"What is?" Blood roared in her ears. Magic burned through her veins, flames pushing up against her skin and warming her fingers.

"You're not afraid of me." Aya stepped back, and a purely feline, wicked smile curved her lips. One that promised death and all the chaos that went with it. "Curious."

Elaine's mouth dropped. A protest rushed to her lips. She was afraid of a lot of things; the Arcan temple, the Grand Matron, the Hunters who pursued her, and of being betrayed. But of Aya? No. The woman got under her skin and stripped past all the defenses, but fear was not what she felt.

"Should—"

Aya's hand shot out, covering her mouth. Sparks skittered down her spine. Her hand reached up to pull Aya off when she saw those steely dark eyes staring at the door. The whites of her eyes vanished.

What the—

Aya pulled away. "Wake Sabra and Tobias."

"What's going on?"

"Go, *now!*" The sudden urgency in Aya's voice made her flinch.

She opened her mouth to ask again, but Aya yanked the door open and vanished outside. Shadows erupted from Aya's skin, wrapping around her in a swirling armor. A chill rippled over Elaine. It was unlike anything she'd seen before.

The door closed behind her, and a split second later, a roar ripped through the air.

Elaine turned on her heel and sprinted to the stairs. She flew up two steps at a time, rushing down the hall where one door was already opening. Sabra appeared, sword in hand.

"She's outside?" Sabra asked brusquely.

Elaine barely managed a nod before the demon strode past her. She hurried on, knocking on all the doors, unsure which room belonged to Tobias. After the third attempt, one opened, and he stood sleepily in the doorway, rubbing his eyes. She opened her mouth when another roar split the night. His eyes widened.

"Stay inside," he ordered, and he moved past her, racing toward the stairs.

"What's going on?" she asked, hurrying after him.

"The ward must've broken again. Monster, my guess," he explained as they rushed down the stairs.

At the bottom, he stopped and turned to her. Worry pinched his face, catching her off guard. No one had given her that kind of concern in years.

"You need to stay inside. We'll deal with this," he said.

"I can help. I'm not defenseless." She lifted her hand, fire sparking among her fingers.

He shook his head. "You're still injured. If you go out there, you'll only get in the way... and if you get in Aya's way, it won't be pretty."

The warning was clear, plus the sprint up the stairs was already taking its toll. Her legs wobbled, nausea pushing up her throat. She hated to admit it, but he was right. The embers snuffed out in her palms, her vision doubling for a second.

"Be safe," was all she said before he turned and strode out, slamming the door behind him.

CHAPTER 6

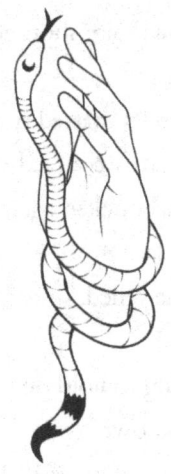

THE HELLHOUND RUSHED AT her, gnashing teeth dripping with venom and burning red eyes. At the last second, Aya dove out of the way, surging to her feet and pivoting to meet the beast as it spun around to charge at her once more. She threw up a shield of darkness and the hound rammed into it with a jolting thud. The shock rippled down her arms, sending her staggering back. Heat burned in her palms as she dropped the shield, summoning more magic to her hands.

The hound scrambled to its feet, shaking its head in a daze. It shook its massive head as if to clear it before shooting forward. Aya sprinted to meet it. Almost as they were about to collide, she dropped low, sliding across the sodden ground. Digging her hand into the earth, she hauled herself up and leaped onto its back.

"Aya!" Sabra's voice cut the air like a blade.

"Summoning circle, now!" she shouted back, clinging on as the beast tried to buck her off.

She sunk her fingers into its matted fur and squeezed her thighs, crouching low. Heavy breaths coursed through her, burning her lungs. The beast roared and bucked again, nearly throwing her off. Curses spilled from her lips.

"Are you ready yet?!" she yelled.

"Patience is a virtue, Aya!"

"You're not the one trying to hold on to a fucking hellhound!"

"You could stab it, you know?"

"No shit but—fuck, can you hurry?" The beast tried to roll, but she yanked on its fur in the opposite direction. "*Sabra!*"

"Gods, you're needy!"

She lifted her head, scowling at Sabra several feet away. The demon offered a wink as she etched a circle of glowing red magic into the dirt. Behind her, the front door opened and Tobias strode out, shifting mid-stride. The hound stilled beneath her, its eyes locking onto Tobias.

Sabra jumped back from the circle. *"Now!"*

Aya opened the floodgate, which was holding back her magic, and thrust it down into the beast. Thick black smoke swirled around them, only stopping at the circle. The beast howled in agony but could not move. From the pit of her soul emerged an incantation, rising from her throat and spilling into the air.

A savage cry tore from the beast as it pawed at the ground, raging against her control. Aya thrust another wave of magic down and—

The hound exploded into dust.

She hit the ground, wincing as her knees took the brunt of the fall. The smoke left the circle and rushed back into her, doubling her vision for a moment. Blinking hard, she battled waves of nausea until the world finally settled. The circle sputtered out and faded away as if it had never been there at all. Her lungs burned as she tried to sit up.

Tobias dropped to her side. "Give me your arm."

She didn't even fight him, lifting her arm so that he could grab her by the waist and lift her. Although she managed to stand, her legs quaked, nearly buckling beneath her. Bile rushed up her throat and she wrenched away from him, emptying dinner onto the grass. Droplets of blood stained the mess, leaving a metallic taste on her lips.

Tobias reached for her, his outstretched hand in the corner of her vision. "Aya—"

"I'm fine." She wasn't, and she knew he wasn't fooled for a moment. Her stomach clenched, threatening to double her over. She squeezed her eyes shut; one hand pressed to her mouth until the feeling passed. Reluctantly, she opened them again, giving Sabra a questioning look. "How the fuck did that get past the ward?"

Sabra glanced beyond her to the ancient woods, frowning. There was no humor or snarky response snapped back. A troubled frown pinched her delicate features. "No idea."

Tobias folded his arms across his chest. "Aya, we've never been attacked before."

First the monster in the woods, then one at the house.

"I know." She straightened up, a cold fury settling in her bones. One tentative step forward and her legs held strong. She headed for the door, but it had already opened. Elaine stood in the doorway, one hand on the frame, the other clutching the nightgown hanging off her slender body. "That's *two* beasts who have come after you in less than two days. Who the fuck are you, and who did you piss off?"

Elaine stepped forward, trying to move out of the way, but Aya blocked her path.

"Why are you sure this has anything to do with me?" she challenged.

Aya scowled. "Our wards are tough, but since your arrival, *two* beasts have gotten through. I don't believe in coincidences." She took a step closer so their chests nearly touched. "You were injured on arrival and I'm guessing you didn't do that yourself. Who is hunting you and why?"

The witch looked away to the woods, silent for a moment. "Everyone."

"*Everyone?*" Skepticism dripped from Aya's lips. "I consider myself to have a slightly larger ego than most, and even I don't believe everyone wants me dead."

A bitter laugh tumbled from Elaine. "I wish it were a matter of ego."

When those gray, weary eyes looked upon her, Aya was rendered silent. She often liked the idea of her enemies broken and beaten, but this was different. It dug at an old wound, and she looked away, unsettled.

"I thought for once, I could stop running."

Almost the same words Aya had said when she first arrived at Purgatory over a decade ago.

Tobias appeared at her side, and she took comfort in her friend's presence, even as her own mind whirred. "At least tell us what you are, Elaine. We can't protect you if you keep secrets from us."

"*Protect* her?" snarled Sabra in protest. "She's—"

"Someone who needs protection," Tobias cut in. The alpha tone radiated from his voice, the air crackling with his power. It couldn't make them submit like it would a wolf, but they felt it all the same. He turned to Aya. "This is what they meant."

That damn message was going to be the death of her. *Protect her.* Aya pinched the bridge of her nose. Of course, the spirits would have her protect the very thing that caused the slaughter of her own people. The irony burned like bitter poison.

She didn't miss the war of agony and fury in Sabra's eyes, or the silence that stretched open like a vast ocean. All she could do was her best to keep Sabra and Tobias safe, that this message wouldn't lead them to harm.

She met his gaze, nodded curtly, and looked at Elaine. "Speak." After a beat, she added, her tone softer, "please."

Elaine lifted her chin. "I'm a Harvest Witch, which means—"

Tobias cursed. "*Gods*—ah, sorry, go on."

The corner of her mouth tipped up. The smile didn't quite reach her eyes, but she was calmer.

An unexpected sting of jealousy swept through Aya's veins. She shoved it down. Tobias put people at ease. That's what he did. Which was why he was the kindest of the three.

"Every temple is bound to one of the seven deities, their patron, as people call it. Every so often, a witch is born with a deity's markings, rather than being tattooed with them when they reach sixteen." Elaine paused and tugged up her sleeve, revealing bare skin. She murmured something and a swirling tattoo appeared, intricately wrapping around her whole arm. "They used to call us Divine Witches, for we were blessed and chosen by the gods. We would bear the marks of more than one god, granting us the divine title." Her smile became bitter. "Now they call us Harvest Witches, marking us as sacrifices so that our powers might be leeched and transferred to a new host. Mine was to be gifted to the crown prince of Vesmir."

Aya shivered at the name she knew all too well.

Tobias took a step forward. "How many of the gods blessed you?"

Elaine didn't answer immediately. Her gaze darted to the woods as if considering the option to run.

Foolish girl.

"Six." Her voice was soft as a whisper. "All but Akaria. No witch has ever served her, for only her descendants, the necromancers served her."

Tobias's voice broke her thoughts with a low whistle. "Well, I can see why the royal family wouldn't want to let you go... and why beasts might be drawn to you."

"So, we should expect more of this?" Sabra asked, glaring at Elaine.

Aya sighed. "I suspect it will get a lot worse."

CHAPTER 7

The following morning, Elaine sat at the table in Tobias's office as he finished examining her now-healed wound. Dappled morning light spilled in from the window, bathing the room in soft light. A warmth lingered in the air. It reminded her of the healing chamber back of her old temple. The stench of burning herbs and the sharp perfume her Grand Matron wore was seared into her mind, leaving her stomach churning.

Don't go there, her inner voice warned, and she banished the memory. The skin was pink, the scar little more than a faded white line. He drew back, silent for a moment, and she tucked her shirt back in.

"The gift of Dianera. Must come in handy," he murmured.

It had been one of the few markings she'd accepted. She could wield the powers of all the gods whose marks adorned her body, but the price was too high. No one was meant to have that much power, and knowing that she was to be sacrificed for it felt like a cruel joke from the gods.

She pushed off the table. "Sometimes."

"And the other gifts?"

"What I have is enough," she said, reaching for her jacket.

A bundle of clothes had been left at her door when she was asleep. When she'd asked Tobias about it, he'd said he knew nothing. Sabra was unlikely to have done it, which left Aya. And *that* led her to more uncomfortable questions.

"So, the gifts are a curse?" Tobias sounded pensive and when she glanced at him, he was reaching for a journal on a side table.

"Not a curse," she replied, pausing before she continued. "The more gifts I accept, the more of a mental toll it is. It just...takes a piece of you each time."

Tobias whistled softly. "Well, that's shit."

Her mouth twitched. "I've made do with the two I've accepted. Arcan's powers give me fire talents, and Dianera's light and healing magic. They've saved my neck more times than I can count."

Something hard flickered in Tobias's eyes. "You're safe here with us. Aya and I won't let anything happen to you."

She didn't miss the fact Sabra wasn't included on that list. A heaviness formed a knot at the pit of her soul. Why had she expected Purgatory to be any kinder?

·····•••··

49

Aya and Sabra were waiting for them out the front when the examination was over. They were standing under the shade of a tree, heads bent together in a low conversation. As Elaine walked over with Tobias, Aya's stony gaze latched on her. Her stomach flipped, twisting into knots. She didn't know what to make of that fire in Aya's eyes.

Luckily, Tobias spoke first. "Ready to go?"

Sabra turned, throwing a glacial look her way. "The Inner District won't be safe for her. She should stay here."

Aya snorted. "I think we established last night that this place isn't exactly as safe as we'd hoped. No, she'll need to hide her magic and for that, we'll need to see Lilibet. We can do that before we seek work."

"I haven't seen her in weeks," Tobias remarked.

"Yes, she grouched to me about that. She was rather upset to find you went to town and didn't bother to visit her," Aya said, shrugging before she went on. "I sent word to her this morning to have the shop shut for our arrival. We should head off."

Sabra released a long string of curses as she held out her hands. "Let's get this over and done with."

Tobias approached first, taking one of the outstretched hands. Aya took the other, leaving an open hand for Elaine. She stared at it, uncertain for a moment. Scowling, grabbed hold and, seconds later, darkness flared up around them, and the world was no more.

· · · · · · · · · ·

Elaine kept her eyes tightly shut while her stomach settled. A cacophony of sounds slammed into her at once, and a myriad of smells assailed her without warning. The firm grip on her hands was released, forcing her to finally pry her eyelids open. A gasp broke from her lips.

Sunlight shone on a cobblestone street crammed with clattering carriages and crowds of people adorned in their finery. Townhouses squeezed together, brightly painted, and lavishly adorned. Ribbons and garlands of flags strung across the road fluttered in the warm, fragrant breeze. A dizzying blend of earthly and floral notes filled the air.

When she'd pictured Purgatory from all the rumors, she'd imagined a dark and poor town falling apart at the seams. But this... this was *thriving*. Energy crackled in the air, sparking across her skin and putting a smile on her mouth.

"This is incredible," she whispered in awe.

"It's not too bad, is it?" Tobias teased, nudging her with his elbow.

She wrenched her gaze from the splendor. "It's certainly not like the stories."

"Is it more wonderful? Charming?"

Aya snorted. "Don't make it sound so fanciful, Tobias. This place is full of monsters."

Elaine hadn't realized Aya was so close, and her heart flipped. Before she could tame her reaction, Aya stalked toward the house they'd appeared in. She looked to Tobias for an explanation. The smile vanished for a moment, returning only when he realized her attention was on him.

"The heart of town is certainly pretty, but don't let this place fool you. Now, we need to get you all sorted before anyone takes notice."

She realized he was referring to her presence, because no one nearby appeared surprised by the fact four individuals appeared out of thin air.

Sabra stood at the bottom of the steps of a nearby house, scanning the street, one hand resting on the hilt of the sword at her hip. At the front door, Aya raised her hand to knock, but before she did, the door swung open.

Elaine let Tobias usher her to the base of the steps as a woman filled the space. Fiery red curls framed a delicate heart-shaped face and moon pale skin. Two long pointed ears jutted out from her hair, the tips glittering with jewels. Her bright blue eyes slid to Elaine, before turning to Aya. A feline smile lifted her rouged lips.

"Well, this day suddenly got a lot more interesting... and it was already off to such a scandalous start," drawled Lilibet.

"Can we come inside before we attract the wrong sort of attention?" Aya asked.

Lilibet rolled her eyes and stepped aside. "Very well."

As Elaine went to follow, Tobias paused, glancing back to Sabra. "Are you coming inside?"

Something flickered in Sabra's eyes before she shook her head. "I'll stay here."

A tense moment played out between them; one Elaine couldn't make any sense of. It broke as Tobias inclined his head and continued up the stairs, taking Elaine with him.

Lilibet led them through a shop front cluttered with shelves and cabinets holding a variety of jars containing colorful salves and spices. The room was filled with the pungent aroma of herb bundles hanging from the ceiling. On a bench sat a one-eyed cat, hissing as Elaine passed. She hurried after the others as they moved into a small area at the rear of the house. Everyone took a seat aside from Aya, who leaned against the wall with her arms folded, watching the others with that enigmatic gaze on her face.

Bright cushions, delicate curtains, and polished tables with a myriad of freshly cut flowers matched the vibrancy of the street outside, and that of the woman herself.

"You were a little vague in the missive about exactly what we are dealing with. I understand now," Lilibet said, chuckling. "A witch. How delightful."

Elaine met the woman's gaze and sat up under her keen scrutiny. A crackle of magic brushed her mind, the nudge of a mental probe against her defenses. The walls she'd constructed around her mind hardened, refusing entry.

After a beat, the feeling faded, and a new sensation brushed over her skin. The hairs lifted. An icy air settled around her, piercing deep into her bones like a thousand little daggers. Her hands closed into fists, gripping the chair tightly as she stared back, refusing to yield.

As quickly as it had begun, it was over and Lilibet leaned back, glancing at Aya with a lifted brow. "I might be able to charm her to appear like a half-blooded fae, but I can't mask her magic enough to make her appear human. Will that do?"

Aya inclined her head but returned to watching Elaine, her gaze unreadable. Heat bloomed in her cheeks, and she looked away. What was it about that damn woman that got under her skin so easily?

There was a rustling of fabric as Lilibet walked over and kneeled before her. The corners of her mouth twitched, the forest green eyes bleeding to glowing amber. Elaine's mouth dropped as a pair of gossamer wings materialized from Lilibet's back.

"You're a fairy," she whispered.

Lilibet winked. "Astute, I see. Now, give me your palm."

She froze. "Why?"

"By the moon, you're even more suspicious than Aya," Lilibet replied. "I need a droplet of your blood—"

"No!" Elaine jumped up.

Everyone in the room froze. Blood roared in her ears. She pressed herself into the wall, wishing desperately that it might swallow her.

"I need a drop of blood to bind to the amulet. It won't hurt. I'm quite gentle." Lilibet said.

"I don't give a damn! No one is taking my blood. Not again," she snarled. Fire sparked through her fingers, and the others took a step back—all but Aya. She remained where she stood, unflinching.

As the blood roared in Elaine's ears, every dark memory of the temple she escaped crashed through her mind. She knew they must be confused by her outburst, but didn't trust herself to speak. A cord was pulled so tightly in her chest that at any moment it was about to snap.

Aya turned to Lilibet. "Do you have another option?"

Lilibet sighed. "Maybe. Come into my office. I might have something temporary until I figure out a better option." The fairy shot her a strange, almost irritated look before she vanished into her office, and Aya followed soon after.

Elaine stared at the door until some of the tension ebbed from her bones, and finally, the fire sank back into her skin.

"Elaine?" Tobias's voice brushed her mind, breaking her trance.

"I won't let anyone take my blood," she whispered. "That was how they were going to take my powers, you see. The day I escaped... the Grand Matron had me tied to a sacrificial table. She was going to slit my throat, drain me dry. That was the only part of me that was worth anything."

His face paled. "Elaine..."

"Blood is power, Tobias, and mine has more power than most."

CHAPTER 8

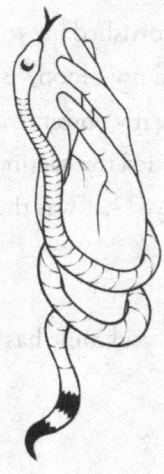

"**Y**OU ALWAYS HAVE A habit of collecting the most unusual guests," Lilibet said as she dug around the cluttered bookshelves.

"I didn't choose this one," she mumbled. A throbbing ache pulsed behind her eye. Dispelling the hellhound last night had left her more drained than she'd realized. All she wanted was to be back at the house, curled under the blankets, half-drunk on a bottle of honeyed wine.

"Then who did?" asked Lilibet conversationally.

Aya stiffened. "It's complicated."

"Well, at least things aren't dull with you," replied Lilibet, pausing for a moment in her rummaging. "Is this going to be a permanent arrangement?"

"It's..."

"Complicated?" Lilibet offered with a wan smile.

"Something like that."

As the rummaging continued, Aya's mind began to stray. Never in her life at Purgatory she imagined she'd be actively trying to keep a witch alive, especially one who bore Arcan's flame. The venom of her past pooled in her belly. How her kin would be ashamed of her.

"Aya," murmured Lilibet.

She started from her reverie and looked up across the room. Those wild eyes, so full of life, were quiet, almost sad, as they met Aya.

"What's wrong?"

"Do you miss them?"

"Who?"

Lilibet straightened up. "Your people."

The air rushed out of Aya as her gaze flew to the door, as if at any moment, the witch might burst through and Aya would be exposed. Even after so many years, old fears never fully left her, and the darkness stirred at the core of her soul, hissing softly.

"She can't hear us. I keep my offices sealed."

"Why are you asking?" Aya's voice was low, scraped raw, like a part of her hadn't been irreparably broken long ago.

"I miss mine."

Aya looked at her friend. A weariness pressed down upon her shoulders as if she carried an unbearable burden of sorrow.

"I'm filled with regret that I didn't leave with them when I had the chance. You're the only one who understands what it's like to be alone."

"We're not the same," whispered Aya. "Your people are still alive. Mine... aren't."

"Mine might as well be with all that stands between us," she replied, taking a step toward Aya. "If you could see your kin again, what price would you pay?"

"I will see my kin again."

Lilibet shook her head. "I'm not talking about death."

"Well, my people are *dead*, Lilibet. All of them. There aren't any fucking necromancers left. I'm the last, remember?" Aya hissed.

The room darkened in an instant, the shadows drawn to Aya as she stared her friend down. Whatever fire burned in Lilibet's eyes was snuffed out, and her friend returned to the shelves. The darkness eased as Aya pulled away, retreating into her mind.

When the roar in her mind eased, she let herself idly study over the cluttered shelves and messy desks. She didn't mean to snap at her friend, but the mention of her people—that unexpected dig at an old festering wound—tore her wide open.

Time, it seemed, hadn't healed that particular wound.

Lilibet gave a cry of delight as she held up a jar filled with polished stones, each reflecting the morning light to splash a rainbow against the wall. "I *knew* I hadn't run out of these. This should help shield your friend for a few days."

"That's it?" She didn't want to be caught in town with Elaine if a charm failed. If Honoria got a whiff of a witch in Aya's care, it'd be hell. She had to figure out her plan in detail first, and how she might use the witch to hurt the Grand Matron of Purgatory's witch temple. "Lil—"

"Oh, stop frowning! I'll figure out a charm without using the girl's blood. It won't be easy, though, or cheap." Lilibet dug out a red stone from the jar and set it aside. Aya watched in fascination as her friend grabbed a leather string from the shelves before setting both in an upturned palm.

"A bottle of Sabra's wine?"

Lilibet whispered into her palm. The thread suddenly wriggled to life, wrapping around the stone, forming a cradle. She lifted the pendant, glowing softly. "Make it three bottles."

"*Three?*" Sabra was going to kill her in her sleep.

"Is that an issue?" There was a teasing glimmer in Lilibet's eyes as they returned to their green glow.

Aya rubbed the back of her neck. "No, but if she stabs me, you're stitching me back up."

"That seems like a fair exchange." Lilibet held out the pendant.

She gingerly took it, surprised at how warm it felt against her skin. "How long do we have before it wears out?"

"See how it's glowing? Once it flickers, you have six hours before it's burned up. The number of days will depend on how much magic you're intending on masking. For now, she'll appear like a half-blood fairy." Lilibet headed for the door and paused with one hand on the handle. "Word of advice?"

"Hmm?" Aya was still studying the pendant.

"Keep that magic of hers hidden. If Honoria gets a glimpse, it'll be war. She'll want the witch and won't stop until she has her."

Irritation coiled in Aya's gut, a snake poised to strike. She straightened up, chafing against the implication. "I can handle Honoria."

Something unreadable flickered in Lilibet's eyes, and she took a step forward. After a beat, she shook her head and moved back. "Be careful, okay?"

Aya opened her mouth to say something, before thinking better of it. Elaine was a witch, which meant the answer ought to have been easy. The silence thickened to a lump in her throat, barring any reply, leaving her uneasy. Her gut twisted.

She never had her answer. Lilibet opened the door to the other room, leaving Aya to follow. Tobias was still at Elaine's side like a protective shadow. His gaze found hers, nudging her mind. Dropping a wall, she let his thoughts in.

Sabra saw Honoria's carriage approaching from a street away.

Aya frowned. *I'm on my way.*

Nodding, she held out a pendant to Elaine. "This will hide your magic for a few days until we find an alternative solution. It won't hurt you."

"And I should trust your word?" asked Elaine.

"I might be a monster, Elaine, but I don't break my word. If you want to be safe from the witch temple, then I suggest you wear it."

Elaine stared at her defiantly for a moment before relenting, and she slipped the pendant around her neck. As she lifted her hair out of the way, the bare skin on her neck was exposed. The moment was over as quickly as it began. Elaine's hands fell slowly to her side, meeting Aya's gaze. The air crackled between them.

"Aya, we should go," Tobias said, a note of urgency touching his voice.

She blinked and managed a nod before moving to the door, glancing back over her shoulder to Lilibet. "I'll have the wine delivered."

"I look forward to it," Lilibet said.

Aya paused for a moment on the bustling street, the warm sun bearing down on her. Her mind churned with tangled thoughts. What the hell was wrong with her? The glaring light reignited her throbbing headache and she rubbed her eyes, wincing. The sooner they locked down a job, the sooner she'd be able to get home and sink into her bed.

Sabra had been right. She should've rested another day. The spell had taken more out of her than she liked to admit.

The door creaked open, and the voice faded away, lost among the demons that haunted her mind. Tobias strode down the steps, Elaine close behind, her shoulders drawn in. The excitement she'd shown at seeing Purgatory was gone. A quiet, reserved girl stood in her place, looking about in caution, hunting for threats. Aya drew her focus back to Tobias, who watched her with a quizzical expression, his mouth a thin line. His eyes glazed over, refocusing a moment later.

"Honoria's rounding the corner now," he blurted out.

Aya studied Elaine. Would the amulet be enough?

A curse shot from her lips as she strode over to Elaine, who backed away but Aya's hand shot out, gently touching her jaw. Elaine glanced up, her eyes widening.

"Please, play along with this. I'll explain later," Aya said quickly.

"What—?"

Aya cut her off with a kiss.

At the softest touch of her lips against Elaine's, something thawed in Aya's heart. Tentative hands brushed her waist, sending shivers rippling across her skin in response. As Elaine moved closer and pressed her body against Aya's, heat roared to life, spilling out across her limbs.

"Miss Sinclair?" a thin, reedy voice drawled.

Aya drew back, as Elaine stared at her in silence. A multitude of replies spilled into her mouth, knotting together. She turned, sliding one arm around Elaine's waist. The girl was stiff but didn't pull away.

A tall woman greeted her, swathed in billowing white robes that somehow never got dirty, and accompanied by other finely dressed attendants. Black curls spilled down loose around her sharp-featured face and cutting brown eyes locked on her. The deeply tanned skin hinted at a life once spent in warmer, more exotic lands.

The Grand Matron of the only witch temple in Purgatory, a faithful follower of the Goddess Dianera, cut an imposing figure. For a woman devoted to a goddess of light and healing, there was little warm and tender about her. Many bowed or dipped their heads when Honoria passed. Only Aya stared, unyielding.

"Honoria, never a pleasure. How fairs your decrepit little hovel?" Aya felt Elaine stiffen to her touch. She tightened her grip on Elaine's hip in a warning and the girl relaxed a little, leaning in close.

Honoria flashed a frosty smile. "Busy. Some of us have honest work to do before Alantorei."

The woman spoke as if Alantorei, a celebration of Purgatory's birth hundreds of years ago by the spirits, was the sole responsibility of the witches. It wasn't; or, at least, it hadn't always been that way, but since Honoria came to power, that was all it seemed to be.

"Must be easy to do without a soul," Aya replied silkily.

Red stained Honoria's ears, her smile slipping for a second. Recovering quickly, her cold gaze slid to Elaine. "And who are you?"

"My lover, Ella," Aya said, pressing a kiss to the girl's forehead. "She's recently arrived in Purgatory and I'm showing her around. I must confess, though, I didn't imagine finding you in this part of town. It's a little far from your cave and the sun is shining today, which I thought you hated."

Tobias smothered a laugh beside her, his mind nudging hers. *Can you stop antagonizing her?*

Bore. She winked at him.

The priestesses beside her were stiff as statues, their hands twitching at the daggers on their hips. Aya wanted them to attack, give her reason to draw blood. She itched for the fight.

"I honestly have no idea what Calix sees in you," Honoria said waspishly.

"Someone who can actually get a job done, unlike others?"

As Honoria's cheeks reddened, a carriage rattled to a stop beside them and the door was thrown open. A well-dressed man with slicked black hair and piercing red eyes stepped out.

Aya had never been so glad for Calix's spies than at that moment. If he'd sent his man Alexios to collect them, it meant there must be a job he wanted them to do. Good.

"Alexios!" Aya pulled away from Elaine to embrace the vampire, who stooped down to meet her.

He grinned at her, fangs glinting. Pureblood vampires like him didn't have an issue with the sun, though the typical sleep schedule of the coven meant they were seldom out during the day. The smile slipped as he faced Honoria, bowing stiffly in greeting.

"Grand Matron."

"Alexios, what brings you here?" Honoria inquired.

"Not you, I'm afraid." He turned his attention to Aya and smiled. "Calix requests your presence. If you'd all like to join me, we'll be off."

Tobias swept past her, climbing up into the carriage, earning a chuckle from Alexios. Aya looked to Elaine, gesturing for her to head in. The others followed. None of them said goodbye to Honoria, who stood glaring at them until the door shut.

Tobias gently touched Aya's knee. "Sabra will meet us at Calix's home."

A sting of hurt pierced her heart. Sabra was distancing herself because of Elaine. Aya understood, but she'd hoped that her friend would trust her. Even with the changed circumstances, Elaine's position at the house would not be permanent. They just had to play it smart for a while and normality would return.

She managed a quiet nod, fidgeting with her hands in her lap.

Alexios tapped the roof and the carriage lurched forward. Once they were out of earshot, he grinned at her. "How is it you spend barely a few hours in town and you manage to bump into that woman?"

Aya sighed. "I honestly wish I could say it was intentional."

Tobias snorted. "You can't resist pissing the woman off whenever you see her, though."

A reply was poised on her lips when Alexios chuckled. "Well, Tobias, if you ever get bored with dodging death, you would have good employment at the mansion."

"A healer to a coven of vampires? Seems like a rather boring job, if you ask me," Tobias retorted.

As the two fell silent, their eyes locked, Aya had the distinct impression of another conversation playing out between the two. She knew Tobias often came into town for nights of pleasure. Had he been indulging in the enigmatic vampire?

She cleared her throat, and Alexios's gaze turned to her. "So, what's the job?"

The smile slipped. Alexios pulled the curtains shut across the window, leaving only a thin band of light piercing through. "There was an attempt on Calix's life last night."

The carriage chilled. Someone bold enough to attack the leader of the vampires? Calix was the very reason peace existed in Purgatory. His influence kept the vampires in check; his deals kept peace with the wolves; and whether by blackmail or his charm alone, he maintained order with the other council members.

Calix *was* Purgatory for all intents and purposes.

"Fuck."

Alexios nodded grimly. "Indeed, which is why he's asking for your help."

CHAPTER 9

T HE CARRIAGE JOLTED TO a stop and Alexios threw open the door. One by one, they filtered out. Elaine was last, staring at the gleaming stone steps and polished marble pillars holding up a grand entrance. Golden doors greeted them, intricately carved with a floral pattern.

She trailed behind everyone, drinking the sights in. Aya paused at the threshold of the mansion, waiting for her to catch up. The kiss flashed in her mind, the taste of Aya's mouth lingering on her lips.

"Are you coming?" Aya asked.

Elaine flushed and hurried forward. As she swept past Aya, the woman's scent brushed over her. She repressed a shiver and moved to Tobias's side. The wolf glanced at her, his brow furrowed.

"Is everything okay?"

No. All I can think of is that Aya kissed me. "Yes, of course. Why wouldn't it be?"

Portraits and vibrant tapestries adorned the towering walls, and a grand staircase dominated the cavernous foyer. Twin statues guarded the base of the stairs, a man and woman in warrior garb, a sword at their hips, carved of polished white stone. Their blank eyes stared back at her; an unflinching, fierce expression immortalized.

She stood stunned by the splendor, a far cry from the backwater inns and hovels she'd taken refuge in after escaping the temple. Her knowledge of vampires was somewhat limited. There had been few books about their kind in the temple archives and on fleeing, she'd done her best to steer clear of any vampire settlements because many of them followed the crueler of the seven gods; Vikra the God of Storms and Seas; and Arcan, the God of War and Darkness.

"Elaine?" Tobias called her name.

"Coming!" she replied, hurrying after the others.

They were led through twisting halls and another ornate door into a large room. One wall was dominated by an immense bookshelf laden with leather-bound books and curios. Several strikingly attractive men and women lay draped on lounges, reclining back with relaxed expressions, their eyes flickering with idle curiosity.

A man rose regally from one of the lounges. He had the same tanned skin as Alexios, differing only with his curly brown hair framing a softer, more youthful face. Golden eyes glimmered, brightening when he spied Aya. His figure was tall and lean, clad in a loose shirt and tight leather pants. To Elaine's surprise, she realized he wore no shoes as he swept over to where they waited.

Calix, she presumed. Aya stepped forward and the pair embraced. As he pulled away, he turned to Elaine. "And who is this gorgeous creature?"

"Elaine. She's the newest member of my team," said Aya.

She tried not to react at the mention of her real name. Unsure why Aya had revealed it here, she remained silent and didn't move, even as Calix circled her with an approving hum.

"Such a beautiful creature. A shame to have you hidden away in that dreary little house in the woods. If you decide you wish for finer things, you would be welcome here," he crooned.

Aya cleared her throat. "As fun as this is, you didn't summon us for a catch-up. Alexios said someone tried to kill you."

A shadow darkened Calix's face as he stepped back, his lip curling in disdain, his fangs peeking out. "A wolf, an exiled one to be precise. We had him imprisoned for a while to determine who sent him, but our methods proved fruitless. He escaped... and, well, things got a little out of hand."

"Your guards killed him?"

"Unfortunately. Leaving us without answers." Calix paused, frowning. "There have been attempts on my life before. That isn't new."

"So why was this different?" asked Aya.

Calix folded his arms across his chest. "This was *inside* my home. Somehow, this assassin got past my wards and into my private chambers. He knew far too much about my defenses."

Aya's brows lifted. "You think a council member might've ordered it?"

"Maybe. Beyond my own people—who I've already checked—only the councilors were ever permitted entry into my private wing, along with yourself and your kin."

"You never thought it might be me?" There was a note of surprise in Aya's voice, catching Elaine off guard.

Calix snorted. "You?"

"I'm flattered. I think." Aya paused.

"Oh, but there is more," drawled Calix. "Alpha Ryker paid me a visit soon after. Apparently, the idiot who attacked me was his bastard son. Not sure why he would have told me. Ignorance would have kept his secret buried."

Something flickered in Aya's face as she snorted softly. "Probably because he knew you'd seek me out, and I am nothing if not efficient at rooting out secrets. My guess is, the truth of their connection would be fairly easy to determine, so by going to you, he opens himself. Clears his name."

Calix inclined his head. "Yes, well, I think out of the whole council he's the least likely to want me dead."

Elaine frowned. "I thought wolves hated vampires."

At once, the pair appeared to remember they weren't the only ones in the room, and turned to her. Calix smiled, bemused by her statement.

"Outside Purgatory perhaps. Here things run a little differently."

Calix took a step forward, and Elaine didn't miss the way Aya moved closer to her. The Vampire Prince didn't miss it either, shooting Aya a grin. "Calm yourself. I'm only answering your curious little pet's question. Alas, I didn't call you here for a history lesson or a lesson on my own deals. My inner circle has demanded I seek protection beyond our coven and to determine *who* is behind this attack. Given the timing to Alantorei, they are rather nervous, as you would expect."

Aya made a hum of agreement. "An attack on you before such an event—or even during—wouldn't look good. Even if they don't kill you, that would undermine your influence."

"Indeed."

"Alantorei?" Elaine blurted out. "What's that?"

All eyes turned to her. Someone from the lounges snorted in amusement. When she realized all eyes were on her, she looked to Tobias for assurance, who began to explain, but Calix raised a hand. He stepped forward, a predatory grin lifting his mouth. "Alantorei, my dear, is the celebration of Purgatory's creation. There's a great deal of showing off from the various factions, and a way to assert who the true powers are in this place."

Aya stiffened, a strange expression tightening across her face. What it meant, Elaine didn't know, and she quickly looked away before Aya caught her staring.

"I see," she said softly.

Calix glanced at Aya. "Have you taught her anything of this place?"

"It's a work in progress," Aya said tightly.

"And you *missed* explaining Alantorei?"

"*Calix,* the job."

71

The vampires tittered. Calix snapped his fingers, the others rising to their feet and shuffling out of the room. When the door had shut, he strode to the closest lounge and leaned against the armrest, crossing his arms across his broad chest.

"As I mentioned, there are two aspects to this job. One, I want protection during the usual array of events I throw every year. Second, I want to find out who is after me. Either by torturing any assailants for information or by your rather mysterious methods of investigations." Calix idly inspected his nails; a steady air of confidence and power rolling off him.

Aya whistled softly. "That's a little more than the usual job."

"I'll triple your usual fee."

Elaine didn't know what that was, but from Aya's sharp gaze and lifted a brow, it must've been a lot. Even Tobias's jaw dropped. Her own heart, still racing, thumped a little harder. Would one job be enough for her to buy a safe place to stay in Purgatory?

Aya eyed Tobias, a silent conversation playing out between them, before that gaze flicked to Elaine. A strange pressure nudged her mind and a voice whispered to her, *this will be a dangerous job. You can say no.*

Elaine kept her face from showing her shock before sending back. *I can do this.*

Satisfied with the answer, Aya closed her eyes and stood, tapping her thumbs together as if in deep thought. An impatient sigh came from Calix.

"We will take the job. Do you still have the body?" Aya asked.

"Downstairs. My people were examining it for clues, but they found nothing."

Aya smiled. The chilling touch sent shivers down Elaine's spine. "Perhaps not. But they're not me."

• • • • • • • • • •

Downstairs, the air was bitterly cold and stank of death. A sour, metallic stench filled her nostrils, twisting Elaine's stomach into knots. Even Tobias's nose wrinkled at the stench as Alexios led them through a long rectangular stone room. Rows of empty stone slabs flanked the open path down the middle. Toward the rear of the room, two veiled women tended to a body. One peeled back a shroud while the other gently poured a little vial of a red liquid into the mouth of the corpse.

"You've never seen someone turned into a vampire before, have you?" Tobias whispered in Elaine's ear.

"I heard it's an incredibly private process." One of the women lifted their head, sensing her interest, so she looked away, focusing on Alexios's broad back.

Tobias made a hum of approval. "It is, which is the mark of trust Calix gives Aya and, by extension, the rest of us. Outsiders aren't normally allowed down here."

At the last table, a young man was laid out. His ashen skin had a faint blue touch to it, and his throat was opened in a bloodied smile. All of his clothes had been removed. It wasn't the first time she'd seen someone naked or dead, but the sight was still unnerving.

Aya, however, moved forward without flinching and began inspecting the body.

Elaine leaned in close to Tobias. "What's she looking for?"

"Watch her and see if you can tell me."

Aya paused at the torso, pressed one hand against the skin, and shut her eyes. Dark shadows reached for her, the same way they had at the house. After a few minutes, they retreated and her hand fell away. The studious inspection continued, pausing over the wrists, neck, and even at the base of the feet. When she finished, she stepped back from the table, confusion pinching her face.

Elaine realized what Aya had been checking for. "She's looking for any signs of demonic possession or enchantments."

"Good. What does the absence of both tell us?"

She was being tested. Pausing, she considered the body and what hadn't been found. From Aya's careful checks, Elaine realized Aya had been looking for marks concealed by spells. How she might've detected them when Calix's people had supposedly checked, Elaine didn't know...

"Nothing concrete. I'm not experienced with demonic possession, having only seen it a few times. As for enchantments, there still *might* be signs. I wonder though..."

She strode forward. This was a matter of proving herself and earning the money she needed for independence. Aya looked up as she neared, silent as Elaine leaned over to peer inside the dead man's mouth.

"What do you see?" Aya asked, her voice soft and curious.

"He's in good health and there's no sign of babbith root, which can be used to coerce." She frowned. "The rest of the body is in good condition, save for the shredded throat, and he's well-fed. There are no scars suggesting he's a soldier or mercenary. Even his hair shows signs of regular grooming. He looks... ordinary."

Any hope she had that he might've been drugged into coercion were dashed.

Aya turned to Alexios. "I've seen enough. Tell me everything you know about him and I'll start making inquiries."

Alexios nodded. "My notes are upstairs. There's not much, I'm afraid. Even Ryker could only afford a few details. Apparently, despite the kid being his son, the bastard kept him at a distance. Likely watching to ensure he didn't spill who his father was."

"I'll let you know if I find anything. When is the first event he wants us to work?"

"The Carmine Ball, two nights from now."

"We'll be there. Don't worry about sending through any layout drawings of the area. I have all that I need."

Alexios snorted. "Naturally. Is there anything you don't have?"

Aya grinned back. "Your heart?"

"If only you enjoyed the company of men, and I women," he said wistfully. With a shrug, he seemed to dismiss the thought. "Do you have a gown for the event?"

A twinkle of wicked delight sparked in Aya's eyes. "Don't worry about us. We'll all be dressed to kill."

Elaine had a feeling the wording wasn't an accident.

CHAPTER 10

THAT EVENING, BACK IN the living room, Tobias appeared
dressed in a loose shirt, breeches, and barefoot. A glimmer of
excitement shone in his jewel-amber eyes, and she wondered idly if
he had that same look in his wolf form.

"Is everything okay?" Elaine asked.

"Aya wants me to test you with a few things before we decide on
your role for the job. Come with me."

Curious, she trailed after him outside. The crackling fire snuffed
out as she passed through the door. Another oddity about the
strange house. The rooms came to life whenever one of them entered. Tobias didn't wait for her as he strode into the woods, vanishing momentarily in the darkness. She hurried after him, plunging in

blindly before her eyes adjusted. Wisps of silver light pierced the veil of leaves, brushing over Tobias's broad shoulders and tousled hair as he walked.

Their footsteps crunched softly over the leaf litter, the only sign of life as a sharp wind whispered through the trees, brushing over her skin. The warmth of the day had long since been sapped from the air, leaving a bitter chill behind.

She was regretting not grabbing her cloak before heading out. Her thin jacket barely kept the icy needles from lancing through her. Even her toes were quickly feeling numb from the cold. She inhaled, calling on her fire magic, and pushed it through her veins. A steady heat filled her, devouring the chill and ache in her bones.

I give thanks to Arcan; she whispered to the sky as they stopped in a clearing. He might be a God of War and Darkness, but his source of magic was fire. A handy ability when traversing frosty climates.

A jewel-lit sky glittered above. Her heart fluttered. It had been so damn long since she'd been able to stop and simply appreciate the beauty of the stars. Being on the run for years meant she'd never had the chance. All her focus had been on survival.

"Elaine," Tobias called.

She pulled her attention away. Tobias stood in front of her, an outstretched hand holding a small dagger. The first test. She took the blade, flexing her fingers around the hilt. It was lighter than she'd expected.

"You showed a keen eye today, but I want to start with your fighting skills. Have you had any training before?"

"No, but I've been in enough scraps to have picked up a few things. What do you want me to do?"

"Draw blood."

Tobias shot forward.

She jumped out of the way with a yelp, scrambling to find her feet as he came at her in a flurry of blows. He had no dagger, but she knew one blow from his fists was guaranteed to hurt. She tightened her grip, pivoting and ducking out of the way. He was fast, but she was touched by the gods and was no ordinary witch.

Rivulets of sweat ran down the side of her face as heavy breaths racked her body. She let him get in close before spinning around and thrusting the blade forward. He jumped out of the way; the metal slicing through the air.

"Good, but still no blood," he taunted, and lifted a hand, beckoning her closer. "Again."

She would never get in close enough to land a blow, let alone keep up the speed for long. Already her strength was rapidly dwindling. She didn't want to call on any of the other talents coursing through her veins. No, she had to do it without them, and by Arcan's grace, she was going to. And she was going to do it without magic to prove a point.

As he rushed at her again, she dropped low, sweeping her leg to trip him. He leaped and landed behind her. In a blink, he had his arms around her waist, pinning her to his chest. One claw pressed against the nape. A thin trickle of blood ran down her skin.

"Got you."

She let a grin pull at her mouth. "Do you?"

"What—"

A sickening crunch filled the air as she thrust her head back onto his nose. The grip on her loosened. She tore out of his grasp, scrambling to get some distance. A low chuckle rumbled behind her as she faced him, watching as he staggered to his feet. His mouth was pulled into a broad smile.

"Still no blood."

"Oh? Are you sure about that?" Her gaze dropped to his forearm and the tiny cut on his arm. A tiny droplet of blood welled on the wound. "That looks red to me."

He lifted his arm, the wound already healing. "Guess you were right about being a scrappy fighter. Let's see what else you can do."

· · · • • • • · · ·

He tested her with hand-to-hand combat, which had her on her ass more times than she liked. Bruises already welted along her skin as they moved on to sparring with sticks. After determining she sucked at that, she was blindfolded and they sparred a little longer. That session was short-lived once she was pinned three times in a row.

Every part of her hissed and complained. She clenched her jaw, refusing to speak up. If she was to make Purgatory her home, she had to prove herself. Through sheer stubbornness, she pushed on until Tobias called for a break. Sweat dripped from his face and there was a red sheen on his cheeks, much to her delight.

She sat down, taking a moment to catch her breath.

"You're not as bad as I thought you'd be," he said with a smile. "Sabra put money on you being worse."

"And Aya?" Heat bloomed on her cheeks and she bit her tongue, wishing she could yank the words back in.

He shrugged. "Aya doesn't make bets."

She had no idea what to make of that, so instead steered the conversation to safer ground. "What else did you want to see?"

"Your fire. How much work have you done with it?"

"Not much. I tried to use it as little as possible. Attracted the wrong kind of attention." She tried to keep the steadiness to her voice, even as her heart raced.

"Hunters?"

Her brow lifted. "You know of Hunters?"

"A few folks have come to Purgatory over the years, told stories about the Hunters of Vesmir. Nasty folks employed by the royal family to hunt down criminals and monsters." Tobias paused, tilting his head. "You don't strike me as either."

She laughed. "I think I'd surprise you."

"You already have. How long were you on the run?"

The smile slipped from her face. "I ran when I was sixteen—the year I was to be sacrificed and my power handed over to the crown prince of Vesmir. I am... oh, I must be twenty-four now? Maybe twenty-five."

"And you avoided the Hunters all that time?"

"I made them think I was dead for a time, which bought me a year or two at first; I was safe for a little while in a remote fishing village, had friends and a home of sorts." Her mind darkened at the memory long buried, and old venom welled in her chest. "Nothing good lasts forever and I was exposed. After that, I ran, barely keeping ahead of them. Every so often, I was able to find somewhere they couldn't find but..."

"They always found you?"

"In the end." She shook off the memory. "It doesn't matter anymore. I'm here."

A heavy silence fell between them, broken when Tobias appeared at her side. "You haven't asked about the kiss. I thought you might want to talk about it?"

The memory burst into her mind like a flash of lightning, bringing a blush to her cheeks. She leaned forward, wrapping her arms around her legs, resting her chin on her knees. Around Tobias, she felt safe enough to let her guard down and talk, but the kiss still left her full of emotions she was scared to examine.

"Is there anything to say?"

A heavy exhale sounded beside her. "She did it to protect you from Honoria."

"She hates witches, and hates me," she said pointedly. "So why protect me?"

No one had wanted to do that for her for years. All anyone had ever shown her was betrayal.

He remained silent for a moment. When she glanced at him, she saw he was frowning. "She was asked to keep you safe."

"By *who*?"

"The spirits." Before she could answer, he continued on, "don't ask why. They didn't explain. It seems they moved you inside our wards when you were out cold, right where you'd be found, then left a note for Aya to protect you."

The spirits had never intervened in affairs in Purgatory before. They were so rare outside of Purgatory, mere stories it felt like. She shifted restlessly on the balls of her feet. In her experience, when someone put that much interest in a stranger, it was never for a selfless reason.

"And that will keep Sabra from ripping my throat out?" She didn't miss the way the blue-skinned demon looked at her, and knew a threat when she saw one. "Or you?"

"You believe I would harm you?" She didn't miss the hurt in his voice and as she opened her mouth to explain, he raised a hand, silencing her. "It's okay. I'm used to dealing with the prickly sort. As for Sabra, she won't act against Aya...as for *why,* that's not my story to tell. For now, consider me your friend."

"Tobias, you should know—"

"You prefer the company of a woman?" He winked at her.

Her ears turned red. "Um, yes. Well, I have enjoyed men and women but how did you—?"

"The kiss... and how you stare at Aya. I won't say how foolish it is and that it will probably lead to heartbreak since I am a rather poor example to follow," he replied ruefully and rose to his feet, holding a hand out to her.

She slid her hand into his, playing over his words when she asked, "and who has your attention that makes you so bad?"

"One who has no idea how much power he has over me," he said with a rueful smile. "Anyway, that is enough for tonight. Let's head back."

They fell into a companionable silence on the return trek. The wind whipped up, rustling the leaves into a musical. The lingering heat from the training kept the chill at bay, though she was feeling the aches build in her body. Luckily, Dianera's healing magic meant she would recover fairly quickly. There would be no sign that she'd even sparred by tomorrow if she was lucky.

By the time the house emerged from the shadows, she was ready for bed. An amber glow lit from the living room windows. Had both Aya and Sabra returned?

Tobias stopped dead at the tree line, his jaw twitching, and his hands curled into fists.

"What is it?" she asked.

He stalked forward. "What the hell is that bastard doing here?" he seethed, his voice dripping with venom.

Who? She wanted to ask, but he was already striding toward the door and yanked it open so brutally that the hinges shrieked in protest.

She ducked in behind him. The warm air washed over her, the smell of herbs and spices filling her lungs... and another scent. Sour. Her nose wrinkled as she took in the scene in the living room.

Sabra hovered in the shadows in one corner, her hand resting on the hilt of her sword. Aya reclined in a chair, her hard gaze locked on the strange male seated across from her. He looked to be in his early forties, handsome, with thick muscles straining against a sleeveless tunic. His hair was long and tied back from his face, showing off a piercing set of amber eyes.

Tobias stood glaring with waves of hatred rolling off him.

"Oh good. Look who's arrived," Sabra sang.

A low growl rumbled from Tobias's chest as he advanced toward the stranger. All traces of the kind healer had vanished. "What the fuck are you doing here?"

The man sneered. "Is that how you greet your alpha?"

"You're not my alpha. You threw me out of the pack, remember?" Tobias snarled.

Elaine remembered Calix mentioning an alpha named Ryker. She inched closer to Tobias, nearly gasping as she caught sight of his eyes glowing gold. Instinctively, she reached for him, an action that wasn't missed by the alpha.

"I thought your tastes were elsewhere," Ryker crooned.

Before Tobias could speak, Elaine moved in front and glared. "Leave Tobias alone."

"Fiery little thing, aren't you? You don't know who I am, do you?" He rose to his feet. "I am Alpha Eddard Ryker of the Purgatory wolf pack and council member."

Aya snorted into her mug. "Only because Tobias stepped down as alpha."

Ryker spun to her. "I came to speak to you about the job you've taken, not to rehash the past."

"You're not my employer. I owe you nothing, and besides, the wolf wasn't one of yours. Which is why I assume you're here," said Aya.

Elaine's mind was still wheeling from the fact that Tobias was a god damn alpha wolf. Even if he didn't hold the position, that power still burned in his veins. Was it because he preferred men? Or had he stepped down and been kicked out for another reason?

"Clarion Ryker was my *son*."

The room fell silent, broken only by the crackling of the fire. The son of the alpha, an exiled wolf, and a failed assassin? From Aya's eerily still posture, she hadn't seen it coming, either. Nor Tobias, who inhaled sharply behind her.

"Oh, we were informed." Aya peered at him over her mug. "That the noble alpha had a bastard son. Did your wife know?"

Ryker nodded slowly, a touch of grief dimming the fire in his eyes. His shoulders dropped. Elaine wasn't sure how much of this was sincere or whether the alpha was merely acting the part of the grieving father.

"She knew... right before she passed."

"And the mother of the boy?" Aya probed.

"His mother was human. The affair was brief. That isn't why I am here. I believe someone made my son do this." Ryker stared intently at Aya. "The last time we spoke he told me he'd found a human girl he loved and was planning to leave Purgatory with her. Apparently, he found a way to do so. He had no reason to attack Calix and I can assure you, this was not done on my account."

Aya, setting her mug down. "So, you want us to clear your son's name? I spoke to Alexios. He tried to stab Calix in his bed. I found no demonic marks or enchantments, forcing him to do it."

"He might have been coerced in another way," said Ryker, a note of desperation in his voice.

"You could be wrong about your son."

"I'm not wrong about this," Ryker insisted.

"Perhaps." Aya rubbed her eyes and yawned. "It's late. One question before you go. The name of the girl?"

"Yrene Caster. She lives in the Red Thorn Refuge according to my men." Ryker stood and strode for the door. For a moment, he glanced back as if he had something more to say. Then, his face shuttered and he swept outside without another word.

The door shut with a rattling clink.

Aya sighed heavily. "I'll head out this evening. Might be worth making some inquiries about this bastard son of his."

Tobias hissed. "We're going to do as he said?"

One brow lifted, but Elaine had the distinct impression that Aya had seen enough of Tobias's fury to show no fear of it. "I'm making *inquiries*. Besides, this job is for Calix and his money. I, for one, would rather enjoy having some facts about all of this—wouldn't you?"

Tobias released a low growl and stalked upstairs with Sabra trailing up after him. The coy smile dropped from Aya's lips and her gaze darkened, landing on Elaine. In a flash, Aya loomed over her, the shadows pulling in around them both.

"Never do that again. Getting lippy with an alpha is not a wise move."

"Not for you, though?" Elaine returned sharply.

Aya leaned closer, her eyes gleaming with power. "No one fucks with a monster like me."

CHAPTER 11

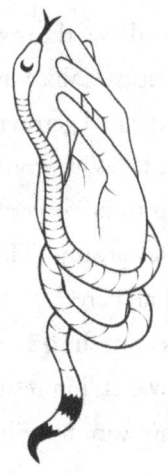

THE REFUGE RYKER HAD mentioned appeared much the same as the others on the outskirts of the Inner District. They functioned as homes for new arrivals, who were told they were kind places, full of kind people who did kind things or those otherwise unattached to any sect within Purgatory.

It was all a fucking lie, and Aya fought the urge to burn every single one to the gods' damned ground. Were it not for the complete shit storm that the act would've created for her, she might've gone through it. Sabra certainly wouldn't have stopped her, and as her old friend gazed upon the towering brick structure, Aya sensed a trickle of destructive ideas whisper through their bond.

"Don't tempt me," she growled.

"You can't say it wouldn't be entertaining," Sabra ventured with a dry smile.

Aya rolled her eyes.

A gloomy gray sky stretched over the town, the distant clouds dark with the promise of rain. At least Calix would keep his party indoors. The man was fastidious and hated getting wet.

Sabra shrugged and asked, "Why would the girl still be here? If my lover was caught trying to kill one of the most powerful men in Purgatory, I wouldn't stick around. Hell, even the Dusk Quarter would be a better option than here."

Aya was inclined to agree, but she'd spoken to some ghosts in the night, confirming the girl was still in residence. "Let's get this over and done with, okay? I don't want to be here any longer than I have to."

Aya approached the door, rapping her knuckles against the door she wanted so desperately to destroy. The door swung open with a keening groan. A scowling woman filled the doorway, swathed in robes that fueled Aya's urge to burn the building to the ground.

"Miss Sinclair, Miss Rook. What brings you to this refuge?" The woman kept one hand on the doorframe, blocking the way. A shadowy aura glowed around her skin—fresh death.

A chill stole into Aya's gut, and she swallowed the lump that suddenly made its way to her throat.

"We're looking for a human, Yrene Caster. I heard she was living here."

A shadow flickered in the woman's gray eyes, her grip tightening on the door frame for a moment. An empty smile lifted her withered mouth. "I'm afraid the girl passed a few hours ago. The poor thing went into labor, but it wasn't a good birth. The little one died as well. Terrible business."

Blood roared in Aya's ears. The darkness pushed up, snarling and snapping, demanding to rip the woman apart. There was no remorse in that leathery face. Any humanity had long ago shriveled up.

Dammit.

Sabra sighed. "What a shame. Oh well, I guess our business is concluded. Come on, Aya. We're done here."

Aya stared at the woman, barely containing her anger. Heat warmed her cheeks, reaching up and staining her ears. Black bled into her eyes, and the shadows pulled in around her. All her wrath surged up from the depths of her soul. She wanted to rip the woman apart and make her suffer, as she no doubt made the souls inside suffer.

The woman shrank back, dread paling her face before she hurriedly slammed the door shut. Sabra's hand settled on her arm. Aya wrenched away, striding down the street. Red hot fury tore through her, shredding her control by the second. All she had to do was turn around and surrender to the dark power within.

It'd be so damn *easy.*

Footsteps caught her up. "Focus on the mission, Aya," Sabra murmured.

••••••••

Predictably, Calix had sent outfits ahead, even though they hadn't been requested. Aya knew, without looking, that they'd all fit—even the one that was signed for Elaine. The man had an eye for detail, and little escaped his attention.

The red boxes, tied off with shimmering red ribbons, sat on the dining table when she returned to the house. As she opened a box bearing her name, Tobias emerged from his office. The anger from last night still lingered in his tense shoulders and pinched expression, as though he were attempting to repress some violent urges.

He forced a smile that didn't quite touch his eyes as he approached. "These arrived about an hour ago. I met Calix's courier at the border before you panic about intruders," he said, opening one of the boxes. "I'm guessing by your 'I want to set fire to someone' expression that the chat at the refuge didn't go well."

Sabra swept past, carrying her gown, and answered. "You could say that. The girl went into labor early this morning. Neither made it."

"That's *convenient*. Is it true?" Tobias replied.

Aya remembered the aura of death that had rolled off the woman. It could've been a lie, a way to keep her out, but her gut said no. She lifted out a shimmering red silk dress. "I'll make inquiries with a few friends tonight to be sure, but they were rather certain the girl was alive when they checked."

"A dead end," Tobias said with a sigh. "Let's hope this party yields some answers. This reminds me... about Elaine. What role do you want her to play? She proved capable with hand-to-hand combat and decent enough with her magic."

"I want her with you, watching the perimeter. The council will probably all be in attendance tonight, and the last thing I want is Honoria getting too close," Aya murmured. She lifted the dress, letting the silken material spill down. As much as she wanted to hate it, Calix had impeccable taste, and knowing the smug bastard, it'd fit like a glove too.

Sabra shot her a withering look. "If you ask me, we should hand her over to Honoria."

"Even if there wasn't the matter of the letter, would you really want to hand her one of the strongest witches alive? We might as well give Honoria our heads, too," Aya said, folding the dress back up. She lifted the box. "You will be with me at Calix's side tonight. Get changed early. We'll head off in an hour to make all the preparations for the party." At the bottom of the stairs, she half-turned back, looking at Tobias. "Let Elaine know—oh, and Tobias?"

"Yes?"

"I'm trusting you to keep an eye on her."

Tobias stared back, unperturbed. "Consider it done, but will you be okay?"

"Me?"

"About Mari—"

"I'll handle her," she replied curtly.

Up in her room, she set the box on the side table and sat on her bed, pressing her head into her palms. Dappled gray light spilled in through the window, too bright for her liking but she didn't have the strength to shut it. Her mind was focused on the looming party. It should be an easy job tonight. All they had to do was to keep Calix alive. It wasn't like he was helpless. The man was one of the oldest vampires in Purgatory, lethal in his own right.

She eyed the box still tied with red ribbon. It was only for one night. She had survived worse. And if Marisol was there, well, she'd make sure it wasn't an issue. Dark laughter bubbled up from the depth of her broken soul, spilling out into the room.

What could go wrong?

• • • • • • • • • •

The gown had been designed with a goal in mind. The delicate red material clung to Aya's body, with two thigh-high slits allowing easy movement. The bodice hugged enough to support her, but not enough to hinder movement. Around her waist, she wore a golden belt with two sheaths for her daggers. An additional gold webbing slid over the dress, with a scabbard for a sword.

At Calix's side as his shadow, no one would mistake what she was. She grabbed her sword from her wall, slid it into place, and headed downstairs. Tobias was fiddling with his tunic, the blood-red fabric tight over his muscled frame. He looked oddly absurd in the finery, cursing as he tried to secure the buttons on his cuffs.

"Here, let me," she said, reaching to help.

He huffed but didn't fight her as she sorted out his cuffs. Satisfied, she stood back to inspect the rest of his attire. Unlike her, he carried no weapons. Tobias disliked using swords and only tolerated wielding daggers occasionally, after some intense nagging on her part. The man was sometimes frustrating, but she loved him all the same.

Satisfied that nothing else was out of place, she stepped back, grinning at his glowering expression. "You look..."

"Like a damn bird."

"A very pretty bird though. Can you move?"

He stretched out his arms in response, squatted down, and stood back up. "Easy enough, but I will shift the second I have to. Calix shouldn't have wasted his money."

A snort of laughter came from the stairs. Sabra emerged, sweeping forward in a shimmering golden gown that clung to her frame. Like Aya's dress, it allowed easy movement, even mirroring the webbing for the sword on her back.

"Well, I for one am not complaining about this." Sabra twirled with a conspiratorial grin. "This is the nicest thing I've worn in such a long time. He must have spent a pretty penny."

Sabra was right. The clothes alone would nearly account for their standard fee. Was that his way of trying to buy their loyalty or perhaps he had some other angle?

Aya stood lost in her thoughts until Tobias's sharp gasp of surprise broke through. She followed his gaze and realized Elaine had appeared. Her stomach flipped without warning, and her mouth felt suddenly dry.

A witch. Remember that.

Her heart stopped as she drank in the shimmering green dress, cut like her own, striking against the pale skin and long, unbound glossy red curls. Intricate swirling tattoos wrapped around the girl's arms, vanishing beneath the dress. Aya had glimpsed witch tattoos before, but those on Elaine stretched over more skin than she'd expected. The marks of six gods on her skin.

"Is it possible to hide these?" Elaine asked.

"Uh... Sab?" Aya glanced at her friend, whose smile had fallen away. "Could you...?"

Sabra's lip curled, the task distasteful, but said nothing as she strode over to the waiting girl. The exchange couldn't have looked any more awkward as Sabra brushed a finger over Elaine's arms. Aya didn't miss the tension in Tobias's body or the way she felt her hand drop to her dagger. Sabra stepped away, the tattoos concealed beneath a glamour.

"Done." Sabra spun around, shooting her a frosty glare before she stalked outside. The door slammed with a rattling thump.

Finally, Aya found her voice. "Let's head off. Best not keep the Vampire Prince waiting."

CHAPTER 12

E LAINE TRIED NOT TO stare at the sheer wealth that assailed
every sense as they wandered through Calix's mansion. Open
doors offered glimpses into opulently furnished rooms or galleries
adorned with portraits. In some vampires draped lazily on lounges,
swathed in shimmering silks and flimsy robes. Statues of naked men
and women, of warriors and deities, flanked the hallways, their polished eyes watching the visitor's every move.

By the time they arrived at the ballroom, she was itching to return
to the house. Marble pillars stood on either side of the large, rectangular chamber, holding up an arched roof. A row of windows ran
down the middle of the ceiling, bright sunlight spilling through, illuminating the polished white stone floor. Flecks of crystal reflected

like thousands of glittering gems. A dais was at one end, holding a single golden throne.

It was a lavish display of wealth. Elaine's gut twisted.

"Did you... is that bigger?" Aya asked incredulously, pointing to the dais. "Did you honestly get a bigger bloody throne for this party?"

"It's lovely, isn't it?" Calix preened.

Elaine didn't think it was possible for his smile to be any brighter.

"It's certainly *something*," Aya drawled.

"The main function will be held here. My men have also been instructed to watch for anyone wandering the halls." Calix paused, frowning. "Must I stay in the chair the whole night?"

Aya snorted. "Not all night, no. But if you want to stay safe, limit your movements unless we're nearby. Sabra will have a thin ward around the dais so no poisonous darts can get through. She'll lower it whenever someone is permitted to approach. As I explained earlier, Calix, this is to keep you safe. Much as I hate to inflate your ego, you are the reason this place enjoys peace. Fuck what the council thinks. You *are* the Prince of Purgatory."

Elaine turned from them, examining the room. Though she knew she was running perimeter work with Tobias, which meant they would be far from the main festivities, she wondered what the party would be like tonight. Tobias said it would be filled with the most powerful of Purgatory's residents, none of whom could be trusted.

She was lost in thought when the ballroom doors swung open with a heavy groan. Soft clicking footfalls greeted her ears. A woman swept in, shadowed by two servants. She wore an emerald green gown that accentuated her golden-brown skin and hourglass figure. Glossy obsidian curls spilled over one shoulder, interwoven with sparkling gems. Elaine found it hard to tear her eyes away from the woman's beautiful face with its high cheekbones and piercing amber eyes.

"Oh, shit," Tobias muttered.

She glanced at him. "Who is it?"

"Marisol, the council representative of the humans in Purgatory... and Aya's ex-lover." Tobias opened his mouth to say something else, but Marisol had approached, bowing slightly to Calix before her gaze slid to Aya. "This should be interesting."

"Why?"

Tobias hesitated. "It's... complicated."

The usual cockiness Aya displayed vanished. For a split second, a flash of something sparked in her eyes that to Elaine, almost looked like...sadness. It disappeared behind an unreadable mask, though she didn't miss the tension ratcheting Aya's body to near stillness.

"Councilor Marisol," Calix said, his sweet voice dripping with polite courtesy.

"Councilor Calix, you've been ignoring my missives and you missed the last meeting." Marisol's practiced smile didn't quite reach her eyes; and as her gaze flicked to Aya, her face hardened. "I see he's employed your services." She turned to Calix. "You should've come to us. We protect our own."

Aya threw her head back and laughed. "Jealous, Marisol?"

Marisol's lips tightened almost imperceptibly, and Elaine knew the barb in Aya's words had hit their mark. "Of *you?* Hardly."

The air thickened with tension, though Calix appeared merely amused by the conversation as it unfolded. His fangs glinted through a barely contained smile.

Marisol bristled. "I don't have time for this." She turned to Calix, her anger bleeding away as if it had never been there at all. "There is some business we must discuss. Might we talk now?"

Calix rolled his eyes. "You're ruining all my fun, but very well, let us talk."

The pair departed, and Elaine released a quiet sigh. So, that was the kind of woman Aya liked?

Aya whistled softly.

Elaine shot a glance at her. The quiet fury that had been there moments before had been replaced by a smile.

"Fucking hell. I let that viper into my bed? I permit you all to slap me if I ever dabble in something like that again."

"Even me?" Elaine murmured.

Aya's gaze turned to her, lingering until it felt like they were the only two people in the room. Her heart flipped dangerously in her chest. The corner of Aya's mouth twitched.

"Even you."

•••••••••

The party was well underway by the time the sun dipped beyond the horizon, plunging Purgatory into darkness. Soft music drifted through the halls as Elaine walked with Tobias on their patrol. They passed several guards roaming the hallways and saw others stationed at the entrance of each room. It appeared Calix was taking no chances.

While normally one to enjoy the silence, a jittery feeling clawed at her from the inside. Twice she had to press her palms into her side to stop herself from fiddling with her dress. She shot a sideways glance at Tobias, but he was a picture of calm.

When they rounded yet *another* corner, she sighed. The way they had planned the job and spoken about it, she'd expected something more, well, *interesting*. Not that she was craving something violent or dangerous to happen, but this, this was ... boring. She released a heavy sigh.

"What do you think of Marisol?" Tobias's voice broke her wandering thoughts.

Her eyes widened one brow lifting. "You don't say a word for ages and *that's* what you start with?"

He snorted, his mouth twitching, and she realized she was being tested. Had she failed? Or was his grin a good sign? When he didn't answer, the restlessness returned, pawing at her to ask him a question, to fill the silence.

"Marisol used to be one of us," he said, shaking his head, as if clearing a memory away. "She lived with us for a few months too, and Aya was happier than I'd seen in ages but her love made her blind."

"To what?"

"Marisol." He paused, turning to her. "She was always ambitious, fierce. It's what first attracted Aya to her, but I think she believed her love might temper Marisol's hunger. To her credit, Marisol *tried* to be content, but the house was too small, and the jobs were not important enough. In the end, she wrote a note saying she said she wanted to make a difference in Purgatory and felt like she couldn't do that with us. She left without even saying goodbye. It broke Aya."

"Why are you telling me this?"

Tobias smirked. "I've seen the way you two stare at each other when you think neither of you is watching the other."

Elaine shook her head. "I don't look at her and I rather think I'm *not* her type."

Tobias held her gaze. "You might be surprised."

"Perhaps when the world ends," she muttered.

"Stranger things have happened. After all, a spirit tasked Aya with protecting you."

Since her arrival at the house, she'd tried to piece together why a spirit might have any interest in her. Spirits were the children of Toriel, the Goddess of Nature and Spirits. Was this Toriel's way of tempting Elaine to embrace the goddess's tattoo?

"Why me?" she finally asked.

Tobias shrugged. "Who can say? The deal Aya struck which created that debt to the spirits was made years ago. It hadn't been called in until now."

"I don't understand. What debt?"

His mouth opened to reply when he stopped, and his gaze alighted on something ahead. She followed it to an open door, from where a cool breeze kissed her skin.

"Tobias—"

He swept into the room. "Do you smell that?"

She followed him, inhaling deeply as she entered. At first, all she caught were the earthy notes of the outside forest... but closing her eyes, she stilled. Recognition stirred in her mind and she spun back to the door. It slammed shut with a deafening bang, and the window dropped.

"Fuck! They're trying to separate us from the others. There's going to be another attempt." Tobias raised his fist to pound the door.

She dashed forward, snatching his hand back. "Don't! It's enchanted."

His jaw ticked, but he lowered his hand and stepped back. "Can you break it?"

She raised a palm to the ward now shimmering invisibly over the wood like a second skin. It was a basic shield spell, the kind any novice witch might conjure. It felt nothing like the ones Sabra wove, which were layers upon layers of ancient demonic magic.

Her eyes flickered open. "Maybe. Move back... just in case."

"Don't hurt yourself."

She walked closer, pulling her hand back to a fist. Heat welled in her chest, a growing storm pushing down to her hands. Tiny sparks leaped across her skin—

And she drove her fist into the ward.

CHAPTER 13

THE WARD SHATTERED INTO a thousand shards of light as her fist plowed through into the door, blowing it right off the hinges. It crashed into the opposite wall, splintering in half before it hit the ground. Silence claimed the air for a moment, and Elaine tried to still her rapidly beating heart. Threads of magic sparked and crackled over her knuckles, dancing over her skin. As she lowered her hand, still trembling from the blow, she stumbled into the hall.

"We have to warn the others," she said, even as her mind still whirled from the magic.

"Agreed. You head to the ballroom and tell them to be on their guard," Tobias replied.

"What are you going to do?"

"I'll follow their scent and try to surprise them from behind. Hurry Elaine. Aya will know what to do."

"I'm not leaving you alone to go after a killer!"

"Aya needs to be warned. What if there are two assassins? Go, now!"

"Fine, but if you get yourself killed, I'll drag you back to this realm myself!" She wrenched away from him and sprinted down the hall.

· · · · · · · · · ·

She threw open the golden doors, plunging into the glittering chaos, a cacophony of music and laughter crashing into her. The heady fragrance of honeyed wine and decadent food assailed her. She slipped through the crowd, ebbing and flowing to the rise and fall of the music. Blood pounded in her ears, pushing her on, as she frantically searched for a way forward

. Where was the bloody dais and why the hell had she been born so damn short?

As she squeezed past a couple who hurled insults at her back, she stumbled into an open space. Aya spotted her from the dais and strode forward, meeting her at the edge. The ward dissipated, and Elaine darted forward. The words spilled from her lips that there was a threat and that Tobias had left to chase a scent.

Sabra was at Aya's side in a flash. "You let him run off after a killer by himself?"

Elaine spun to her. "I didn't *let* him do anything! You've known him longer than me. Do you really think I could tell him what to do?"

Sabra's mouth opened in protest, but Aya's cutting glance silenced her.

"She's right and you know it," Aya said tightly. "Find him. I'll stay with Calix."

"Where do you want me?" asked Elaine.

"With me—"

A scream cleaved the air.

She pivoted to the chaos, the crowd scrambling to the edge of the room, parting like a severed neck. A woman stood in the center of the room, soaked in blood. In one hand a sword wreathed in black flames. At her feet, a man lay dead in a puddle of blood.

"Elaine, Sabra, with Calix, *now*." Aya swept past, drawing her sword in a fluid arc.

"You heard her, get up here," Sabra growled.

Elaine stumbled to Calix. A few of his vampire guards had closed ranks, drawing in to protect their leader. Sabra's arms were wreathed in ribbons of shadows, her black eyes burning with power. Another ward shimmered up, thicker than the one before.

Elaine watched as Aya prowled forward, holding her sword in one hand. The room darkened in her wake, as though she were devouring the light. Aya had called herself a monster... and at that moment, she looked the part. A creature forged of darkness; elegant, wicked and downright lethal.

The woman looked up and raised her sword.

Aya burst forward.

The two collided in a series of blows, metal clangs sounding across the room that had surrendered to silence. The cries of the guests had ceased and those that hadn't run through the doors watched on, hungry for blood.

Aya moved effortlessly, parrying off blows and ducking, never stopping. She was like a ghost, her feet barely touching the floor, as she launched into her attacks. Bearing down on the assassin, she was relentless, a warrior of death.

Her opponent matched every blow, and the pair moved in a blur. Aya dodged the swing of the sword, but as she surged up, the woman dropped low and drove her fist into Aya's gut, sending her staggering back. Elaine stepped forward. A hand clamped around her wrist.

"She's fine. Don't interfere."

Is she really, though?

The fight shifted and Aya was pushed back toward the crowd, barely holding off the flurry of blows. The attacker bore down on her with a ferocity that left Elaine's heart thundering against her ribs.

Aya dropped low, pivoting out of the way before surging up with a burst of speed. She lunged at the attacker, grinning wickedly, as if she'd gotten them right where she wanted. Any trace of exhaustion melted away, as if the warrior within was finally exposed.

"*See.* Aya has this handled." Sabra released her.

In a flash, Aya got behind the woman and swung the sword low, slashing at the back of the woman's knees. She dropped to the ground with a blood-curdling scream. Elaine's heart froze in her chest as Aya rushed the woman, ripping the sword out of her hand and driving her fist into the back of her head. The attacker dropped to the ground.

Aya's head lifted, meeting her gaze across the room. Her stomach somersaulted, uselessly churning over as she stared back. Though blood splattered on Aya's skin and her dress was torn to ribbons, she was every inch a monster dripped in death. Those dark, fathomless eyes, once a luminous gold, homed in on her.

At that moment, there might well have been no one else in the ballroom. Time froze and not even the sound of breathing broke the silence. Her heart refused to beat, as if she too had become an immortal creature, bound to this strange woman wreathed in darkness.

Aya's gaze snapped to the side of the dais. The moment shattered like glass.

Elaine turned, and time resumed.

A vampire stepped onto the dais. One of Calix's men, she reflected later, adorned in his uniform. His dark, empty eyes latched onto the vampire leader.

He exploded forward.

Elaine threw up her hands by instinct; fire roaring up from the ground in answer, forming a wall. The vampire surged through, cleaving her shield like a dagger. Fangs glinted first, stealing a note of alarm right through her bones. She tried to step back. Every sense howled to flee, to cry out, to do something, but her body refused.

She tried to scream—

A dagger slammed into the side of his head with a soft thunk.

He crashed into her and the back of her head smacked the ground. She tried to breathe but the weight of the vampire's body crushed her lungs. Panic gripped her heart, its frantic thump trying to pump blood through her veins. She raged against her body, begging her chest to expand, to desperately gulp in the air it needed. Blackness nudged the corner of her vision.

A face appeared above her, a warm hand on her cheek. Gentle, soothing. The shadows retreated and her vision cleared, and Aya's face sharpened into focus. Her heart flipped once more without warning, leaving her breathless for a moment longer.

Those terrifyingly beautiful eyes pinched, her mouth a thin line. There was anger there but it lacked the heat she'd seen before; something else softened it, a gentleness she hadn't expected, and left her reeling as words spilled from Aya's lips.

"You fool. Why did you have to throw yourself in front of Calix like that?"

She tried to muster any kind of reply, but the words never came. As her head rolled to the side, she caught sight of Aya's hip where one of the daggers was missing.

"I—" Oblivion claimed her, and she felt no more.

•••••••••

Elaine's head pounded as she emerged from the haze of sleep. It felt as if a thick sludge had pinned her down, rendering her too weak to move. As she pried her eyes open, taking in the shadowy outline of her room, a little more strength returned. The pressure eased on her body, and she forced herself up, even as her muscles hissed and protested. A low whimper stumbled from her lips as she pressed her hand to her forehead.

Moments later, footfalls approached the other side of her door and it swung open. Tobias swept through, freshly changed back into his loose shirt and breeches. Dark shadows lined his eyes, but as he sat at her bed, taking the time to check her over, a little tension ebbed from his shoulders.

"How do you feel?" he asked.

"Sore. Is Calix okay?"

Tobias's lips twitched. "He's fine."

The door opened again. Aya stood in the entrance, silent as death, watching her with unreadable dark eyes.

Tobias gently touched the side of her head, turning it to inspect where she'd hit it against the stone. "I forget how easily witches of Dianera can heal."

"It's not the first injury I've had, and it probably won't be my last either," she murmured, forcing a smile.

Aya turned sharply, and the door shut with a soft click.

Why did she come to see me? Is she angry?

"Don't mind her. She was worried." Tobias's voice brought her back to the room.

She blinked. "*About me?*" she asked incredulously.

For a moment, it appeared as if he wanted to say more, but instead, he sighed and continued to check her injury. Once he finished, he left her to rest. She sank into the pillows, staring up at the ceiling, mulling over Aya's strange actions.

CHAPTER 14

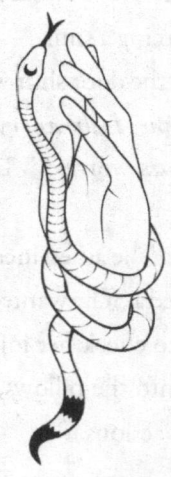

"I DIDN'T THINK YOU'D leave so soon," Sabra remarked as they descended Calix's dungeons the following morning.

Aya ignored the statement. She was painfully aware that Sabra hadn't missed her lingering close to Elaine's room, waiting for the witch to wake up. Or that she'd scarcely slept since the party. The truth was, she had little understanding of her actions, only that she'd needed to see the girl wake, and know that she was okay. She couldn't get the sight of the vampire lunging for Elaine out of her head.

It was absurd. Fretting like an absolute fool over a witch.

The memory of her people quickly stifled any thoughts of it, and her heart hardened.

The damp, stale air wrapped around them. She inhaled deeply, scenting death in the air. It called to the depths of her soul, awakening the darkness within. While the rest of the mansion, with its clean halls, pristine rooms, and fresh air made her feel uncomfortable, among the shadows, she was home.

At the bottom of the stairs, Alexios greeted them. An air of exhaustion hung over him. Vampires needed sleep, same as everyone else, but it appeared he'd had none since the ball.

"How is your friend?" he asked conversationally as they continued down the dimly lit hall.

Torches burned steadily in their iron baskets, lighting the way.

"Recovering. How fares your guest?" She didn't want to talk about Elaine, not with Sabra and certainly not Alexios.

"And Tobias?" Alexios inquired.

Why the interest? "He's fine—the assassin?"

Alexios's gaze darkened. "She's awake but hasn't said a word or touched the water we gave her."

She nodded, though her mind was far away. "Did you get anything off the body of the guard?"

"No, same as the wolf. Calix is pissed about that by the way."

Sabra snorted. "Aya saved his life and he's *mad?*"

"Aya doesn't have shit aim and he knows it." Alexios scowled back.

A biting retort died on Aya's lips. All night she'd stayed up, pondering *why* she'd dealt such a killing blow. In the end, she'd determined simply that she had seen Elaine staring down death—and had intervened. Simple as that. Calix was a fool to think there was anything more.

Sabra released a low hiss. "Well, Calix can go shove his pissy attitude up his—"

"*Sabra,*" Aya growled.

"What? You know I'm right. He should thank us." Sabra folded her arms across her chest. "Keeping him alive is the point, right? If he dies, this whole land goes to shit, and I, for one, *am* old enough to remember what it was like when he wasn't in power."

The reminder of the tenuous balance they danced upon hung over Aya's neck like a blade.

When Aya blinked, they arrived before a black metal door. Alexios fished out a key and pushed it into the lock, opening it with a rattling click. A witch light sputtered to life in the ceiling, devouring the darkness and illuminating the tiny space. The woman she'd fought was sitting on the floor, resting her back on the wall. Chains were fastened around her ankles, with cuffs securing her hands together. Around her neck, a metal collar which was linked to the chains on her ankles.

"This seems... excessive," she remarked.

Alexios slid her an arch look, as if to say, *you know how Calix is.* He shrugged. "I do as commanded. Now, I shall leave you here. Sabra, might I have your aid with something?"

"Aya, do you need me?" Sabra asked.

She shook her head. "I'll be fine. I won't be long."

The pair left her in the cell. She stared at the wreck chained to the floor, wondering where the savagery in those eyes had gone. What sat in its place was a cowering, wide-eyed young woman, pressing back into the wall as if it might swallow her whole.

"W-who are you?" The soft voice was scraped raw, as if she'd spent the night screaming.

Aya tried not to think about the tactics the vampires used.

"Aya Sinclair—have you heard of me?"

What little color was left drained away, and her head bobbed. "Yes."

"And you understand why I am here?"

Again, a nod and Aya crouched down, studying the frail creature before her. "You're not the one I fought. Maybe in body, but in mind? Someone did this to you, made you their weapon. Tell me who."

"Why should I trust you?"

Aya's brow lifted. "Do you have any other offers I should know about?"

"No." The woman's head dropped. "The last thing I remember was walking down a dark alley and the next thing I know, I'm here, accused of trying to kill that vampire. That's all I can tell you."

Aya had known liars and killers and traitors for much of her life. This woman wasn't one of them. She didn't need the dead to whisper that.

"What's your name?" she asked.

The woman laughed softly, a hollow, broken sound. "Yuna Falloway."

Normally, Aya didn't ask the names of folks like Yuna—it made things too personal when the ugly side of her work happened. But this was different. Yuna was a victim like so many in Purgatory who fell to the machinations of others. Just one more she couldn't save.

Even if Calix granted Yuna amnesty, the rest of his coven wouldn't stand for such an attack to go unpunished.

"I can make things easier for you when the time comes," she murmured.

Yuna lifted her chin, and the fear had shrunk behind a resigned, sad smile. "I knew the second I woke up that I wasn't walking out of here. At least I don't have anyone who will be sad when I'm gone. That has to count for something, doesn't it?"

Aya lowered the walls of her mind and pushed out a probe, hunting for anyone that might be close by. Silence answered her, and she shuffled closer to Yuna. "My people believe that death is not the end, that Akaria waits for us in the realm beyond this one. You will find peace there and the warmth that you should've had in this one."

Yuna's eyes widened. "Your *people?* But that would mean you're a—"

"A necromancer, the last living descendant of Akaria's mortal daughter, Iska." Aya brushed the tangled hair from Yuna's face, tucking it behind her ear. "I can help you pass on. It's about all I'm good for, I'm afraid... but, before that, I need answers. If you let me into your mind, I might see who did this to you. I can make them pay."

Yuna chuckled a low, hollow sound. "I've never had anyone care enough to avenge me before. How do we begin?"

"May I take your hand?"

She gingerly reached for the outstretched hand, smoothing her fingers over the palm. Closing her eyes, she slipped into Yuna's mind and plunged into the inky darkness, the bitter chill stealing into her soul with icy tendrils, coiling tightly around her heart. The first layer was a whirl of chaotic, fearful thoughts, broken with flashes of broken memories.

The darkness fell away, yielding to a sprawling meadow beneath a cloudless blue sky, the warm sun on her skin. The sweet note of blossoms saturated every breath. Frowning, she dropped and slammed her fist into the ground. The earth shattered into a thousand shards, sending her tumbling once more into an abyss.

Memories slammed into her thick and fast, a screaming cacophony. Pain blistered through her consciousness, tearing it apart at the seams. A soundless scream tore from her as she fought to hold on, the howling rage and panic tearing her apart.

And amid the chaos, several voices cut through the darkness like a blade, a single message uttered clearly.

"I speak your true name in my cause. Be my blade and strike the one I seek. Let no one know this truth."

Magic exploded all around her, a scalding rush of heat against her skin. She ripped herself free from Yuna's mind, choking back a scream. Blood roared in her ears, drowning out all else. Her mouth filled with dust as she pressed her palm to her forehead. After several deep breaths, her hand fell away and she looked upon the young woman, whose face had twisted into a frozen look of agony.

A blank expression stared back. A trail of blood ran from the corner of both eyes, nose, and ears.

Yuna was dead.

CHAPTER 15

THE HOUSE WAS ALIVE at night, and Elaine was wide awake with it. Walls flexed with labored breaths, and floors creaked and groaned. Shadows danced by bands of moonlight spilling in from the shuttered windows. A gentle wind stole through the halls and doors, rattling locks and rustling curtains. It felt as if the home was anxiously awaiting the return of Aya and Sabra.

Elaine was downstairs, digging around the shelves in the kitchen for a mug, when the front door swung open. The low screech pierced the veil of silence.

Aya walked in, shutting the door and locking it. She pressed her forehead against the wood, a heaviness seeming to weigh on her shoulders, dragging her down.

Elaine went to take a step forward but caught herself. What comfort could she possibly offer that Aya might accept?

It felt like an eternity before Aya turned to face her.

A breath eased. The house creaked. A little of the restless magic ebbed away.

For a moment, Elaine forgot how to inhale. A multitude of greetings lodged in her throat, each more useless than the last. Dark shadows clung beneath her piercing gaze, the moonlight catching those beautiful eyes.

Aya pushed off the door and glided toward her, silent as a wraith, and carefully maneuvered around Elaine to dig out two mugs from the cupboard. She picked up a pitcher, wordlessly pouring some water into both before pushing one back to Elaine.

"Thank you," Elaine murmured, and took a gentle sip.

Aya nodded absently. A strange quietness hung about her, shadows crowding her gaze. She poured more water into the pitcher. "Can't sleep?"

"About as well as I usually manage." Elaine bit her lip. "How did it go with the assassin? Did you learn anything?"

"She died." There was a heaviness in those words that struck at something deep in Elaine's gut—sympathy.

Because in that small reply, it offered a glimpse at a humanity Elaine hadn't seen before. A softness beneath the hard, cynical exterior. Something she hadn't expected at all.

"Do you want to talk about it?" she murmured.

Aya's gaze snapped to her, slicing right through her defenses. "You don't think I killed her?"

Elaine had seen her share of killers, many of whom had pursued her, and though she had glimpsed the same nature within Aya, she didn't believe Aya had slain the assassin. But still, she asked, "Did you?"

Aya was the one who looked away first. "No. Not that it made any difference. Whoever did this to her left a trap in her mind, killed her the second I started digging around."

"Could you have saved her?"

"No. She had no mark. There was nothing I could've done." The quiet grief threw Elaine off, and the shadows that crowded Aya's gaze rendered her silent.

The front door swung open once more, and Sabra appeared, wiping her hands against her breeches. "The wards are good, no monsters. We should be—" Sabra's mouth snapped shut as she glimpsed Elaine. "Oh, you're awake," she said with a glare.

"*Sabra,*" Aya warned.

"Relax. It's been a hell of a night. I'm going to bed," Sabra said, heading for the stairs. "I have some more sleeping draughts if you need some?"

"I'll be okay," Aya replied.

"Suit yourself." With that, Sabra left them and Elaine was alone with Aya once more.

She studied the war of emotions on Aya's face, as the mask had fallen away and she was finally glimpsing the real woman beneath. Without the snark and bravado. A band of moonlight cut over that hard, unyielding face, and her stomach flipped. There was something terrifyingly beautiful and utterly haunting about Aya Sinclair.

She didn't know what to do. This revelation was the last thing she expected.

"You did all you could," Elaine said.

Aya gave a smile that didn't quite reach her eyes. "But it wasn't enough."

"That is simply how it is."

Aya stared at her with renewed interest. "Spoken from experience?"

"More than I'd like." Elaine set her mug aside, pausing there for a moment as she pressed her palms against the bench. "I've never been very good at saving people or many things, really."

"Then what are you good at?"

There was a quiet note of teasing, so faint that Elaine nearly missed it as she shot Aya a look. A retort poised on her lips as she swallowed it down and picked her answer.

"Running."

••••••••••

At dawn, Elaine was woken by Tobias. He instructed her to dress for some more training and to meet him downstairs.

"And hurry," he said, closing the door.

Blinking groggily, she mumbled an 'okay' and hauled herself out of bed. By the time she dressed and stumbled her way outside, wincing as the bright light crashed over her, Tobias was approaching with two horses.

"Where are we going?" she asked as she took the offered reins.

"A little ride. I want to show you something. If you're going to stick around in this place, you should understand it better."

"What about Aya and Sabra?" She hadn't heard them come home, though Tobias seemed unperturbed by their absence.

Tobias swung up into the saddle, settling comfortably with one hand resting on his thigh. "Aya sent word. They ducked back into town to check over a few things. We'll meet them at Calix's mansion later. He wants to go over the next few events before Alantorei."

She hauled herself up. "Do they think there might be some clues about her body?"

"Maybe. We're trying everything we can right now. That one of Calix's trusted guards was affected is concerning."

They set off at a brisk trot, breaking quickly into a gallop. Elaine had learned how to ride after escaping the temple, stealing a few mounts in her time, but it had been nearly two years since she'd last been on a horse. She'd forgotten how freeing it felt. The wind whipped her hair, the sun on her cheeks, the power of the horse beneath her as it stretched out. Hooves drummed steadily against the road, crunching every so often on a twig or through a pile of leaves.

The ancient forest wound around them, teeming with life. Birds flittered and darted among the leaves, singing softly. A rabbit darted across the road, vanishing among the thicket. The breeze whispered and moaned, rustling the leaves and bushes, whipping up eddies of dust across the road.

She crouched low and flicked her heel. The horse shot forward, thundering past Tobias. Lost to the rush of the wind, galloping along the twisting road, she was *free*. Lifting in the saddle, she released the reins, squeezing her thighs tightly to hold on. Eyes shut, a wild smile lifted her mouth.

The horse jerked to a stop, rearing up. Gasping, she grabbed for the reins. As she tried to soothe the startled horse, a wolf emerged from the trees, larger than any she'd seen before, with russet fur and glowing amber eyes. A small package hung from its teeth.

Her heart slammed hard against her ribs and heat rushed down to her palms in response, embers sparking over her skin.

Moments later, Tobias trotted to a stop. "Alpha Ryker, what do you want?"

The wolf snarled, dropped the package, and darted off into the woods. Elaine slid from the saddle, watching cautiously as Tobias unwrapped the bundle. It was a leather-bound book with a note attached to it. He handed the book to her and read the note.

She leafed through the pages, frowning at the text. It was in a language she swore was familiar, but she couldn't pin down where she'd seen it before. A cursory glance over the pictures inside, detailed drawings of plants, and several symbols that reminded her of spell marks, made her realize what it was.

"It's a grimoire," she said.

Tobias hummed uneasily. "Ryker said one of his men found this at the house his son was staying at. It was a box of possessions he thinks was from his son's lover."

"But I thought the girl was human? This belongs to a witch though I don't recognize the insignia," she murmured. Six of the seven deities were etched on her body, and she knew of Akaria's symbol, and it was none of them.

So, who did the owner of this grimoire—if it didn't belong to the girl—worship?

Tobias frowned. "Not sure. I always understood the power witches possessed was directly linked to whatever deity they worshipped. Is there any way a witch could gain power from another source?"

She frowned. "Not to my knowledge. Why would Ryker give us this? Should this not go to Calix?"

"My guess is he's aiming at keeping Aya on his good side. Whether to hide any sinister part in this scheme against Calix or to prove he's not involved, I'm not sure."

"You say that as if he is afraid of Aya?"

Elaine was getting the distinct impression this was a trend with many of the folks in Purgatory. Just how powerful was Aya? She'd still not figured out what exactly her mysterious benefactor was, only that she wasn't human.

"The wise ones are wary of her. Aya has earned her reputation."

She stared at him. "As what? Some terrifying monster?" Before he could say anything in response, she asked, "What exactly *is* Aya?"

"Someone you don't want as an enemy."

"That's not an answer."

A coy smile teased his lips, as if her growing frustration and confusion was infinitely amusing to him. A sentiment she didn't share.

"*What* Aya is exactly is a secret you have to earn. Now, come on, we should keep going."

"Where are we going?" she asked as she returned to hers, stashing the book into the saddlebags. She swung up into the saddle.

He clicked his tongue and the horses broke into a trot. "You'll see. Now, try not to race off again. We're almost there."

••••••••••

After a few more minutes' ride, they reached a sprawling clearing set against a cliff's edge. Four stone pillars guarded the corners, half-covered by beards of moss. Strange magic hummed in the air, ancient, stirring the power in her veins. The dawning light stretched out from the distant horizon, sprinted across the sprawling woods and the vast Inner District of Purgatory, and reached up to the clearing. A balmy warmth spread over her skin, and she closed her eyes, surrendering to it for a moment.

She inhaled deeply, savoring the rich earthy tones and delicate floral notes perfuming the air. Bumps rippled down her arms, lifting the hairs. Awareness prickled through her chest as she dismounted, moving into the clearing slowly.

"What is this place?" she asked softly.

It felt like sacred ground, like the prayer gardens of the Arcan temple. None but the Grand Matron and a few select witches were ever permitted there. Once, as a small child, she'd snuck inside. She'd felt more alive than anywhere else in the temple. When she was discovered, they'd whipped her until her back ran red with blood. Though the physical scars were long gone, the ones buried below lingered, and ached even now after so many years.

"Aya found it a couple of years ago. She sometimes meditates here, but we mostly use it for training. This place is... special to Aya. She only agreed to you coming here this morning." He paused for a moment. "She doesn't want a repeat of the ball, so we're here to train."

Right after our talk this morning, thought Elaine. A warm glow washed over her. "So, where do we begin?"

He smiled at her. "I'm going to teach you how to throw a punch because, frankly, you're awful and scrappy."

CHAPTER 16

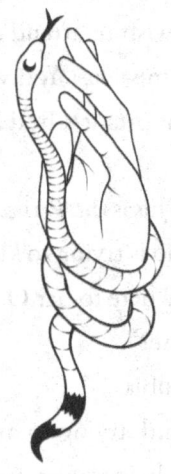

WHEN AYA RETURNED TO the house, a missive from Calix for the next event was lying on the dining table. The white paper was neatly folded with a glossy red seal. Even as she reached for it, she knew what was contained within.

Dread coiled in her gut as she tore the seal and scanned the contents.

The ceremony for the choosing of this year's Veil Queen will take place at the temple of Dianera. Honoria has agreed to temporarily

*rescind your ban so that you and your team may act as my guards for
the event.*

Footsteps sounded on the floor. Tobias reached over and plucked
the invitation from her hand. He let out a whistle. "Honoria actually
lifted the ban?"

"That's what it says. I knew the ceremony was coming up, but I
thought Calix might not wish to attend given the attempts on his
life." She glowered at the missive. "You would think for a man so
aware of his own damn importance, he'd actually take care to avoid
being assassinated."

Tobias rolled his eyes. "This is the *Prince* of Purgatory. Regardless,
the faster we figure out who is trying to kill him, the better."

"Oh, do you have somewhere to be? Or, rather, with someone?"

"And if that were the case?"

Aya's brows shot up. "Tobias..."

As she stared at her friend, trying to make sense of what he was
about to say, swept into the living room, pausing at the table to pluck
the letter out of Tobias's hand. Her dark eyes widened as she read the
contents. "What is this? She rescinded the ban? For all of us?"

Whatever Tobias had been about to say was gone, as he smiled
brilliantly once more.

Aya nodded. "It appears so. I'm sure Honoria wasn't happy, but
you know what Calix is like. He probably gave her little choice.
That man is the only reason the witches don't have more control
in Purgatory. If Honoria had her way, this place would be a very
different place."

"Well, this should be fun. Are we putting on any money on how badly this will go?" Sabra asked.

Tobias rolled his eyes. "I'm not betting anything. I always lose."

"Coward." Sabra looked at her, a teasing glint lighting those dark depths. "What about you?"

"I'm with Tobias. I never win against you." Aya leaned against the table with a wry smile. "Now, there is work to be done. Sabra, can you head into town early? Speak to Calix and ask him where he's stationed his guards. We don't want a repeat of what happened last time."

And like that, the mood shifted, and the humor was sucked out of the room. Sabra's smile fell, but she didn't argue. "Consider it done."

"We'll take the horses and meet you there. If you finish early, can you check over the wards the witches have set? They likely won't let us set any within the temple. Everyone needs to be on their best behavior and prepared for trouble. The mental trap left on the latest assassin ensured they couldn't share any useful information. If someone tries to attack Calix, grab them and bring them back here. Is that understood?"

Tobias and Sabra nodded. The latter touched her arm, giving it a tender squeeze.

Sabra turned to go. "I'll head off now. See you this afternoon."

Aya looked at where Elaine had been standing. The witch was gone.

"How did Elaine's training go?" she asked Tobias.

"We covered a lot of hand-to-hand combat and whatever else I could teach her. It would help if someone decent with a sword spent some time—"

"No."

Tobias smirked. "Why not?"

"You know why."

A war of unsaid words raged between them. Tobias was the first to look away. "After you killed that vampire, I saw how you looked at her. Would caring for her be so bad?"

A flash of movement caught her eye. Elaine stood at the foot of the stairs. Aya's gut twisted nervously. Ever since their talk in the kitchen, something had shifted between them, and she didn't like that one bit.

Her heart stuttered, catching on the question. She couldn't breathe, couldn't think for a second. All she saw was her mother's defiant smirk before her head was cut off, and her sister's furious shouts before a sword was driven through her heart. They were dead. Her people were dead. She slammed the memories away, feeling the hot sting of tears. The funeral ceremony had left her more vulnerable than she realized.

"Aya—"

She flinched at her name, stepping back. "How can you ask me that?"

"It's not a betrayal to your—"

"Don't you *dare* finish that sentence," she hissed.

Pity softened his gaze and she hated it. He didn't understand. But how could he? His people were still alive, even if he'd left them.

She pinned him with a warning look. "Know this, Tobias. I will *never* fall for a witch."

CHAPTER 17

I WILL NEVER FALL *for a witch.*

The words roared through Elaine's mind as she numbly changed into the dress Tobias had given her. There had been no promises of affection and Aya made clear her feelings about witches. So why did it bother her so damn much? Hell, it wasn't as if it was the first time someone had scorned her for what she was.

A witch, one whose powers brought nothing but pain and destruction; one who was constantly hunted and certainly no temptation for anyone seeking an easy life. Hell, Aya's rejection wasn't her first...but it was the only one she realized bothered her.

When she headed downstairs, Aya was back to her normal self. Her swaggering, carefree air had returned. She lounged by the cold fireplace, leisurely eating an apple. Elaine looked away and hurried over to Tobias. He was fiddling with the buttons around his cuffs, and muttering angrily.

"Do you want some help?" she asked.

He sighed, dropping his hands. "I bloody hate wearing this stuff." He cut off suddenly, his ears reddening, and shot her a sheepish look. "Are you okay?"

"Of course. Why wouldn't I be?"

He looked down at his feet. "No reason."

Had he known she was in the hallway when Aya said those words? With a frown, she finished helping him, and stepped back.

Aya rose from the lounge and tossed the apple core into the fireplace. "We were waiting for you. Let's go."

•••••••••

The temple stood in a sprawling garden, proud among weeping willows and manicured grass. Towering pillars held up a grand entrance, gleaming in the afternoon sun. The sun emerged from the blanket of clouds, bathing the grounds in swaths of golden light. Rows of blossoming flowers edged the paths. Climbing plants wrapped around a myriad of statues and stone seats.

They arrived an hour before the first ceremony, so the grounds were quiet, save for a small group of vampires and witches gossiping by the gilded doors. Calix was surrounded by his most trusted guards. Alexios stood at his side, one hand resting on his sword. The prince's second in command glanced their way, stilling for a moment before inclining his head in greeting.

Aya hadn't said a word since they'd arrived; that was until she locked eyes with the witches and released a colorful string of curses that made Elaine blush.

"Deep breath," Sabra whispered.

"Easy for you to say."

Elaine turned to get a closer look at the group of witches. Honoria stood in the middle, stiffening as they approached. A shadow of cold fury darkened her ethereal face. It was an expression she'd seen many times on her own Grand Matron, back at the Arcan temple. Even the distance between them seemed insufficient, and Elaine itched to turn tail and run.

Honoria's gaze could've withered even the strongest man; it slid to Elaine, and the hatred was replaced with piercing interest. Elaine understood the look. Even with the pendant warm against her skin, masking what she was, she still felt exposed.

"You're one of us. Lift your head." Tobias gently touched the small of her back, pushing her forward.

She hadn't realized she'd slowed her pace and shot him a warm smile. "How are you so calm?"

He leaned in close, his breath brushing the shell of her ear. "Because I know that despite all her airs, Honoria is afraid of Aya."

"Enough to leave me alone?" she laughed nervously.

As he pulled back, he nodded sagely. "Aya's the only one who's ever dealt a blow to Honoria, one the Grand Matron will never forget."

"What did she do?" she whispered.

"*Tobias.*" Aya's cold voice shattered the moment. "Later."

He pulled back with a sigh.

Whatever he'd been about to say would have to wait. They'd reached the entrance. Calix glided over.

"Please, let us proceed inside. You should appraise yourself of the area," Calix said, gesturing for them to follow.

As they passed through the golden doors, Elaine gasped in awe. The first room was a long rectangle with a tall, arched roof held up by rows of pillars on either side. Two enormous glowing witch lights hung in delicately woven metal cradles, throwing swaths of near-sunlight across every inch of the room with scarcely a shadow to be seen.

Rows of pews flanked a clear path down the middle of the room. At the far end, on a dais, was a statue of the temple's deity; Dianera. She stood in polished mottled white and black stone, her flowing robes appearing as delicate as silk. A jeweled blue bird was carved on her shoulder, with one green and one golden eye staring back across the room. Thenia, the Soul Bird; who ferried those who succumbed to sickness or injury to Akaria's domain, the Eternal Realm.

Calix led them toward the statue where several chairs of glossy wood with tall backs and curved armrests were set out. "This is where the council will sit during the main event. All the guests will come in through the main entrance and must remain seated the whole time. When the ceremony is over, they will depart. We will not leave until the area has been cleared. I trust this meets your approval?"

Aya nodded before turning to the room. "How many guests?"

"One hundred and fifty-three."

"I see."

Calix merely smiled at the frosty tone. "I cut it as best as I could, but you know how some of the older families are in this town. The Veil Queen is a prestigious title and it does well to garner favor with the new queen, not merely to receive favorable blessings during Alantorei but also—"

"Don't waste your breath on her, Calix. Aya here has never truly appreciated these events or ceremonies," Honoria said primly.

Sabra snorted, and even Tobias chuckled beneath his breath. Elaine wondered what the joke was. She looked at Aya, who wore a coy smile that didn't quite touch her eyes.

"I'm always amazed at how much you think you know about me," Aya said silkily. "One would think you were, shall we say, a little obsessed?"

Heat flamed Honoria's cheeks. "Don't make me rescind—"

Calix stepped between the two. "Now, now, perhaps you could refrain from killing each other until *after* this delightful affair is concluded?"

Aya smiled serenely. "I don't know what you're talking about, Calix. I'm on my best behavior."

"I'm afraid your words inspire me with little confidence." Calix turned to Honoria. "Please accept my apologies, Grand Matron. Now, if you might excuse us? There are some private matters I wish to discuss, and I believe your witches have some work to attend to before we begin."

Honoria bowed, a mask of calm returned once more, and retreated. As they went to exit back through the main doors, Honoria glanced back, a look of hunger on her face. Elaine stiffened as the woman's gaze landed on her. It was a look she had seen on so many witches in the past. She lifted her chin, as Tobias instructed, and stared back.

A challenge gleamed in those chilling depths... and Elaine answered it with a bitter smile. *Give it your best shot, Honoria. You will not have my power.*

CHAPTER 18

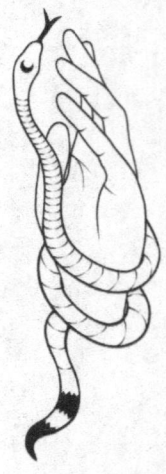

T HE LAST OF THE guests trickled into the temple, shoes clicking and shuffling over the stone floor. Hushed voices eddied through the air, and several times Aya caught her name being uttered. It had not gone unnoticed that she was in attendance, even standing behind Calix. No doubt it would fuel the gossip of Purgatory for at least a few days.

Aya kept her gaze on the procession before lingering briefly on Honoria. She scarcely trusted the Grand Matron *not* to try something to drive a wedge between Aya and Calix. The witch was opportunistic, so Aya would need to keep her guard up.

Once the last arrivals were seated, Honoria rose from her chair and glided to the middle of the dais. She began the welcoming speech, thanking Dianera for her unending protection of Purgatory. Aya chafed at every word. Dianera had no role in creating their home. In fact, she was pretty sure the goddess didn't give a damn about the place at all, let alone the witches who professed their love for her. It was the spirits who forged this haven, and by their will and protection, it remained safe. At least from outside threats.

When Honoria finally finished, the rest of the ceremony flowed on as it always had. Some of the wealthier and more prestigious gave speeches of prosperity, and others thanked them for their tireless work to better Purgatory. It was all bullshit, as far as Aya was concerned. Eventually, it concluded with several songs to Dianera. When the music tapered off, Aya stood grinding her teeth and flexing her fingers. She released a sigh of frustration as Honoria rose once more and reclaimed her position on the dais.

"Esteemed guests and fellow council members, it is time for us to reveal who Dianera has chosen as this year's Veil Queen." There was a rustling of fabric before Honoria fished out a sealed letter from her robes, holding it out to the crowd.

The guests leaned forward, hunger in their eyes. Whoever was to be revealed would be the focus of political interest for the next twelve months. Last year, it had been a banshee, who had sequestered herself away when the pressures got too much. There was even a rumor the girl had stabbed a noble who wouldn't leave her alone until she agreed to back him in some scheme, but as Aya knew, not all rumors were proven to be true.

Honoria tore the letter open. "Why, Dianera truly blesses us. I introduce the new Veil Queen... Councilor Marisol Torren."

The air was ripped from Aya's lungs. *No.*

Marisol rose delicately from her chair and swept forward. A hand slid over hers, but she couldn't look away to see who. All focus was on the dais where Marisol kneeled before Honoria, a picture of smiling serenity, as a crown of thorns and bones was nestled on her head.

All hopes of keeping her interactions with Marisol at a minimum were shattered.

"Fuck."

•••••••••

Once the ceremony concluded, the guards were instructed to wait outside the temple. Aya and her group, however, could stay. Honoria and Calix were in a deep discussion, but Honoria had erected wards so none of them could hear a damn word.

I still have the power, Miss Sinclair—remember that, Aya imagined Honoria saying.

"What do you think they're discussing?" Sabra ventured idly.

"I'm trying not to think about it," Aya replied.

But it was hard. The ceremony had gone off without a hitch, and no one had threatened Calix's life. Though she'd been reluctant to leave him alone, she knew Honoria wasn't dumb enough to hurt him in a room with the two of them.

So, the waiting continued. Much to her dismay, Elaine appeared the most relaxed, talking in a low voice with Tobias. The two had quickly become thick as thieves, and she wasn't sure how to feel about it. Jealous? No. Tobias was allowed to have friends, though she wouldn't have minded had he chosen someone a little less... well, *her*.

Frowning, she leaned back against the wall, her arms folded across her chest. Seriously, what the hell was being discussed, and why was it taking so damn long? Normally she didn't mind the quiet jobs, the long stints of waiting around. But now, she was in a witch temple, and that was enough to make her skin crawl.

"So, Marisol is the new Veil Queen," Sabra murmured.

Aya pinned her with a withering look. "I know. I was there."

"Do you want me to poison her? Not to kill her, but I could make her shit herself for a week. Something to ensure she doesn't appear at events or—"

"Leave her." Aya picked her battles if she was able to. Starting a war with Marisol, who had already shown her true colors, was not one she was interested in. "She's not worth it."

That was what she told herself, anyway. But as she'd watched Marisol be crowned, she wanted to rage and scream and lash out with everything she had. Old wounds reopened and salt rubbed in. She'd *loved* her, and Marisol walked away because Aya hadn't been enough. Right on the day that Aya planned to tell Marisol what she truly was.

"But what she did to you, to us? She shouldn't get away with it," Sabra said heatedly.

Aya blinked, realizing that Sabra had kept going. She cast her friend a weary look. "Can we continue this conversation later?"

Sabra tilted her head. "There was nothing you could have said or done that would have made her want to stay."

"I'm aware. She left a note."

"I went after her that night," said Sabra.

"What?"

Sabra waved a hand. "We didn't speak. I followed her to the council building and snuck in. I watched as she was voted in as councilor, though it wasn't made official until later."

Aya turned to her friend, aching and angry, and stunned all the same. "You never said anything."

"You were so *angry* back then. It was as if you were sixteen once more and we were both leaving the Dusk Quarter. I thought if I told you that, if you believed Marisol betrayed you for the council, you'd burn the place to the ground." Sabra paused, a dry smile tugging at her lips. "Whilst that *was* tempting, the last thing I wanted was to fuel your pain."

There was no argument on her lips. Aya knew the depth of the rage burning in her veins and how quickly it could consume her. It was her constant companion, lingering at the core of her soul, slumbering away until it was awakened once more.

Aya stepped forward, gently touching her friend's arm. "No secrets. Not between us."

As the silence returned between them, Aya leaned against the wall once more. She drummed her fingers, itching for the day to be done. Being so close to witches, especially one who wanted her dead, chafed at her nerves.

Her mind wandered in its boredom, lost to the reaches of her turbulent thoughts and twisted memories.

"Smoke!" Tobias's voice thundered through her mind.

Aya exploded into action, surging off the wall. She turned to the source of Tobias's cry as the blackened smoke billowed toward them. The distant crackle of fire rapidly approached, the acrid stench already brushing her noise. Another scent threaded through it. She shot Sabra a look but her friend already summoned darkness to her hands.

"Is that what I think it is?"

"Hell Fire."

"Fuck."

Sabra spun to the door, drawing her fist back for a blow when Aya stepped forward.

"That's warded by a witch. You can't break that—"

"Neither can you!"

Aya tried to argue but in a flash, Elaine was at their side. Light blazed around her fist.

"Step back!"

Aya grabbed Sabra, wrenching her out of the way as Elaine plowed her fist into the door. A thundering bang rattled the world, leaving Aya's ringing viciously. Biting back the pain throbbing through her skull, she stumbled to the doorway as Calix filled it.

"What's going on?"

"Hell Fire! We have to go, *now!*"

Honoria appeared beside his shoulder, glowering for a split second until she, too, beheld the billowing that was rapidly closing in.

"Time to go!" she shouted.

Aya sprinted down the hall. The others followed close behind, boots thumping against the stone. Heat thickened, every breath burning over her lips, and as they rounded the corner, she heard the roar of Hell Fire. It was closing in. This magical fire was no mindless inferno. No, this was summoned with a target and moved wherever it wished.

A predator forged of fire.

They entered the main hall, which was thankfully absent of guests. Aya leaped from the dais, sprinting down the central aisle to the door when a force slammed into her. Air whistled in her ears as she went flying, crashing into the chairs with an agonizing thump.

She scrambled up, fighting the pain that splintered across her chest, every breath suddenly hurting. It felt like she'd broken a rib, or possibly several. There was no time to waste. She staggered to where the others were waiting. Honoria moved to her side with an expression of fury.

"What the hell is this?" the Grand Matron seethed, raising a hand wrapped in ribbons of light to the ward.

The shield shimmered, but remained. Her face paled. If Aya wasn't so damn skeptical, she might've thought the look of fear was genuine.

"Can you... break... it?" Aya wheezed out, wincing as darkness nudged her vision.

A metallic taste rushed up her throat, pooling in her mouth. Fuck. She doubled over, a cough racking her body. Something warm and sticky dribbled down her lips. Wiping it with the back of her hand, she stilled. Blood stained her skin. Every breath hurt. The amount of air she was getting in was fading, and fast.

Honoria strode to the shield and pressed her palms against it. White light erupted around her, ribbons spilling from her form and swirling at her feet. It brightened, forcing Aya to look away. Tobias was in front of her in a flash, one hand cradling her face. She batted him away as the light dimmed and lifted her head to Honoria.

The woman thrust her palms back into the shield, shattering it into a thousand shards of light, crashing down around them. The victory was short-lived as the flames spilled into the hall. The raging blue inferno rushed down the dais, advancing toward them.

"Everyone out! Follow me!" Honoria shouted.

Calix dashed past her, out the door first. Honoria was close behind. As Aya took a step toward her, her gaze hardened as if an idea had come to her. Aya recognized that look and called out, "Oh no you don't!" Too late. The doors slammed shut, sealing them inside.

Aya let out a savage scream, staggering to her feet and stumbling forward when a pillar cracked and chunks of stone fell, crashing down. A hand yanked her out of the way as a stone smashed into the spot she'd been standing. Elaine released her grip and stepped aside as Sabra thundered, "Did she fucking trap us here?"

Aya straightened up, even as her legs wobbled, threatening to give out. A wall of blue fire advanced toward them. She shot Elaine a look.

"Can you control it?"

"I don't know. I've fought nothing like this before!" Elaine said.

The flames were nearly upon them and thick smoke choked the air. Aya doubled over, coughing blood onto the stone floor. Damn Honoria. They'd be dead in moments if they couldn't stop the flames.

"T-try!" Aya forced out, reaching for Elaine's hand. "*Please.*"

Elaine nodded, and ripping the pendant from her neck, she tossed it aside. Aya watched as the girl stepped toward the fire, throwing up her hands. A blue glow burst from her, and she dropped low, slamming both palms onto the stone.

Ice exploded from within her, a wall shooting upward, crashing into the ceiling. The Hell Fire slammed into it and Elaine gave an agonized cry, the sound tearing at Aya's heart. This was not a witch who wanted her dead, but one in pain *for* her.

More bloodied coughs racked her body. In the depths of her mind, a gentle melody bloomed, pushing up through the darkness, spilling through her veins.

A cold presence slipped into her mind. *Protect her.*

"Keep going!" she roared into the chaos.

"It's not working. I can't stop the flames..."

Aya grabbed Elaine's hand, even as dark oblivion sank its talons into her mind. "Yes, you *can.*"

Cracks ripped up the wall.

"By the gods, witch. Do something!" cried Sabra.

The ice shattered into snowflakes and the fire rushed forward. Elaine threw up her hands, light erupting from her palms to create a shield surrounding them. The Hell Fire advanced but could not break through the protective barrier. She staggered to her feet, throwing her hands out wide, and passed through the shield into the flames. The inferno wrapped itself around her in a vortex of blue fire, devouring her.

"*Elaine!*" Aya roared in anguish.

The inferno raged and a cacophony of screaming filled the air, drowning out all else. Time slowed as the vortex started shrinking and the flames were drawn inwards, colliding with a single point—Elaine.

The witch threw her head back. A final scream ripped the air, and the fire was no more. Blue embers still danced over her skin, and as Elaine turned to face Aya, her once gray eyes glowing an icy blue. Those cerulean depths burned through Aya, stealing the air as she tried to speak, to think. Gone was the frightened witch. In her place stood a goddess.

Elaine's eyes suddenly rolled back into her head, the light blinking out. She swayed and hit the ground.

"Elaine!" Aya crawled across the floor, reaching for her. Her fingers brushed the girl's skin, still warm to the touch. Shakily, she checked for a pulse, releasing a released breath as a faint beat tickled her finger. She was alive. Out cold and likely exhausted from all the magic she'd used.

"Aya! Elaine!" Tobias staggered over, one arm still looped around Sabra.

Aya tried to speak but darkness surged up, and she crumpled to the ground, the abyss swallowing her whole.

CHAPTER 19

As Elaine emerged from the depths of sleep, every part of her screamed, muscles crying out. Prying her eyes open, she tried to speak, but her mouth was dry as a desert, and her throat felt like it had been scraped raw. A half-strangled sound squeezed from her lips.

From nearby came a rustling of footsteps and a shadow fell over her. A warm hand brushed her cheek, and an earthy scent filled her lungs, even as they whimpered from the pain.

"Elaine?" A low voice brushed her ear.

She knew them... right? But before she could get an answer, or let her vision clear, she slipped into oblivion once more.

•••••••••

When she woke again and forced her eyes open, the world was clearer. She realized she was back in her room, the pale morning light trickling in through the open window. The curtains were drawn back and a cool breeze whispered in, brushing her skin.

Without warning, the memories of the Eternal Flame and their near-death crashed into her. She sat up intending to get out of bed, but her muscles screamed in protest, and stars flashed across her vision. The world tipped forward, spinning for a moment, as she sat there a thin sheen of sweat glistening on her skin.

Aya!

The last thing she remembered was Aya calling her name. Then nothing except the flames. The darkness.

Pressing her hand to her face, she closed her eyes, trying to make sense of the memories and arrange them into some kind of order. What had she done? The fire had been closing in...and then what? A cold chill slid down her mind, a single memory taking hold—calling forth a wall of ice.

"Oh, *no,*" she cried, pressing her fist into her mouth.

She'd sworn she would never summon the magic of another deity. Her soul was already burdened by wielding the powers of Arcan and Dianera. Now another had a claim to her soul.

Dropping her hand, she turned her mind inwards, latched onto the luminous blue thread that now twisted among the fire and glowing orb of white light. Vikra's power flowed through her, icy tendrils shooting down her arm. Her eyes flew open. A tiny rose forged from ice rested in her palm.

Without thinking, she threw the rose, watching as it smashed into the wall, scattering frozen shards across the floor.

The door flew open. Tobias filled the space, his eyes wide. "You're awake!"

It took her a moment to find her voice. "How long was I out?"

"Far too long." Tobias sat on her bed, taking her hand. Fragments of ice clung to her fingers. "Vikra's magic?"

She managed a mute nod. The last thing she wanted to talk about was her power, so she pulled her hand away. "How's Aya?"

The light in his eyes dimmed. A sense of panic tightened her chest, squeezing out the air. Tobias stared at his hands in his lap. "She's not in a good shape. I've stabilized her as best as I can, but..."

"*But what?*"

"I think she has some internal bleeding or some organ damage. I'm not sure. She *should* be healing, but something is wrong. I can't even risk taking her on horseback into town and Sabra is also too drained to transport anyone. She tried and collapsed," he muttered. His gaze lifted, and she knew what he was asking, though conflict warred in his eyes. "Elaine..."

"Help me up." She swung her legs over the side, wincing as her feet hit the ground.

"You should rest—"

"And if she dies?" She cut him a look and looped her arm around his waist. "At least let me see if I can help, please. After that, I'll rest. I promise."

He nodded and helped her out of the bed. It was a slow shuffle across the room, and in the end, he scooped her up and carried her.

She didn't have the strength to complain, biting her tongue as he ferried her into Aya's room.

It was the first time she'd seen it, and it was certainly not what she expected. Chaos and color. Bookcases filled to the brim, clothes strewn around the room, and a desk that scarcely had any clear space. A stack of half-finished paintings leaned against the wall, a jar of brushes on the floor next to them.

Wrenching her gaze away, she looked over at the bed where Aya lay, her hair spread across the pillows. The sheets were peeled back, exposing Aya's bandaged body. Sweat glistened on her skin and she turned her head restlessly against the pillows. Elaine's heart thundered against her ribs as she saw how labored Aya's breathing was.

Tobias carried her over, gently lowering her onto a chair beside the bed. She reached out, gingerly setting her palms on Aya's bare stomach. The skin was a dark mottled red and hot to the touch. Aya groaned as Elaine gently pressed down with both hands. She closed her eyes and slipped within, letting instinct guide her. Calling on Dianera's light with its healing properties, she released it into Aya's body. A warm glow spread throughout, mending fractures, sealing torn ligaments, and repairing damaged organs.

Heat built in her head, and the pressure intensified to a sharp throb.

Just a little more. There! It's done.

Wincing, she withdrew and removed her hands, placing them in her lap. Aya was already breathing easier, and a little color was back in her cheeks. Elaine picked up a cloth from the side table and gently dabbed the sweat away. An expression of peace lay on Aya's face as she slept. There was no trace of the warrior who had fought the assassin at the party, nor the woman who had roared out her name as if she was terrified something might happen to her.

She was losing her mind. Aya had made it clear what she thought of witches and of *her*.

"Are you okay here for a moment? I need to check on Sabra." Tobias asked, oblivious to her warring emotions.

She mumbled a nod, still cleaning Aya's face when he left. Then she was alone with her thoughts. Yet the memory of Aya screaming her name wouldn't abandon her mind. It clung on, sinking talons deep, until she set the cloth aside and grabbed her knees, staring at the floor.

Why did she have to give a damn what Aya Sinclair thought of her?

She wanted a home, a family, a place all her own. Yet every time she'd reached for those things, they were snatched away or went up in flames. Perhaps she was not meant to have those things. Not in this lifetime, anyway.

"E-Elaine." The sound of her name brought her back to the present.

Aya's eyes fluttered weakly, her mouth barely moving.

Elaine stood up to call for Tobias when Aya opened her eyes. "Elaine?"

"I'm here," she answered.

Without realizing it, she gently touched Aya's hand, ready to pull away the moment Aya showed her touch was unwelcomed.

"I've never had a witch save me before. They're usually always trying to kill me." Aya smiled weakly.

The question of Aya's story was poised on her lips when a soft snore reached her ears. Aya had fallen asleep. Over and over, she toyed with her final words, trying to decipher their meaning.

When it was clear that Tobias would not return, she rested her head on the bed. She needed a few moments sleep and she'd heal again.

Just a few moments...

CHAPTER 20

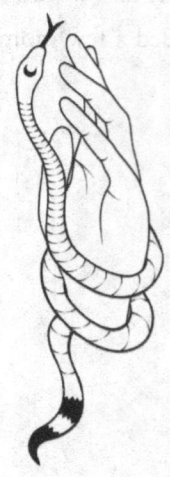

T HOUGH AYA'S BODY THROBBED in every place imaginable, and her mouth felt as though it was filled with dust, it was preferable to waking up on the floor, soaked in sweat from a nightmare.

She raised her hand to wipe the sleep away when it brushed against something warm and soft. Sparks skittered up her arm, her heart flipping as she rolled a little to the side, seeing clearly what, or rather who she'd touched.

Elaine.

The witch was sitting on a chair, resting her head on the side of the bed. One cheek rested on the covers, letting Aya see her face, at peace in sleep. Dark circles lingered under her eyes, and there was a paleness about her that Aya didn't like. A few strands of her red curls had fallen across her brow, and Aya's hand itched to brush them away.

She traced the shape of Elaine's face. The curve of her jaw, the slope of her nose, the constellation of freckles across her cheek and brow. She rued the fact she'd never noticed them before.

Entranced, she didn't notice the door open until Tobias approached the bed. Heat rushed to her cheeks as she looked up at him as if caught doing something she shouldn't. The smirk on his mouth showed he'd noticed.

He helped Aya up to sit. "How are you feeling?"

"Like hell, but okay." Aya glanced at Elaine. "How long has she been here?"

"Since yesterday," he said softly.

"And she ended up in my room?" When he didn't answer, she wrenched her gaze from Elaine. "Tobias?"

"You weren't in good shape and... she healed you."

Ice slid into her veins. The debt to the spirit had been to keep Elaine safe, a task she was failing at. But as quickly as the anger sparked in her chest, heating her cheeks, it dimmed. She could see the worry in Tobias's eyes. He never would have asked Elaine to use her powers if he hadn't thought it was the only way to keep her alive.

She sucked in a sharp breath. "How bad was it?"

"You nearly died."

She had gotten close to Akaria's embrace, to being reunited with her people, and she hadn't even realized it. Another cruel reminder of what a failure as a necromancer she was.

"Why not move her back to her bed to rest?" she asked numbly.

Tobias snorted softly. "I tried. *Twice.* She grabbed your hand, refused to let go."

Her gut flipped. It was all wrong. She had to hate her. Everything was spiraling out of control. It was messy and unfamiliar, and she didn't like it one damn bit.

"Take her back to her room."

"Aya—"

"*Please,* Tobias."

Aya's distress compelled him to move, the fight bleeding from his shoulders. When he stooped to scoop up Elaine, and the witch reached for Aya, she pulled her hand away. She watched them leave, and once the door shut, she hunched forward, pressing her face into her palms. In the quiet of the room, her sister's voice rose from the dark memories she'd buried so deeply.

Know this, witch, I am a child of death and you will never defeat us. We are children of Akaria and we are eternal.

Aya's hand fell away, the tears spilling down her cheek. "Please forgive me."

The darkness didn't answer. It never did.

•••••••••

Luck wasn't on their side the following morning. When Aya headed downstairs. Sabra and Tobias were arguing over what their next move was, now that Calix had requested them for a job in two days. Meanwhile, Elaine sat at the dining table, staring at the flickering pendant, her face white as death.

Fuck.

"We need to get into that refuge. Let me break in and I'll find out whatever secrets they're hiding," Sabra said.

Tobias threw his hands up. "Elaine's pendant is flickering. We have to go to Lilibet's."

"I think this job is a *little* more pressing, given that Honoria tried to kill us."

"We don't know she tried to kill us. Calix was with her. Logically, the priority was to protect him." He sighed heavily.

Sabra snorted. "Open your eyes, Tobias. I think it's a bit more than that."

Elaine lifted her head as Aya walked past, the shadows beneath her eyes giving Aya an urge to place a hand on her shoulder. Her fingers flexed, and she pressed her palm to her thigh. It felt as if the girl's piercing gaze bore holes in her back as she approached the arguing pair.

She forced her attention away.

"Why don't we divide our efforts?" At that, the pair stopped and faced her. Loathe as she was, she knew what job she was going to—even if it left her gut in knots. "I can take the refuge with Sabra. We'll dig up what we can on Yrene and perhaps find why she was there and not at the house Clarion had. While we're doing that, Tobias, you take Elaine to Lilibet. It's best if both are done at night, anyway."

The unspoken truth about Elaine hung in the air. Since her temporary pendant was failing, they had no choice but to return to Lilibet—either to obtain another temporary one or hope that she'd found a more permanent solution.

The doors had been shut during the attack, so Honoria hadn't seen Elaine wield her magic. Questions would arise in time though, and the spirits command pulsed through Aya.

Protect her.

But it seemed she was the only one who was fretting over *that* task, while the others stared back with a mixture of pity and concern. Sabra even reached out, but Aya shook her head softly, the hand falling away. Elaine was still in the room and Aya wasn't in the mood to divulge her demons to her, certainly not about her time in the refuge. A cold whisper of a memory bubbled up, the mocking laughter of a woman echoing in her mind, and the echo of nails sunk into her arms sent pain prickling along her skin.

She blinked, driving the memories away. "Can you send Lilibet a message that you're on your way?"

"Of course, I have no intention of appearing unannounced. I still have a scar from where she once threw a book at my head." He smiled sheepishly.

Sabra snorted. "You don't have a scar. You heal just as well as us."

"A *mental* scar. It was quite traumatizing."

"Such a big scary wolf, brought down by a *book*."

Aya caught the retreating sound of footsteps and saw the retreating figure of Elaine heading up the stairs. A frown deepened her brow. Before she realized it, she had already walked after her.

She stopped outside Elaine's room. Even as she raised her hand to the door, her heart pounding, mouth dry, she wondered what the hell she was doing. With a heavy sigh, she stepped back, turning to leave. The door creaked open.

"Aya?"

Drawing a deep breath, she forced herself to face Elaine. "You know we won't let Honoria take you right?" she said gently.

Elaine's grip tightened on the door frame. "Because you don't want her to have my power."

"That's not—"

"It's okay. Really." The weary smile said otherwise. "I know you're under some sort of obligation to protect me, much as you don't want to. At least that's more than anyone has done for me before."

Elaine turned and stepped back into the room, as if needing the distance between them.

Heat burned Aya's cheeks as she followed into the room. "You shouldn't be so accepting of that."

"As opposed to what? Hoping for things I've never had and probably never will?" Elaine turned to face her.

Aya closed the distance and raised Elaine's chin until their eyes met. Though Elaine's words had been soft, weary even, fire glinted in those jeweled depths; enough to steal Aya's breath away. It took her what felt like an eternity to utter the words burning her lips.

"There is a warrior in you. I look forward to the day she appears."

CHAPTER 21

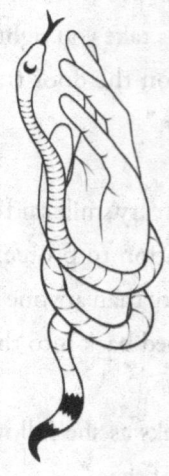

UNDER COVER OF DARKNESS, Aya and Sabra teleported into the back garden of the refuge. Dark shadows stretched out from a dead tree and twisted toward the starlit sky. What ought to have been a haven for those in search of peace reeked of death. Aya sensed the dead stirring close by, drawn by her arrival. She stared at the looming structure, so similar to the one she'd escaped years ago, and wondered, not for the first time, how she might burn it all down.

When she had first arrived at Purgatory, she had been assigned one just like this. It was all they could do for an orphan without family, money or any pack to join. After all, the hunters that had found her wandering the woods, starving and burning with fever, hadn't known what to make of her. She appeared human, but when they had tried to help her, she lashed out and threw one through the air as if he weighed little more than a rock. It had marked her as something distinctly *not* human. Beyond that, she'd kept her mouth shut.

Aya learned from a young age what it meant to be a necromancer—hunted, seen as less than, and worth a king's ransom.

"Aya?"

"Hmm?"

Sabra was at the back door, gesturing to the handle.

"Is it locked?" asked Aya.

"No, they left it free for us to wander through," Sabra drawled.

Aya kneeled before the door. "One day I am going to teach you how to do this."

"Why? You do it so well," Sabra replied with a wink.

Aya dug out her tools and made quick work of the cheaply made lock. She stood and pushed the door open. A loud creak split the air, stealing the breath from her chest. One hand dropped to the dagger at her hip.

"There's no one there," Sabra announced, sweeping past.

"*Sab.*"

"This isn't exactly a place crawling with guards."

A shadow darted ahead of Sabra. Aya threw up her hand. Shadows flared around her fingers as a ghost was jerked back into a band of moonlight.

It was a woman, scarcely twenty, with a tattered dress and skin absent from both arms, revealing her bones. The ghost girl stared, furrowing her brow. "You're here. When you asked us to find the girl here, I expected that to be the end, especially now given well..."

"There was a change of plans," Aya replied.

"And the demon?"

Sabra snorted. "I can see you."

Surprise flashed in the girl's eyes. "What?"

"Don't meet many demons, do you?"

Aya cleared her throat. "As *fun* as this all is, can we please return to the task at hand? If you could let us know where the girl's spirit is, that would be good."

It shouldn't have been possible for the ghost to appear paler than death, but she managed it as she stepped back, shaking her head. "That isn't possible, I'm afraid."

"Why not?" Aya asked.

"Her spirit isn't here. Yrene vanished soon after she died."

"That's not possible," said Aya. "No one moves on that quickly. Even at peace spirits will linger for at least several days." The only time she'd ever known it to happen sooner was with a necromancer's intervention—or if someone had stolen the spirit.

Someone didn't wish to risk the chance of the dead speaking. Whatever secrets Yrene knew, she had taken them into death and onto wherever her soul now slumbered. All she hoped was that Akaria was kind to the girl, her lover and their infant.

"That is all I know. I'm sorry," the ghost replied, breaking Aya's wandering thoughts.

She chewed her lip, mulling over what to do next. Sabra cleared her throat.

"We should check out the records the matron keeps. Might get some more information on this girl," Sabra said.

In an instant, the ghost was gone and nothing but shadows wrought by beams of moonlight dancing in the empty hall. She couldn't bury the unease twisting in her gut like a knife, that after so long, she might be exposed.

A hand brushed her upper arm. "Aya?"

"I'm fine. Let's get this over and done with."

•••••••••

The matron's office was on the top floor.

Refuges were constructed from the same design, a way to cut costs back in the early days of Purgatory. They were all cheaply made, doing little to hold back the cold once winter sunk its talons into the land, and the heat when summer descended without mercy. A cold chill whispered through the creaking halls, stealing what little warmth gathered in unseen nooks.

Aya approached the black metal door. A single padlock hung from the handle, gleaming silver in the moonlight. The small window to her right offered just enough light as she kneeled, digging out her lock-picking kit.

Sabra stepped aside with a grin, giving Aya enough space to work. The corner of her mouth twitched as she shimmied the pin in her hand, and the lock came free, falling into her hand. After setting it back on the door, they entered the room.

A small, cluttered office greeted them. It was filled with tables heaped with children's toys, a brush or comb, bangles, vanity mirrors, and jewelry. As she moved about the room, running her gaze over the chaos, she lifted a simple ring, gasping as a rush of emotions exploded in her head. The ring fell from her hand, clattering across the desk as she realized what all the items were.

Mementos of the dead, tokens of those spirits trapped in the halls.

It appeared that whenever someone died in the refuge, this matron took something of theirs as a keepsake. Something one might do if they had a hand in their deaths, or liked reminders of the misery they inflicted.

Her hands curled into fists. She wanted to rip the flesh from the woman's bones. Make her suffer like the dead bound to the refuge.

"Are these what I think they are?" Sabra asked, holding up a little stuffed doll.

"Yes." She stepped back from the desk, not trusting herself from flipping it in a rage or throwing every damn object at the wall, or tearing apart everything within reach. She felt the urge to destroy tear through her soul, leaving her hands curled into tight fists, nails biting deep into her palm until she felt the trickle of blood along her skin. "Let's see if we can find something useful. There may be something belonging to Yrene here."

She dug into the chaos strewn across the tables, doing the best she could to shut out the memories of those who'd lost their lives. They came thick and fast, but none belonged to Yrene. It was maddening. All those tokens of the dead, and none were the ones she was after.

She thought about trying to call in some ghosts to help, but quickly dismissed the idea.

It would be too cruel to let them see what was inside, even if she could get them inside. And on the slight chance that happened, she imagined none of them would stick around for very long. That she understood.

A heavy throb pounded behind her eye as she moved onto the next table. A feeling of hopelessness seeping in from all the tokens she kept touching. She paused, drawing back. Sabra seemed unaffected, and she thought she probably ought to let the demon keep searching. There was a danger in handling such items too much.

But she couldn't leave until they found something tangible. Something she might have control over, given the second she returned home, all she felt was herself slipping. Closer to madness, to disaster, to Elaine, and it terrified her.

"Aya!" Sabra hissed softly.

Sabra stood holding a book. As Aya looked closer, she realized it was a simple diary. She took it from Sabra's grip, gasping as Yrene's memories poured through her. Flashes of her life with her lover, tender moments stolen together in shadowed halls, the sight of her curled up on a musty bed with his arms wrapped around her. Both their hands resting on her swollen belly.

The image faded, leaving a warmth lingering in her belly. For a moment, she felt the baby within her, though the feeling quickly dimmed. Just as well. It was an unnerving experience.

Shaking her head, she opened the book and frowned. It was written in the same strange text as the grimoire, which she'd assumed was some sort of ancient language. She leafed through the pages, hoping to find something she might be able to read. A few drawings of Clarion, rather well done, dotted the pages. The depth of love and adoration was clear in every line. In the last few pages, the writing grew scratchier as if whatever Yrene was saying was a desperate final plea. She brushed a finger over the words, fear coiling around her heart.

Icy tremors slithered down her spine.

Whatever was in the final pages had left Yrene fearing for her life and that of her baby. She handed the diary back with a shaky hand, telling Sabra what she'd learned.

"Kind of coincidental that the girl died in childbirth? What if the matron had something to do with it?"

Aya glanced around the mess, considering the same thing. "I think that if the matron *is* involved, she's merely a pawn. This office doesn't belong to someone who is scheming to tear Purgatory down from within. My guess is, the girl knew enough that whoever is behind all of this couldn't let her live."

CHAPTER 22

THE NIGHT WAS COLD, and a breeze nudged Elaine up the steps to Lilibet's door. Her heart thundered in her chest, leaving sharp breaths racking her chest. She couldn't shake the memory of Lilibet approaching for blood, making her feel like a cornered animal, ready to lash out. A hand slid around hers, squeezing softly, breaking her reverie.

She flashed Tobias a nervous smile as the door opened.

Lilibet ushered them wordlessly inside. Elaine didn't miss the way she glanced down the street before shutting the door softly, lingering for a moment with her back to them. What had the fairy so rattled? Even the wings that folded down her back trembled.

"Is everything okay, Lil?" Tobias asked.

After a minute, heavy with silence, Lilibet turned, with a smile that didn't quite reach her eyes. "Nothing to worry about. I am glad you have come. I was going to send word to Aya about having Elaine come in for her pendant. But when I heard about what happened at the temple I let it rest for a few days so you had time to recover."

A lie, if ever Elaine had heard one.

"How much did you hear?" she asked, relieved her voice was steadier than she felt.

Lilibet swept past them, waving a hand. "Bits and pieces at first. I heard you guys were trapped in a temple with Hell Fire. How you managed to survive it is a wonder. You really are a powerful one, aren't you?"

Elaine shifted on the balls of her feet at the remark. All her life, she'd been seen for the power in her veins and little beyond that.

Tobias saved her a reply as he gently nudged her forward. "Let us continue the talk inside."

She managed a shaky nod and followed Lilibet to the back room. There were dozens more plants in the room, though they were in varying stages of decay and none had any blooms. Cushions were scattered across the floor, and there was a damp stain on the floor. The sweet note of jasmine tea lingered in the air.

Lilibet left them waiting on the lounges and slipped into her office. Elaine caught the sound of clinking glass on the other side of the door and the soft tread of boots on the carpet.

"How much does Aya trust Lilibet?" she murmured to Tobias.

"They have known each other for nearly as long as Aya has been in Purgatory. I think they met in one of the refuges when Aya was around eleven or twelve? I'm not really sure. Aya doesn't talk about that time of her life much." Tobias paused for a moment before he continued on, "I only met Aya when she was eighteen. Much of her life before that isn't discussed."

Elaine had seen the worry in their eyes when Aya had said she'd be going to the refuge. Aya had spoken steadily, but Elaine had picked up the tiniest note of tension in her voice.

"The refuges, they're not good places, are they?"

Tobias's jaw tightened. "No. The council keeps them open because it houses all those who don't have a pack or temple to join. It deals with the misfits, so they don't have to."

Her gut clenched at the thought of Aya being a child in a place like that. No wonder she was so hard and cold at times. "So, they know all about the terrible things that take place and they let them happen so they don't have to do any extra work?"

"That's Purgatory for you."

"Tobias is right," Lilibet said as she returned to the room. "This place will eat you alive. How you survive is based on the friends you make and the alliances you form. That's how Aya, who pisses off Honoria by merely existing, has lived for years without losing her mark. By being smart, and having the right allies. It's by no accident that she's friends with Calix."

Lilibet swept forward, holding up a golden ring. It was simple, with a small red jewel embedded in its center, glinting softly beneath the witchlight. She held it out to Elaine. "This will drain a little blood out of you while you're wearing it, but it will mask who you truly are. An ingenious design, if I say so myself."

Tobias leaned in. "Nice work. Where did you learn to make it?"

"My witch friend taught me. Don't tell Aya, though. For obvious reasons."

Elaine shifted uncomfortably, biting her tongue.

The pair regarded each other with a silent exchange, a secret between them that Elaine wasn't privy to. She pushed down the stab of envy and reached for the ring. But her fingers brushed it, knocking it from Lilibet's hand. The ring hit the ground and rolled under the couch. Elaine kneeled, muttering a string of apologies as she tried to see where the ring was hiding, when another glint caught her eye. A pin lay near the ring, the symbol on its head staring back at her. She stretched further, gasping as a tremor of magic touched her fingertips.

There was no mistake. It was the pin from Honoria's cloak.

"Is everything okay? Can you see it? I can lift the couch," said Tobias with concern. "Hold on—"

"No, no, it's fine. I have it."

She grabbed the ring, scrambling up to her feet, trying to hide her panic with a thankful smile. Her heart moved again, slamming hard against her ribs. As she slid the ring on, a heavy feeling settled over her, the usual hum from her magic near silent.

"I can feel it working," she murmured.

"Good. This will last much longer than that pendant. So long as you keep it on, it should work fine." Lilibet turned to Tobias with a warm grin.

Perhaps there was a perfectly rational explanation for Honoria's pin to be there. She was overthinking it. Anyway, without the pin in her possession, she doubted anyone would believe what she'd seen. Aya especially. Why would she believe a witch, even one who saved her life?

Elaine was painfully accustomed to folks believing the worst of her.

··········

Only later, when they were riding their mounts through the quiet streets, did she let herself breathe once more. She tried to get her thoughts in order and consider what she'd seen. If she concealed what she'd seen and the lie exposed, any trust she's built would be destroyed in an instant...and if told Aya what she'd seen?

Who knew what she would do?

"Elaine?"

She blinked several times, looking up. "Yes?"

"You've been awfully quiet."

Her gaze dropped to her hands, clutching the reins so tight her knuckles turned white. Forcing herself to loosen her grip, she pressed her palms flat.

"How much does Aya trust Lilibet?" Before Tobias could reply, she added, "I can see they are friends but...is it, well, does she trust her like she does Sabra and yourself?"

Tobias tilted his head. "I'm not sure, honestly. Lilibet was never offered a room here, so I suppose that answers it...but Aya has known Lilibet since she arrived. Time like that creates deep bonds."

And you have only been in Purgatory a short while, her inner voice whispered.

"I see."

"You shouldn't worry about Lilibet selling you out to the witches. She wouldn't risk crossing Aya like that."

"But didn't Honoria visit Lilibet that first time I came to town?"

The day Aya kissed her for the first time.

Tobias's brow knitted together. "That *was* strange, but Honoria *is* a council member. I'm sure there was a rational explanation."

"Because Lilibet wouldn't cross Aya?"

"Exactly."

It should've calmed the doubts gnawing in her mind, but her gut said otherwise.

Even when they were back at the house, and he led the horses away to settle them for the night, her mind was still a turbulent mess. Tobias glanced back over his shoulder. Their eyes met in the moonlight, as if he sensed the war raging in her mind.

A lump lodged in her throat, and she swallowed it down, turning quickly and striding inside. She didn't let herself stop until she was back in her room. The door shut, and she sank to the floor, resting against the door. A shaky breath raced through her as she drew her knees to her chest, burying her head between her knees.

It'll be fine. It'll be fine. It'll be—

The air rushed from her lungs, blood roaring in her ears. Sharp breaths stuttered over her lips. The darkness closed in, sinking deep into her mind and soul. And as she lifted her head from her knees, tears spilled down her cheeks. She pressed her hands to her face, trying to stem the flow, which only made them fall harder.

You're not safe.

She won't believe you. Why would she?
No one ever believes you.

CHAPTER 23

T HE HOUSE SLIPPED INTO a strange calm in the days—and weeks—that followed. They finished two more jobs, simple dinner parties, without incident. The leads they had on whoever was behind the attacks had dried up. Neither the diary nor grimoire yielded much, despite Elaine's attempts to decode it. She'd managed merely a few lines, and that was mainly guesswork.

All was too quiet for Elaine's liking. It felt awfully like the calm before the storm.

More than once, she tried to bring up Honoria's pin and ask about Lilibet's relationship with the witch. But every time she brought the words to her mouth, they failed to find freedom and she sulked away, angry with herself.

A sentiment shared around the house.

Aya had grown increasingly irritable, disappearing with Sabra for hours on end. Tobias said they were trying to hunt down leads but from the frowns they returned with, it wasn't yielding anything useful. Elaine was used to being alone even so. There were times she craved connection and conversation.

Tobias sometimes left during the night without warning, returning as dawn crept over the forest. Before she had any chance to ask where he had been, he would drag her off for a training session in the clearing with the stone pillars. There they idled away the hours. Sun or rain, they sparred and went through endless sets until the sweat dripped from her body. Despite the pain and exhaustion, she tried to learn from him, adjusting her form as best as she could.

One morning, as she was thrown to the ground yet again, she seethed in frustration. Why couldn't she get it already? No matter how hard she fought, she always ended up getting her arse kicked during training.

A shadow fell over her. Tobias grinned, one hand held out in a peace offering. "You *are* getting better."

"Am I?" All her aches and bruises screamed otherwise.

"Oh, come on. I'm not landing as many hits as before. I know you might not believe it, but you are improving."

"Not fast enough," she grumbled.

His brow dipped. "In a rush to be somewhere?"

"I want to be useful," she replied, glancing away with a pause. "I want to be more than my magic. That I am capable of defending myself."

"Your magic is a part of you."

She laughed dryly. "I wish it wasn't. All my life, all people have cared about is my magic. That's *all* they ever see. I mean, all Aya sees me as a witch. I'd like to prove I'm more than that."

Tobias reached for her and drew her into his arms. Elaine stiffened, but then allowed herself to relax against his chest.

"You don't have to prove anything. I see you as far more than a witch with remarkable powers. You're my friend and you have a place here with us. As for Aya, she might just surprise you."

She snorted. "The day Aya Sinclair says she doesn't hate me will be the end of the world. You'll see."

Even as the words spilled from her lips, the sight of Aya reaching for her, calling out her name, as the Hell Fire threatened to destroy them, her heart squeezed sharply. It meant nothing. It *had* to mean nothing because if it didn't, she was in bigger trouble than she liked to think about.

He finally pulled away, grinning. "I look forward to watching you be proved wrong there."

••••••••••

Aya sat at the dining table when they returned, a missive resting in her hand. The fireplace crackled softly, throwing a buttery glow across the space, catching the wispy strands of Aya's hair around her face. She didn't stir up as Elaine drew closer, or even when Tobias headed into the kitchen, noisily rummaging for mugs.

Elaine paused at the end of the table. "Another event?"

"The festival of Alantorei is tomorrow." Aya sounded quieter than usual, the hard tones in her voice lacking. A memory of something darkened her face.

"Well, we knew it was coming up. The missive is a little late though," remarked Tobias.

"My guess is his own people tried to convince him *not* to attend. I asked Alexios to try but it seemed that was a failed attempt," said Aya, glowering at the missive. "And now we're to attend. This ought to be delightful."

Alantorei, the festival celebrating Purgatory's creation. Elaine remembered Calix describing it and wondered why Aya had seemed so uneasy. He'd said that she seldom attended the festival, which struck Elaine as odd. Aya appeared the type who would enjoy a party; the wildness and opportunity to surrender to heady desire.

She pulled out a chair and sat. Though she wasn't sure what encouraged her to stay, only that the expression on Aya's face gave her pause. It lacked its unreadable mask, giving a glimpse into the woman beneath the practiced exterior.

"What's our role?" she asked.

Aya blinked, glancing up as if she'd just registered Elaine's presence. "There's some small ceremonial stuff where we'll hang around as Calix's personal guard. After that, Calix will return to his mansion. He doesn't stick around for long after the lantern ceremony, does his own back at the mansion, and celebrates with a private affair. We won't be required for that."

If that's all, why do you seem so damn troubled?

"I've been meaning to ask, what happened after the first attack? I noticed he has different personal guards. Why the new ones? Is that why he's not asking for one of us to be around him all the time?"

"He had Honoria establish new wards in his mansion and check over his new guards. We are only needed for those public venues where the wards are less effective or there are more openings for attacks." Aya's frown deepened, and she leaned back in her chair, burning a hole into the wood with a troubled look.

Elaine still hadn't told the others about the pin under Lilibet's couch. The fairy was one of Aya's old friends, so why would she be believed over someone like that? Tobias *might* think she was being honest, but she doubted he would side with her over Aya. Besides, she had no proof it was anything nefarious, anyway.

Even so, the words found their way to her throat. She swallowed them away. "I didn't think he trusted the council? Or is Honoria the exception?"

Aya sneered. "He said he's testing her. Still, a dumb game to play with her. He should wait until we have more information, not that we have much of that."

"I'm sorry I couldn't translate the journal, by the way."

A flicker of confusion pinched Aya's face. "Don't waste time worrying about that. It was a thin hope you might translate it, anyway. We know very little about Yrene. Ryker gave us her grimoire—at least, we assume it belonged to her—but that doesn't offer any insight. We're right back where we started."

Tobias made a grumbling sound. "That is not saying much. Someone is trying to kill Calix—albeit in a very poor attempt—turning random folks into assassins. Then there is the matter of Yrene, a pregnant witch who possessed a mysterious grimoire none of us can make sense of it." He rubbed the back of neck with a groan. "I don't like the stink of this. This whole situation makes me think we're only scratching the surface with whatever is going on."

Aya cursed beneath her breath. "The fact Calix is being targeted—whether he is the end target or a means to an end—means that whoever we are dealing with is smart and powerful. I just wish I could make sense of their goal. The first attack tells us they had inside knowledge but the ball attack struck me as odd. First the woman, whose mind was trapped, and then the vampire who was, we think, spelled into attacking. A feat that isn't easy in itself."

Elaine was slowly beginning to understand the strange place she found herself in, and she too had the impression she was a pawn in a much grander scheme. The real question was who the real powers were.

"If Calix is a means to an end, what would be the ultimate goal? You speak about him as if he is what holds this land together. Is the desired result chaos and a new power claiming dominance?" She frowned at the floor. "That seems far too obvious."

When she looked up, Aya was frowning at her. "If the goal was that, how does Yrene tie into this? Or is her role purely coincidental, and she's only linked to this whole mess by her lover?"

Elaine shook her head. "Unlikely. You mentioned her soul was taken from the refuge, that such an act is entirely intentional. My guess is she knew something. Her grimoire might hold the answers we need."

"I hope so," was all Aya murmured back. "Because this isn't the end and I'm afraid of where this will lead."

••••••••••

In the twilight hours, where only a ghostly breeze whispered through the house, Elaine crept downstairs. Her bare feet made no sound over the mood, save for the occasional plank that creaked as she hurried to the kitchen. Sabra left a pitcher of water out on the bench. Elaine dug out a mug and poured a drink. She was tempted to try and start a fire, if only to boil some tea but the effort was too much.

She lingered there in peaceful silence when the stairs creaked. Her gaze snapped up. Aya approached, blinking blearily. She was clad in shadows and a thin shift that hung off her full figure. A band of moonlight washed over, capturing every curve and dip. From the swell of her breasts to the flare of her hips, she was a goddess of the night.

And she stole the breath right from Elaine's chest.

Aya's gaze snapped wide and she stopped dead. "Elaine? Why are you up?"

"I wanted a drink." She held up the mug in her hand. "Did you want one?"

The burning stare seemed to pierce right through her very soul, leaving the air crackling between them. Her mouth dried. She refused to squirm but warmth flared through her blood anyway, pooling low in her belly. What was it about this woman that made her want to drop to her knees, to beg?

Seemingly oblivious to her torment, Aya nodded curtly and closed the distance. At the last second, little space separated them. Elaine's breath hitched. Aya fished out a mug and reached past Elaine, their arms brushing against each other. The hairs lifted up in a flash, gooseflesh rippling up her arms. She quickly schooled her features as Aya stepped back, pouring her glass.

"Is this to be a thing between us?"

Elaine blinked. "What do you mean?"

"Twilight meetings in this kitchen." Aya set the pitcher aside but didn't move away. "Was it a nightmare?"

"Um, no. That would imply I could sleep."

"Speak to Tobias. He can create a sleeping draft. Works a treat."

A pregnant silence settled between them. Honoria's pin appeared once more in her mind, demanding the question be uttered. There weren't any likely interruptions and it was the best time to ask. A chill stole down her spin, curdling the fear in her belly.

"Aya? How much do you trust Lilibet?"

In the blink of an eye, Aya was stiff, her eyes dark, guarded. "She and I have known each other for years. Why?"

"Honoria was there that day. The first time I met Lilibet."

Aya's gaze hardened but she didn't answer at first. Her jaw twitched, leaving Elaine to wonder if Aya had been uneasy over by the event. A tiny flicker of hope sparked in Elaine's chest.

"What are you asking?" Aya asked softly.

Elaine set the mug aside and gripped the bench. "When Tobias took me back, I found something...a pin. It looked like—"

"Careful with your next words. Lilibet is my friend."

She straightened up. "All I wanted to know is if your friend works with Honoria at times."

"Even if she did, it is purely for council work. She would not betray us." Aya took a step closer. "She wouldn't do that to me."

"But would she sell me out?" She didn't bother to hide the unease in her voice.

Aya's gaze narrowed. "Even if she did, do you think I would let Honoria take you?"

Elaine felt the weight of those simple words, hearing the sheer defiance dripping from them. She broke away first, unable to bear the intensity of the stare.

"And what would you do if they tried? If she betrayed you?"

At that, Aya was silent but there was a storm brewing in her eyes.

CHAPTER 24

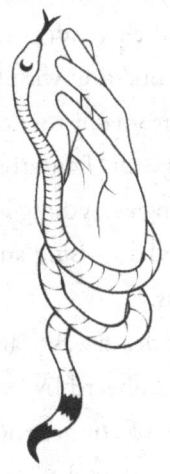

ALANTOREI HAD ARRIVED AND Aya was in a dark mood.

The conversation with Elaine kept replaying over in her mind, forcing her to return to questions she'd buried. Lilibet wasn't the type to betray her. She'd had more than one chance to do so over the years. There was no reason for that to have changed.

Right?

By the gods, the witch is in my damn head.

She blinked, trying to drive the madness away, and instead focused on the event.

The festival of Purgatory's birth, the day the spirits forged the shield surrounding the land. To reinforce the safety of the dwellers, they had created the marks affording protection to all those who took refuge within its boundaries. The only price of which, permanent residency and no chance to leave.

A small price, apparently, for safety.

A myriad of stalls with their vendors sprawled out across a large field under the starlit sky, bursting with wares and barrels of honeyed wine. The delicious aroma of roasted meats, pies, sweet tarts, and candied fruits filled the air. Lanterns hung from posts, lining the makeshift streets, casting everything in a golden glow. Laughter and song spilled into the night, rising and falling with the distant symphony of the musicians.

The veil between life and death was nearly gone, and ghosts spilled into the fray, unseen and unheard by everyone except for Aya. It ought to have been a time of connecting to the dead, celebrating their lives, and remembering who they had once been.

As she stood in front of Calix's tent as a private meeting took place within, she surveyed the festival with mixed emotions. The others flanked her, but only Sabra shared in the silence. Elaine and Tobias murmured to each other in low voices, and a thread of envy coiled in her gut. She wished she could gaze upon the event with anything but rage and pain and all the ugliness that stained her soul.

Old memories of past festivals bubbled up. The sound of her mother's songs, sweet and ethereal; her eldest sister practicing death chants; the smell of her father's cooking; and her brothers, grinning and laughing, as they dashed among the furniture in robes two sizes too big for their tiny frames. She'd always hung back in the shadows, jealous that her powers were dormant back then.

But after so many years, those memories blurred at the edges, and even the voices faded.

Time had taken everything from Aya, and it continued to carve away at her broken soul.

· · · • · · • · · ·

When the meeting was over, Calix swept out, his red-cloak billowing behind him. He flashed her a smile, his fangs catching the light of the lantern, his eyes glowing red. A faint sheen of blood stained his lips. Alexios was at his side, along with several human feeders who trailed out in a giggling cluster, vanishing into the festival. Aya didn't miss the lack of blood on Alexios's lips, but it was Tobias who spoke first.

"Not hungry, Alexios?"

The vampire smiled serenely. "I already fed."

"Oh?" A frosty note chilled Tobias's voice.

Before Aya could make any sense of it, Calix clasped his hands together. "Time for the lantern ceremony. We should go now. I would like to get the best seat and once this is all over, head off."

She repressed a shiver. The ceremony. The council threw one every year to mark the creation of Purgatory, and the damn thing was to be led this year by Marisol. Normally she could pretend to enjoy herself for the sake of Sabra or Tobias. However, after how the last one went, she wasn't so sure.

As they trailed behind Calix, carving a path through the crowds toward the center of the festival, something inside of her pulled tighter. Every breath strained against her ribs. Oh gods, she couldn't do it. She'd thought she could, but she was wrong. Blood thundered in her ears, a storm unleashed, determined to consume her completely. The muscles in her body screamed for her to stop, even as her mind pushed her on, at war with itself. Over and over, her soul pleaded to turn around, retreat to the safety of the woods and her home. The darkness whispered for her, beckoning with a gentle, outstretched hand and a promise of peace.

Her control was slipping as the last of the stalls fell away, yielding to a sprawling clearing. A large crowd had gathered, unlit lanterns in hand. The distant music tapered off, yielding to a growing silence. Her gaze drifted to the wooden dais where a single figure was already seated. Her breath hitched.

Marisol sat resplendent in her golden dress, shimmering like a goddess in the light, her hair woven with jewels. The human counselor appeared entirely *in*human, achingly beautiful, and a reminder of when Aya dared to love.

A memory flashed through Aya's mind. Marisol in a plain blue dress, hair braided down her back, smiling at Aya. They were lovers for only a few months, but Aya plunged in deep, her heart beating loudly whenever Marisol was around. The words 'I love you' had danced on her lips, and as she'd pulled Marisol in close, the lanterns lifting into the sky, she'd leaned in. Her lips had opened, the declaration filling her chest until it wouldn't be denied any longer.

Marisol had kissed her, and the words were devoured. She'd felt Marisol's love at that moment, thrumming between them like a brilliant star in the sky.

There had been no sign that Marisol was anything but content.

"Can we stay like this forever?" Marisol whispered on that night, smiling so brightly, she was a burning star; glowing, breathtaking, and stealing every moment of sanity Aya had left.

So of course, she'd grinned and replied so earnestly, "for you, I can make a thousand moments like this one."

"And what price do I have to pay?" teased Marisol.

"Kiss me every day."

Marisol's brow lifted. That glimmer of amusement sent Aya's heart tumbling from her chest. "Even when I'm mad at you?"

"Even then."

A heavy sigh, dramatic and fighting to contain a laugh, came first before Marisol replied, "very well, if that is the price I must pay."

What a lie it all was.

She blinked the painful memory away, her chest aching as if it had been carved open once more. Looking up as they approached the dais, she met Marisol's stare. It was then she realized she'd never been able to read her at all, that she'd been played for a fool. No matter her attempts to find a reason, she was denied the truth at every plea. For all she was able to conclude, she'd been betrayed for power and position.

And it all ended in a note, a few curt words, and left on the bed they'd spent so much time in together.

"Aya?" Elaine's voice cut her reverie like a knife.

They had arrived at the dais. Calix took his seat, leaving them to shadow his throne.

"Lift your chin. It's her loss, not yours." With that, Elaine stood on the left of Calix, right between him and Marisol.

Aya couldn't shake the words from her mind, even as the rest of the councilors arrived and took their seats. The growing crowd filled the clearing, the soft chatter fading away until a heavy silence claimed dominion. Marisol rose regally from her throne, her skirt brushing the floor as she swept to the edge of the dais. A priestess stepped up, carrying an ornate lantern in her hand, and handed it to Marisol.

Aya wanted to be anywhere but that damn ceremony. But as Marisol's voice ceased, and her lantern lifted into the sky, sparking the procession of others rising into the night, all she could see was that memory.

Her heart cracked in two all over again.

•••••••••••

Calix announced he was tired, and requested Sabra return him to the mansion. The pair vanished in a plume of smoke. Aya sighed in relief, the tension bleeding from her shoulders.

At last, the night was over.

She wanted to get out of there, even if that meant walking back to the house on foot. It'd take a few hours, but it'd be a way to clear her head.

Maybe then she wouldn't be such a mess.

Tobias clasped his hands together. "Well, now that we're free for the night, I'm going to head off. There is someone I am to meet. Do you need anything from me?"

Aya recalled Tobias's interaction with Alexios. Was her friend seeking the comfort of a certain vampire?

He grinned, eyes lit with magic, and she shook her head. He bent forward, kissing her cheek before striding off into the glittering festival.

Once he was lost by the crowd, she was alone with Elaine, who shifted on her feet, glancing toward the party. A hunger blazed around her, the air crackling with magic. Elaine might not be aware of it, but she was responding to the thinning veil and the ancient power that thrummed through Purgatory. She was a creature forged of magic, blessed by the gods.

Aya's heart softened. Elaine looked so damn excited by the revelry. She sighed. A few hours would not hurt. She'd survived worse and for saving her life, Aya would endure the discomfort.

"Come on, let's go." Aya started to walk toward the glowing tents and singing crowds, her heart squeezing.

"What?" Elaine squawked, hurrying after her.

As she fell into step beside her, Aya threw a dry look. "I can't exactly leave you to wander around alone, now can I? Who knows what trouble you might get yourself into?"

"As opposed to the trouble I seem to find myself in when I'm in *your* company?" Elaine replied.

Aya snorted. "I don't know what you're talking about." Nervousness skittered through her chest and she hurriedly asked: "Well, would you like to see the festival?"

All thoughts of the past and Marisol bled away as Aya stared into Elaine's eyes. There was pain there, but also a spark of hope that caught her off guard. It lured her in, perhaps against all better judgment, as she awaited Elaine's response.

"I want to see everything," Elaine whispered, gazing upon the festival with a look of longing.

"Very well, little witch. Lead the way."

Elaine's piercing stare plunged deep into her soul. A thundering flutter of her heart and she swallowed back the urge to grin, denying the euphoria skittering through her body.

It was a dangerous line she was walking. She knew it and she didn't care.

And deep in her mind, her sister's voice rose from the dark.

"Be brave, little sister. You have a heart. Let it sing."

•••••••••••

They visited dozens of stalls, tasting everything they could until their bellies ached. Aya didn't mind one bit. The skewered meat, tiny sweet pies, and candied fruit were better than she remembered. Warmth filled her body, the dizzying cacophony of noise no longer bothering her as it had before. Even the memory of Marisol had retreated to the darkness. All her focus was on the witch who darted excitedly ahead of her.

Those wild red curls danced as she moved, capturing the lantern light like a waterfall of fire.

Every so often Elaine turned to her, smiling brilliantly in the glow of a festival. Even with the ring dampening her magic, Aya glimpsed the power blazing within her. There was fire in her eyes, a strength that met the pain of her past with defiance.

Before she knew it, they arrived at the heart of the festival. The bonfire blazed high into the sky, plumes of smoke twisting together in shimmering ribbons of gray and white. Barefoot dancers floated across the grass, skipping, jumping, and singing. Their voices lifted into the sky, tangling with music that sang out from a dais nearby.

Elaine spun to her. "Dance with me?"

Instinct screamed at her to say no. It was one thing to walk the grounds with a witch, to lower her guard, but to reach out and take the offered hand? Her heart thudded against her ribs so hard that she feared it might tear out of her chest.

"I—"

Elaine stepped forward, far too close for Aya's comfort, their breaths mingling for a second, and took Aya's hand. The touch sent sparks shooting up her arm. Her breath hitched. She was mad. She couldn't do it. No, she had to pull away.

That was what she kept telling herself as Elaine pulled her across the grass, stopping in the middle of the dancers. As the crowd writhed and swayed, the heady air wrapping around her and the warmth sinking into her skin, she stared into Elaine's eyes. Gods, they had been piercing before, but as the wild madness played out around them, she looked like a creature of desire.

Instinctively, she reached out, taking both of Elaine's hands and raising them high above their heads. She stepped in close, their chests touching, firelight blazing across their skin.

"This is madness," she whispered.

"But isn't it glorious?" Elaine replied.

Their hands slowly dropped. Aya gently brushed Elaine's bare arms, the hairs lifting in her wake. A moment of stillness poised between them, the world holding its breath for a second. Time stopped.

The music shifted. Her hand rested on Elaine's hip, and they swept together, swirling across the grass. Embers skittered overhead, a thousand tiny glowing gems lighting the night as they danced. Drawing in and pulling apart, they never lingered too far away. Hands brushed bare skin, breaths mingled, a heady rush consuming them both.

All her focus was on Elaine, on the way she moved, effortlessly and ethereal in every step. Aya drew her in close, pressing her chest to hers, one hand running down the length of Elaine's spine. The girl shivered at her touch, leaning in close, lips almost connecting.

The music changed again. Elaine pulled away, stealing Aya's breath with her, and kicked off her shoes, joining in on a line of dancers. Aya couldn't look away, and the witch knew it, staring back with a molten gaze. There might've been no distance between them, the rest of the world tumbling away, until Aya swept forward, pulling Elaine back into her embrace.

They swayed together, hands intertwined, mouths inches apart. Aya couldn't look away from her lips, remembering at that moment how they had once tasted, and how she wanted to do it again. A hunger to surrender to the night, to lose herself in Elaine, burned through her, an unstoppable inferno raging within her soul.

"Are you going to kiss me, Aya?" Elaine whispered, the warm breath caressing the shell of her ear.

The reply died on her lips as Elaine pulled back, the firelight flickering in her eyes.

Aya stepped back, taking Elaine's hand in hers. "Come with me."

Elaine didn't argue as Aya pulled her out of the clearing. What she wanted wasn't for prying eyes. A molten heat filled her veins, compelling her to the forest that backed the festival.

She pulled Elaine with her into the darkness, their bare feet crunching on the leaf litter as they plunged into the ancient forest. Magic pressed against her skin. Akaria's power flowed through her, filling her with every step. When silence finally arrested the air, and all traces of the festival were devoured by the night, she spun, pushing Elaine back against a tree.

A gasp broke from Elaine's lips. "Aya—"

She crushed her mouth to Elaine, silencing whatever might've been said. The witch softened in her arms, pulling her into a warm embrace. Desire exploded between them. Hands clawed desperately at clothing, trying to peel it away and get at the heated skin beneath. Shivers racked her body as Elaine's fingers pulled up her skirt, trailing across her thigh. A shuddering breath ripped from her mouth as she bent lower to press kisses along Elaine's jaw and down to her neck. Still, the girl's dangerous little hand lifted higher, moving inwards, and Aya groaned as she reached her goal.

Heat coiled in her core. Her hand dropped, desperately seeking the slit in Elaine's dress, until she could push the fabric aside. She cried out as Elaine found her center, circling it with agonizing slowness, teasing out the moment. Sparks skittered through her body.

Her mouth found Elaine's once more, plunging in for a bruising kiss as her fingers found Elaine's slick heat.

Aya wrenched away with a wicked grin. "Do you want me to stop?"

"Don't you fucking dare."

Her lips brushed the shell of Elaine's ears. "And if I dare? How shall you punish me?"

Elaine pulled away, breathing hard, rolling into Aya's hand. Together they writhed, pressed hard against the tree, chasing the dizzying heights of pleasure. Gasps and moans rose into the air, tangled with their breathless cries. The tension ratcheted, coiling into her body until she felt her control slip. Dark magic spilled into her veins—

Aya threw her head back with a roar as the magic erupted around her. Elaine thundered on, pushing her beyond oblivion until seconds later, she cried out and slumped against her. For a moment, neither of them moved, breathing hard against the tree. Sweat glistened on her skin and her heart pounded hard against her ribs, shattering all rational thought.

"That was...that..." Elaine chuckled into the crook of Aya's neck, shaking softly.

"I want to taste you." Aya leaned in, kissing her hard until Elaine swayed. "May I?"

Elaine stared back, her gaze unreadable for a moment before she gave a nod. Aya kneeled, gently pushing up Elaine's skirt, who watched her through heated eyes. She leaned in—

A bolt of pain exploded in her chest, splintering outwards. Her head jerked back with a scream. Darkness howled through her soul, squeezing her heart hard. Something was wrong. Dread sank into her gut.

She tried to breathe, to suck in air, but no matter how hard she tried, she could only sit there, her chest burning until understanding dawned.

No, no, no!

Aya scrambled awkwardly to her feet, swaying as her legs quaked, threatening to give out. Another wave of agony crashed into her, shooting through her limbs. Sharp breaths racked her body as she spun, stumbling forward.

"Aya! Aya, what's wrong?" Elaine called out, hurrying after her.

"Sabra! She's—" The words were cut off as a blast of magic burst through her chest, the screaming agony clawing against her ribs. Darkness nudged the edge of her vision. Hands grabbed her upper arms, steadying her. Blinking, her vision cleared. Elaine stood in front of her. All traces of their passion were erased in worry.

She tried desperately to will the pain away, to clear her thoughts. If anyone had hurt her friend, she'd slaughter those responsible, even if it cost her mark.

Finally, she found her voice. "Sabra. She's hurt."

CHAPTER 25

T HEY SPRINTED THROUGH THE words, back to the festival.
Elaine kept one hand on Aya, ready to catch her if she stumbled. Darkness rolled off her in thick waves, pressing against Elaine's skin.

Once they burst through the tree line, the silence struck her like the crash of a wave against the shore. No music, no singing, and no hint of life. All was silent. The lanterns flickered, but there was a stillness about the grounds as if the world held its breath. Aya seemed to know where to go, darting through the stalls, leaving Elaine to follow.

Up ahead a small crowd clustered around a single point.

Elaine chased Aya across the grass, plunging through the fray like a knife, and as some watchers hissed at the intrusion, others shrank back when they spied Aya. It was the first time she had glimpsed their fear of Aya. Although none knew the depths of Aya's magic, they understood all the same that she wasn't entirely human.

The crowd parted and Elaine stopped dead in her tracks.

Sabra was on the ground, her chest torn open. A puddle of black blood stained the ground. Aya released a broken scream, dropping beside Sabra. She reached for her friend, cold as death to the touch, and struggling for breath. An icy wrath pooled in her chest.

"Who did this?" Aya asked in a voice cold as death.

A man stepped forward. "I saw a woman attack her and run off. That's all I know."

Whispers rippled across the crowd, though Aya appeared to have no concern for their interest. Elaine's magic hissed in her chest, pushing up against the binds placed by the ring. It burned her finger, but she didn't care. Sabra was in pain, which meant Aya was, too—and that cut Elaine deeper than she expected.

"Elaine, I need you!" Aya pleaded.

She kneeled beside her. The bloody sight of Sabra's mangled chest turned her stomach. It looked like she'd been clawed open. The demon's eyes flickered precariously, the light in them dimming.

Aya grabbed Sabra's hand, squeezing so hard her knuckles turned white. "I'm here, Sab. I felt you calling me. Please don't die."

Elaine reached for the ring on her finger. It was clear Sabra could not heal herself. Whatever had been done to her was blocking her ability. There was only one thing left to do.

She pulled the ring off and took hold of Sabra's hand. Closing her eyes, she tore down her walls and drew from the well of Dianera's magic. It roared from the pit of her soul, coursing through her body. White light erupted around her, blinding all who stood nearby.

Gasps filled the air, but she didn't care. She focused her mind and pushed all her healing energy into the wound. At first, nothing happened, for every defense that Sabra had attempted to deny her entry.

"Let me save you!" she cried, driving another wave of magic into Sabra's body.

The walls cracked and her power surged in. Elaine clenched her jaw and dug deep, holding on as more energy poured through. Muscles stitched back together, flesh remade, and what was broken was made whole once more.

The light dimmed and all her energy rushed out of her at once. Dizziness swept over her, sending her swaying to the side. A hand shot out, an arm sliding around her waist, holding her steady for a moment. The surrounding chatter grew louder, drowning out her thoughts, making her head pound until a single voice cut through it like a clap of lightning.

"*Silence!*"

A shiver rippled down her spine. She blinked, her vision clearing, as the crowd parted. Honoria emerged, her hood pushed down, staring at Elaine with wide eyes. It was then she realized that during the healing the crowd had been driven away. No one else remained except for a small group of witches and the other councilors.

All eyes were on her. The game was up.

She had exposed herself, something she tried her best not to do. Still, she didn't regret it. She had made her bed and would lie in it.

With the ring gone, the Grand Matron could see all the raw magic swirling around her. Ribbons of light still tangled through her fingers, wrapping up her arms like gauntlets.

Aya's grip tightened on her and she took comfort in that touch as she looked down, breathing a sigh of relief. Sabra was out cold but breathing deeply, her blue skin untarnished and looking as if it had never been ripped open at all.

"You hid a witch from me?" Honoria said with a hard look at Aya. "She belongs with her people. Not with you." The woman's gaze slid to her, cold as a winter's storm and she was a child again, back in the Arcan temple facing the Grand Matron's terrible wrath. "Whatever she's told you, she isn't to be trusted. Aya Sinclair *hates* witches and murders them. Did you know that?"

Her heart froze in her chest. It had to be a lie. A lump lodged in her throat as she looked at Aya, who stood staring at Honoria in unmasked loathing, the hatred raging like an unending storm. No words of rebuttal came, only a sneer that spoke volumes.

Aya's gaze hardened. "I've killed *one* witch and she deserved it." She pulled away from Elaine. "I may be a monster but, here's the truth, *Honoria,* so was your sister. Even until the bitter end when I drove my sword through her heart and severed her head."

Elaine's mouth filled with ash.

Honoria's gaze slid back to Elaine. "By the laws of Purgatory, as the Grand Matron, you are a child of Dianera and I command you—"

"*No.*"

Hushed whispers rippled around her. Elaine squared her shoulders, meeting Honoria's glacial expression. She was not afraid because she wasn't alone. Aya remained steadfast by her side, facing the threat with her.

"I said—"

"I *know* what you said," Elaine snapped and lifted a hand, fire sparking to life through the ribbons of light. "But I am no child of Dianera. I took no oaths and swore no allegiance. I am God-blessed, a Harvest Witch. I owe you *nothing* and I have not spent my time escaping the clutches of people like you to simply return to chains."

One of the counselors tittered behind her. Marisol swept forward and Aya stiffened, cursing so quietly that Elaine couldn't make it out. Instinctively, her hand shot out, grabbing Aya's. For a moment, Aya didn't respond, her body poised with tension. Elaine squeezed and Aya threaded her fingers in response.

"Elaine, you should know that witches in Purgatory without the temple's protection aren't treated well. It's the way things are here."

"Is that a *threat?*" Warning dripped from her voice. Ribbons of fire and light danced across her skin.

Marisol stopped dead, not moving any closer. "No, but you should choose your allies carefully. Aya might have the protection of Prince Calix for now, but how long will that last?"

"I'm right here," Aya mused.

A look of fury darkened Marisol's eyes. "The normal procedure is to bring her into town, but you hid her from the council. This is to get back at Honoria, isn't it? Let's not pretend as if you'd do this for any other reason."

Anger bubbled up in Elaine's chest like molten metal, scorching her throat, and spreading up her face. They all thought so little of Aya, even those who were once supposed to love her.

Her mouth opened, a protest rising to her lips when Aya laughed. It was a cold, brittle sound, like glass shattering. "Jealous, Marisol?"

"Don't be ridiculous. I'm not—"

"Did you even tell the council we were together? That you liked the way—"

"This isn't the time to discuss such things. You have only ever sought power and to reap vengeance on the witches. Your hatred knows no end, Aya. That's why you live out in the forest, where none but your misfits and the dead tolerate you." Marisol's voice dripped with venom.

"*Enough!*" Elaine threw a hand to the sky, light erupting upward and exploding outwards. Sparks rained down, a thousand tiny diamonds tumbling down around them.

A hush descended upon them all.

She released Aya's hand, stepping between her and Marisol, forcing the councilor to face her. "I belong to *no one.* Not a temple, nor anyone who seeks to take my power. I am with Aya and her family because they have shown me more kindness than *any* of you or any witches that I have met before this place. Do you really think I would throw it away for your promises of security?"

Marisol's gaze flickered to Honoria, a silent exchange unfolding between the two before the Grand Matron shook her head. She turned to Elaine, her features pinched. "Very well. Your decision shall be respected. A formal letter of excommunication will be delivered, stating your status as an unaligned witch within Purgatory."

With that, the tension bled from Elaine's shoulders, and she battled the urge to grin. The somber expressions of everyone around her suggested that perhaps being happy wasn't the best course of action. She dipped her head, bowing slightly, and stepped back to Aya's side.

"Aya! Elaine!" Tobias shouted from across the field.

As she turned to the sound of his voice, he came running over. His tousled hair, swollen lips, and disheveled attire spoke of what he'd been doing. The second his gaze snagged on Sabra, she watched the joy drain from his face, and he shoved back those who blocked his way.

He kneeled and scooped Sabra up in his arms. He faced Elaine, nodding. It was clear he knew what she'd done, and the implications of her actions.

Elaine cast a cold glance at Marisol. "We're done here."

CHAPTER 26

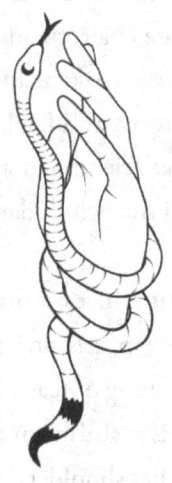

A YA FELT LIKE SHE was sixteen again, sitting by Sabra's bed, anxiously waiting for her to wake up. Back then, they hadn't been friends, and their bond was newly forged. A deal made of desperation and loneliness. She possessed every intention to let Sabra have a life within Purgatory without her—after all, who would want to be friends with someone like her? A wild, angry girl whose fury rivaled Arcan, the god of war's vicious nature?

Sabra had, apparently.

They'd chosen the house in the woods, heavily warded and away from prying eyes. It became their haven, the one place their true natures might be let loose. Sabra was the first person she'd dared to tell what she was, and the darkness that haunted her. Sabra had told her all that she'd endured at the hands of Honoria's sister.

Murdering her had been easy after that.

Now she sat in that same chair, beside Sabra's bed. Her powers stirred once more. The beast awakened from its den, prowling up to the surface, gnashing teeth and hackles raised. If the attacker responsible for hurting her friend had appeared at that moment, she would've unleashed all the hellish darkness within her, and she would've liked it.

At some point, Tobias came in, carrying a tray with some food for her. He set it down on her lap, refusing to move until she finished the stew and drank the hot mug of tea.

"She'll be okay. Sabra is a stubborn ass. This won't keep her down," he said, squeezing her shoulder.

She set the mug down on the bedside table. "Why did they do it? Why hurt Sabra?"

Tobias sat down beside her, the bed dipping under his weight. By instinct, she leaned against him, resting her cheek against his shoulder. There was warmth in his presence, a tenderness she ached for. In it, she felt a brief glimpse of peace.

"Whoever did this, we will make them pay," he murmured quietly, a promise of violence dripping from every word.

She smiled. "How blood thirsty of you."

"I'm a wolf. I protect my pack."

As his hands pressed against his thigh, she grabbed one, threading their fingers together. "That include a witch, too?"

"Of course." There was a pause as he pulled away, forcing her to straighten up and meet those storming eyes. "They will come for her."

"Let them try."

• • • • • • • • • •

At some point, she fell asleep. Jerking awake from the syrupy darkness, she bolted upright in the chair, heart pounding. Sabra was sitting up, staring back with a guarded look. Relief ripped open the floodgates, as she yanked Sabra into her arms. Before she could stop herself, tears spilled down her cheeks like liquid fire, but she was beyond caring. All that mattered was that Sabra was safe, alive.

Sabra was a statue in her arms before she leaned in, resting her cheek on Aya's neck. For a moment, neither of them spoke until Aya pulled back to wipe the tears away.

"I'm okay, Aya," Sabra said.

Aya punched her softly in the arm. "*That's* for scaring me. You nearly died."

"I must give my thanks to Tobias—"

"He didn't save you. Elaine did."

Sabra's mouth dropped open, leaving her gaping like a fish before her voice filled the room. "Did you ask her?"

Aya had seen the look on Elaine's face when she had healed Sabra. There had seen no hesitation when she'd taken off her ring and exposed herself to the vultures of Purgatory. All for a demon who had shown no kindness to her at all. Simply because it was the right thing to do.

A bitter laugh choked out from her. "Ask her? Sabra, I could barely string a word together when I saw you dying, or did you forget that we're linked? I felt you leaving and I was a fucking mess."

Sabra had fallen silent, drawing away with a pensive look in her eyes. The thoughtful look on her face gave Aya a flicker of hope. She sat back in her chair, waiting for her friend to speak.

"Why did she save me?"

The question remained unanswered. Aya had an idea, but it wasn't an answer Sabra was ready for. She had to come to that on her own and believe it.

Instead, she rose to her feet and kissed Sabra's brow. "Perhaps we were wrong about her."

With that, she headed out, feeling the burning stare of her friend on her back.

········

Tobias was curled up on a chair in his office, Yrene's diary in his hand. He was so absorbed that Aya's arrival went unnoticed. The room was a mess, a far cry from its usual order, with books scattered across his table. Magical texts, spell books, and a few journals she knew were stolen from an apothecary in town. She reached for one.

"There's nothing in them even I can read," Tobias grumbled.

"Oh?"

He closed the book, set it aside, and reached for a folded letter on the desk beside him. "A letter arrived for you. It's from Calix."

Her breath caught in her throat. Even without reaching for it, she knew what was going to be inside. Reluctance burned through her fingers as she plucked the letter and ripped it open. A curse broke from her lips as she threw the letter on the table.

"He's requesting a private meeting," she said.

"That's not as bad as I thought. I mean, when it had arrived by messenger at the ward I thought..."

She knew what he'd assumed. Closing her eyes, she pinched the bridge of her nose. A thousand scenarios were already unfolding in her mind. It wasn't the end of the world, but their lives were about to become infinitely more difficult. She'd survived worse. They all had. But that didn't make the oncoming storm any easier.

"I'm right, aren't I?" His voice broke into her thoughts.

Her hand fell to her side. "Probably."

"What will we do?"

She rubbed the back of her neck, hating the uncertainty that clawed at her gut with sharpened talons, shredding her control to ribbons. "I have no idea. I really don't."

• • • • • • • • • •

The mansion loomed before her like an executioner. As she slid down from the saddle, handing the reins to an attendant who scurried over, she marched to the front door. A light rain drizzled miserably that evening, the darkening clouds sominously.

Unease twisted down her spine.

The front door yawned open with a groan. Alexios met her with a grim expression. He gestured her wordlessly inside. Releasing a heavy sigh, she trailed in after him. Questions tangled in her mouth, but she knew it was pointless asking him anything. The meeting was a formality.

At Calix's office, Alexios offered her a reassuring smile before pushing the door open. He murmured a gentle word of encouragement before shutting the door behind her.

The office was exactly as she remembered it, organized and smelling of lavender oil. Calix stood by the window, his back to her, hands interlaced behind his back. Even from where she stood, there was no missing the tension in his body. She moved to the desk, her footfalls scarcely making any sound across the rugs. She didn't sit, instead resting one hand on the back of the chair, waiting for the words she knew were coming.

"You know I have no choice in this," Calix said softly.

She rolled her eyes. "Don't lie to me. You can do that with everyone else, but not me."

At that, he turned. Shadows crowded his eyes, making him look his age for once. His shoulders dropped, giving the air of an old man the burden of his rule too much.

"Why didn't you tell me?" he asked.

"Tell *you* I had a Harvest Witch in my possession? Don't insult our friendship by playing the fool now. It's beneath you."

His gaze narrowed. "You've never trusted me."

"Don't insult our years of friendship," she retorted. "I trust you but I know the position you are in. Do you honestly think I wanted you in that position where you'd be between Honoria and me?"

"You should have given me the choice!"

She spun away with a curse. "And I want her safe!"

A heavy silence consumed the room. Her heart thundered against her ribs, every blow a knife through her chest. She closed her eyes, snarling at the slip. For years, she'd always been so careful with her words, but since Elaine's arrival, something within her was unraveling. Her mind was fraying at the seams, leaving her more unsure of herself than she'd felt in years, and she hated it.

"You actually care about the witch," he murmured in wonder.

"It's complicated," she said after a pause. "And I didn't want to add to your situation. We still don't know who is trying to kill you, and I hate it. You are the reason this place hasn't gone to shit."

"You remember the time before, don't you?"

"How could I forget." She turned to him, her heart slowing. "It was your speech on the council steps that gave me the courage to leave the refuge."

"Ah, yes, you went to the Dusk Quarter after that, didn't you?" Before she could answer, he continued, "you certainly made quite the reputation there. I wanted to hire you a few times but... well... you were so young and..."

"And?"

He smiled ruefully. "The incident with Honoria's sister. Once you exposed the horrific experiments she was conducting, it made things easier for me to force Honoria into an alliance. She wasn't too happy you killed her sister though, which made it a little difficult to do business with you."

Aya shuddered as memories of Sabra, chained and broken in the witch's basement, flooded her mind.

"But you're still going to fire us, aren't you? Even with this threat hanging over your head?"

He reclined in his chair, a grimness settling over his porcelain features. "Honoria is spinning this story that you harboring a Harvest Witch is part of a scheme to cause chaos in Purgatory, possibly to overthrow the council."

"*What?*" She took a step forward, and his hand snapped up, stopping her. "That's bullshit. You don't believe her, don't I?"

"It's not a matter of whether or not *I* believe her. The rest of the council is inclined to do so. My power can only do so much," he replied ruefully.

As much as she hated every word, she knew he was right, and she certainly enjoyed alienating herself from the rest of Purgatory. Keeping everyone at a distance ensured her secret was safe, along with those she cared about. It hadn't caused issues—until now, that is.

"Should I expect them to come for me?"

"For trying to kill me? Maybe. I can state I don't have any evidence to support that claim, and that I believe your evidence. However..."

"If she supplies any evidence that does support that, you can't protect me?" She already knew the answer before he nodded, and she pinched the bridge of her nose. "I should have never taken this job."

"I am sorry for this. Truly."

For all their years of working together, she knew he wasn't lying. Calix never intentionally wrangled her into things that brought her harm—certainly not like this. He protected her, gave loans when needed, went above and beyond. It was why she'd readily agreed to his mission.

As far as apologies went, it was honest and still every bit as shit as it felt.

She rubbed the back of her neck, trying—and failing—to work the knot out. "How much time do I have?"

"I can't say."

"Can't or won't?" When he didn't answer at first, her hand fell away and her chin lifted. "Which one is it?"

He rose slowly from his chair, reaching for the glass of blood on his desk. "You should go, Aya, warn the others of what's to come."

"And then what?" She dared to take a step toward him. "I can't leave. None of us can. That's the price of life in Purgatory. Even if we could, there is nowhere any of my family could go, least of all myself."

"Then prepare for what comes next." He inclined his head as he lifted his glass. "Goodbye, Aya."

The heaviness pressed so fiercely upon her shoulders, stealing the breath from her lungs, she turned and stalked toward the door. Her mind churned with a dark and terrible future looming before her, threatening everything—and everyone—she cared about. How had everything crumbled so damn quickly, slipping through her fingers like running water?

As her fingers brushed the handle, a broken gasp cut the air. Something clattered as it hit the ground, and a split second later, a heavy thump. She twisted sharply on her heel, freezing dead in her tracks.

Calix, on the floor, clawing at his throat. Bloody foam spilled from his lips, a gurgled plea bubbling through. Aya surged into action, sprinting across the room. She threw herself to his side, reaching for him when he threw his head back with an agonized scream. Heart pounding, she tried to think what to do, but saving people wasn't something she know much about.

Another cry ripped from his bloodied lips as a thin trickle of red ran from the corner of his eyes. His eyes flew to hers—scared, pleading. A wordless cry poised on her lips, the frustration roaring through her soul like a guttering cry. His pale hand lifted, shaking as it grabbed hold of hers, squeezing for only a second.

His eyes widened further as a final cry was choked off, and he slumped to the ground, his hand falling away.

For what felt like an eternity, she sat there, holding the body of her friend. Every instinct of survival screamed for her to move. *Get up, get up, get UP!* But her body refused, and she stared, her mind a cacophony of chaos.

She barely noticed the door creak open until a figure filled the space, and she lifted her head.

A guard stared back.

The reality of the scene slammed into her, and finally, that sense of survival seized her and she scrambled up.

The guard looked to Calix, paling, before he shot her an accusatory glare. "What have you done?"

More guards filled the hall behind the first, and Aya realized the fight Calix spoke of was happening a lot sooner than either of them thought.

Aya straightened up, frowning. "Don't suppose you'd believe I had nothing to do with this?"

CHAPTER 27

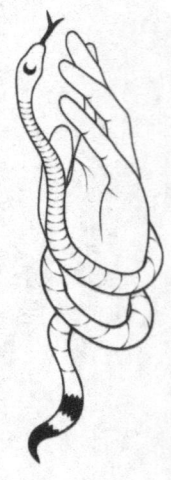

A LL HELL BROKE LOOSE.

The guards exploded forward, surging into the room with ringing cries and swords drawn. Aya twisted on her heel and hurled herself through the window. Glass shattered, tearing at her clothes and skin. Wind screamed in her ears as the ground rushed to meet her. As her feet hit the ground, she rolled forward and burst up to her feet.

As bellowing sounded off from above, she dashed across the garden. Something hissed past her head, slamming into the ground with a muted thump. An arrow. Before she could react, another sliced the air past her cheek, the feathers cutting her skin. The sting bloomed along the wound as she threw herself behind a tree and sucked in the air, trying to steady her focus.

She was dead—or worse—if they caught her.

If they hadn't believed her before that she was innocent, there was no chance now that she'd run. She knew many people already saw her as a murderer, so the idea of her killing Calix wasn't so farfetched. Blood already stained her hands.

She knew the mansion like the back of her hands having studied every inch of the vampire's home. Curious about what secrets he might hide, and also because it was her habit. Never ally yourself with someone in their home without knowing every escape route. Everyone was capable of betrayal, even those closest to you.

Her hand dropped to the daggers strapped to her hip. She sorely regretted not bringing her sword, but she'd been expecting a firing, not someone trying to murder her.

Heavy footfalls thundered closer, a death march on its way. Shouts sounded out, spilling into the garden. Taking a deep breath, she pulled out her daggers, kissing the cold metal with a prayer to Akaria. No one stabbed her in the back and got away with it. Today would not be the day she died.

"Give up, Miss Sinclair. You will not escape this mansion alive."

"People have been trying to murder me since I was five. You really think you are the ones who will succeed?" she drawled.

Silence answered. It was now or never.

Her eyes fluttered shut, and she turned her focus inwards to the raging storm of darkness within her soul. A cold chill slid over her skin. The awareness of everything around her sharpened to absolute clarity. Over a dozen guards filled the courtyard, inching closer; the scent of the grass, damp with recent rain; a bird that rustled in the branches above; someone in the house shouting an alarm.

She stretched out her hands, calling on the power. The wall containing it tumbled down and at once, the raw magic thundered upward and ripped down her arms. Her eyes snapped open as darkness exploded from her palms.

A hush descended over the courtyard.

"This is your final warning. Let me leave and I might let you live," she shouted.

"You think you can stop us?"

"Yes."

Laughter rippled through the guards.

"You're outnumbered," one replied.

She snorted. "And you're outmatched."

May Akaria show you mercy. Or not. I don't care.

She threw herself from the safety of the tree, bolts of darkness ripping from her hand. Two tried to move, but even with their vampiric speed, they stood no chance. The power bore through their chests, tearing them wide open. Aya leaped into the fray. Their eyes widened, and the looks of confidence shattered into fear, realizing at last what she truly was.

Bodies dropped in her wake, and even as they tried to flee, she descended on them with the wrath that sang in her blood. No mercy held her back.

Once she plowed through the last vampire and his body hit the ground, she stopped. Heavy breaths shuddered through her chest, sweat glistening on her brow. Droplets of blood stained her lips. She reached up, wiping it off with the back of her hand. She surveyed the carnage, feeling no guilt. They had been offered a way out. Their fates were on them.

As the bells rang out across the mansion and the distant shouts grew louder, she ran toward an open door and headed inside. She broke into a jog, hurrying down the halls she knew by memory alone. The magic thrummed in her blood and she itched for more bodies to drop, to surrender to the monster within.

When she came to a locked door, she stepped back and kicked her foot into it. Wood shattered against the wall.

Fuck.

She shot a glance back down the dimly lit hall, then burst through the doorway, plunging down some steps into a kitchen. The place was usually empty during daylight hours when many of the residents were asleep.

There was no time to appreciate the rich aroma of spices hanging in the air, not when a headless ghost sat on the table, or its missing appendage rested on a nearby bench. Two blank eyes stared unseeingly at her, and the body turned as she hurried through.

A few turns later and she stumbled outside. A low stone path ran alongside the tall wall looming over her, leaving shadows to gather thickly even in the afternoon light. The rain drizzled steadily and soon soaked through her torn and bloodied shirt. She tipped her face to the sky; the rivulets running slick down her face, washing the blood away.

Shouts came from nearby, so she took off down the path. The wind whipped up, lashing her skin with a thousand icy needles. Heavy footfalls rumbled on the stones, rushing ever closer. Her heart thundered as she flung herself around the corner, darting through the narrow paths and vegetable gardens.

The guards closed in.

She burst into the stable yard, the looming shadow of the barn stretching out toward her. Puddles rippled in the heavy rain, muddying the ground. Aya sprinted to the barn, reaching for the handle when an arrow hissed past her head, slamming into the door. The men spilled into the yard, their shouts rising into the air.

"The next arrow won't miss," shouted one of them.

A hiss stole from her lips as she turned slowly, raising her hands in surrender. Over twenty men now circled her, armored, and bearing swords or bows with arrows knocked. All were aimed at her. A crack of thunder split the air, and lightning erupted across the sky, splashing everything in a flash of white light.

"It's over Aya. You're surrounded," a guard said, approaching from the line of his men.

Heavy breaths shuddered through her as she considered her options. Her blood still hummed with magic, the death from the garden slaughter singing within her soul.

A cold breath fanned her neck, the ghostly sensation of a hand sliding over her shoulder. Dark magic prickled beneath her skin, lifting the hairs along her arms. It was a presence she knew all too well, for it had been with her from the moment her powers had first awakened.

You are the last of my descendants, Aya. You will not die today. Fight back. You must protect the witch, Elaine Tormelin.

The men closed in, taking her silence as surrender.

She closed her eyes, heart pounding. *As you command, Akaria.*

The walls fell within her, and the darkness pushed up, rushing outwards. Her eyes opened, arms were thrown wide. She felt the ghosts who stalked the halls of Calix's home, and those who lingered in the nearby streets. She stretched out her mind, entreating them to come to her aid.

Come to me.

Within seconds, spirits milled protectively around her, their ghostly presence a shield between the guards and their mistress.

The men stopped dead. Their fear dripped into the air. There had always been rumors of what Aya was, but no one had ever glimpsed the true depth of her power. She pointed one hand to the men, and they stepped back in terror.

"W-what are you?" one asked.

She took a single step toward them. "Death."

Shadows exploded from her chest, the roar of Akaria's magic erupting into the night, a storm unleashed. And as lightning split the sky once more, she released the monster chained within. The spirits leaped forward and the carnage began.

CHAPTER 28

NIGHT HAD FALLEN, AND the storm that had settled in grew heavier with every groan of the house as it battled against nature. Heavy winds battered the house, lashing the windows with rain. The walls creaked and groaned, fighting to stand strong. Elaine curled up by the crackling fire, a blanket wrapped around her body. A thin band of light peeked from beneath Tobias's office, and she could hear the occasional shuffle of footsteps along the floor.

She kept her gaze on the front door, digging her nails into her palms. It had been hours since Aya left and there had been no word since. While she knew it would take time to ride into town and back, she couldn't shake the feeling something had gone wrong.

Her mind churned with ugly possibilities. Flashes of Aya hurt or dead. No matter how hard she tried to shake them away, they returned increasingly vivid until she swore she could taste blood on her lips.

"You're being absurd. She's fine," she muttered, throwing the blanket aside and standing.

The warm air wrapped around her as she stalked into the kitchen, digging out a mug and the pitcher of water.

Gentle footfalls brushed the floor as she poured a drink. Thinking it was Tobias, she reached for another mug when Sabra appeared in the doorway. Wrapped in a thick robe, her blue skin was pale, and her dark eyes locked on Elaine. Her impenetrable gaze lacked its usual fire as she stared at Elaine, stripping her to the bone. She lifted the extra mug, setting it on the bench.

"Do you want a drink?"

Silence arrested the space. Sabra's dark gaze slid to the raging storm outside. "She should be back by now."

"Can you sense her? Is she okay?" The questions were out before she could stop them.

"She's alive," was all Sabra said, but Elaine didn't miss the quiet note of worry in the words.

"You're not sure?" Elaine asked.

Sabra hesitated. "I can't sense her sometimes. Calix's home is full of protections, so that can affect it; if Aya doesn't want me to know, she can shut me out; or if someone is actively blocking the bond and I can't get through."

Silence settled between them once more. Should she talk more? Something had shifted in her relationship with Sabra, and she didn't know where that left her. She preferred the venom. At least she was used to that.

"How does that work, this bond you have with her?" The second she asked, and Sabra's eyes widened, she cursed internally. "I'm sorry. That's prying of me. You don't need to—"

"I want to thank you," Sabra murmured.

Elaine's gaze darted up from the mug. "*Thank* me?"

"Why did you do it?" Sabra turned to her, pinning her with a searching look. "I wasn't exactly nice to you. Hell, neither was Aya. You could've…"

Elaine set her drink down and leaned forward. "It was an easy choice. You needed help, so I gave it."

They fell into a heavy silence as Sabra averted her gaze to the fire. Elaine longed to know how a demon came to be in their world, what the story was there, but she didn't know how to voice her curiosities. She was uncertain of Sabra, and of this gentleness that now filled the pregnant air between them.

Sabra released a shuddery breath, as though something within her pulled taut and finally snapped.

"I was ripped from my realm nearly sixty years ago, and spent the following fifty years imprisoned by a witch—Honoria's sister." Sabra's voice was scraped raw, agony dripping from every word. "I was so broken and lost when Aya appeared one day. This scrawny, vicious little creature with this look of horror in her eyes as she saw me. Not for what I was, but for my state, for the chains that bound me. She freed me, then asked if I wished to return to my realm or stay. There was nothing left for me to return to, so I chose the latter. Aya became my anchor."

"And the spirits offered you a place in Purgatory?"

Sabra laughed harshly, the sound like shattered glass. "No. Demons are not of this world and they were not interested in permitting me to stay, even with me being properly anchored ensuring I wouldn't lose control of my powers."

Elaine's gaze flickered to the mark on Sabra's shoulder, the same as the one that etched the inside of her wrist. "Then how did you get that?"

"Aya struck a deal. At that time, we both believed that debt would have been called in but as time passed, there was no request—until you, that is." A dry smile teased Sabra's mouth.

"I'm not like—"

"I know," said Sabra gently. "To the shame of my poor behavior, I know that now. Still, Aya has just as much reason to hate your people—well, more if I'm being frank—and she's softened toward you. Not simply because she wants you in her bed."

Fire burned right through her cheeks and up her ears. "That's not why she, why, uh..."

One brow lifted in response. "I know Aya better than most. She's never looked at anyone the way she looks at you."

"Even Marisol?" The words were out before she could drag them back in.

"Even her." Shadows flittered across Sabra's face as she looked away once more. "That human never deserved Aya."

Elaine didn't want to talk about the human counsilor, nor whatever the depth of Aya's feelings toward her might be. It was a lesson in pain and one she wasn't much in the mood for thinking about.

"I trust the witch who held you was properly punished?" she asked.

If Sabra was thrown off by the question, she didn't show it.

"There is a reason why the smart ones in Purgatory know to fear Aya Sinclair."

Elaine opened her mouth to reply but suddenly twisted to face the door. It flung open, slamming hard against the wall. A gust of wind howled through, whipping droplets of rain across the floor. A bloodied figure staggered inside, rain-soaked and with their clothing torn.

Aya.

Elaine rushed forward as Aya's legs buckled, and she dropped to the floor. Catching her before she hit the ground, Elaine slipped her arm around Aya's waist. Damp hair clung to Aya's bloodied face, her eyes were fully black and unfocused. Ribbons of shadowy magic rolled off her trembling body, the cold chill brushing Elaine's skin and soaking deep into her bones.

Sabra hurriedly closed the door after a worried look outside. "She's alone."

Aya shuddered in Elaine's embrace, whispering in a tongue she hadn't heard before, but that somehow struck a chord buried deep within her. A name was poised on her lips, caught only by the rapid beating of her heart.

Tobias appeared and lifted Aya out of her embrace.

Wrenching away from him, Aya staggered up to her feet. The black ebbed away, revealing the golden hue of her amber eyes, and the shadows retreated into her body.

Elaine had seen some of Aya's powers before, but this was different. A chill filled the air, and something familiar stirred at the fringes of her mind. Suddenly, all the hatred Aya bore for witches made sense, and why Aya had seemed to despise her when they first met.

It was a power she'd only heard about in stories and whispers, snatches heard from the very witches who joined soldiers on a country wide purge... Monsters, the witches of her temple once claimed, needing to be destroyed.

As the understanding twisted her tongue into knots, and she struggled to speak, Sabra asked, "Whose blood is that?"

"It's not mine. Guards...they tried to stop me but I didn't let them." Aya raised a shaking hand to her face. "Calix is dead."

Both Sabra and Tobias gasped. No one said anything, only the sounds of the crackling fire filled the silence.

At last, Elaine found her voice. "You're a necromancer."

Aya stiffened. All eyes fell on Elaine, the weight of their gaze bearing down, ripping the air from her chest. Shadows reached out to Aya as if drawn by her.

"That's why you... why I..." A knife twisted in her gut, bile rushing up her throat. Now she understood what she represented to these people. She was going to be sick. No wonder her presence had barely been tolerated.

Aya moved closer. One finger lifted Elaine's chin, making her meet that near-black gaze. "We will talk about this, I promise, but right now, we have to move. The council believes I murdered Calix, which means they'll be on their way here."

Elaine's heart pounded. "Where are we going? I mean, where *can* we go?"

But Aya was already pulling away, striding to the stairs. She looked at Sabra and Tobias, who shared a silent exchange. It was Sabra who answered.

"We're going where the council cannot follow."

Elaine's chest constricted painfully, the old fears whispering she was once more about to lose a home. "Where?"

There was an expression on Sabra's face that might've been fear. "We're going to the Dusk Quarter, the place where monsters dwell. It's the one place the council won't go—for now. Not even for a murdered council member and a Harvest Witch."

•••••••••••

No sooner had she gathered a spare set of clothes, the grimoire, diary, and a few personal items, was there a knock came at her bedroom door. She glanced fleetingly about the space that, for a short time at least, had become a haven.

The knock rattled her door again, breaking her reverie.

"Yes?"

"Can I come in?" Aya's voice whispered through the door—tentative, wary.

Her heart froze in her chest, barring the reply for a moment. She swallowed it down heavily. "Of course."

Aya slipped inside, gently closing the door. She'd changed into fresh clothes and a clean cloak settled on her body. Twin daggers were strapped to her thighs, simple and lethal all the same. It was almost as if the bloody sight from the kitchen was merely a dream. There was no hint of the darkness she'd glimpsed before either, nothing but an air of uncertainty in Aya's eyes as she closed the distance between them. The blood of the guards was washed away, but she still glimpsed it in her mind anyway.

Elaine flinched as a slender hand peeked from the folds of the cloak, lifting to her cheek. Hurt flashed in Aya's face as she dropped her hand.

"Are you afraid of me?" A quiet note of pain lay in those words.

"No!"

A beat of silence but something loosened in Aya's body. "I had no choice. If I'd let them take me, they might've broken me and found out what I was. It would have been a death sentence and not only for me."

"You did what you had to." A sentiment which had kept her alive for years on the run.

Aya turned away sharply, raking her fingers through her wild curls. "I can't say I forgive all witches. A part of me will never forget the faces of those who killed my family. It was that hate that kept me alive when I'd lost everything and everyone I'd ever cared about."

The world beyond that room faded away. The truth of what Aya was didn't scare her, nor did she think for one moment that she had killed Calix. She closed the distance, reaching out tentatively, brushing her fingers on Aya's hand.

In a flash, Aya turned and pressed her mouth to hers. The heat of their kiss exploded through her, thick with longing and desperation. Fingers dug into her hips, pulling her close as if Elaine might vanish. She reached up, clutching Aya's shoulders, returning in earnest. Breathless, wondrous, just as it was every time they collided together.

It was over too soon. Aya pulled away and pressed their foreheads together. "I don't want to take you to the Dusk Quarter."

"Why?"

Aya closed her eyes. "I wasn't a good person when I lived there." She gave a bitter smile. "Not that I am now, but I was worse then. The things I did. I don't want you to look at me like—"

Elaine's fingers caressed Aya's cheek. "Like what?"

"Like I'm a monster."

Something deep in her soul broke as the words spilled from her lips. "You don't scare me." She cupped Aya's cheek, staring into those fierce and wild eyes. "And if you're a monster, then so am I."

"You're not—"

"I've killed people, Aya. Some who deserved it, others who didn't. But I did it because I had to survive, just as you do every day." She leaned in close, their breaths intertwined as their hearts danced as one. "That is who we *are*—survivors."

The world grew quiet around them once more, neither making any move or sound.

A knock at the door broke the moment, and it was Tobias's gravelly voice rumbling through. "Aya, Elaine?"

"Yes?" Aya replied.

"We need to go. Sabra is out the front."

There was a retreating sound of footsteps, and they were alone once more. Elaine pulled away first, grabbing her cloak from the end of the bed. As she tied it around her neck, she moved to grab her bag when Aya looped it onto her back. She cast one final look at the room, wondering if she would ever see it again.

"Come on, we need to go."

She shut the door, reluctantly pulling away. They'd return, all four of them, because this place had become her home, and she'd be *damned* if she let anyone take that from her.

CHAPTER 29

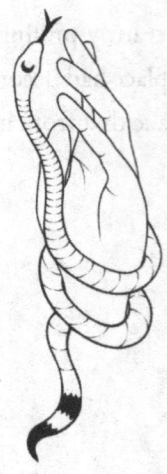

THE DUSK QUARTER WAS nestled deep in the mountains that guarded the western edge of Purgatory. The labyrinth of caves ran deep underground, with dozens of enormous cavern supporting small settlements. Unless you stood at one of the several entrances that led inside, it was almost impossible to know it was there. Those from the main town at the Inner District never ventured to the Quarter, a sentiment returned in kind.

Out front were two statues, spirits whose faces had been worn smooth by time. All that was discernible were their feminine bodies, half-covered in an ancient beard of ivy. Their hands stretched upward, appearing to hold up the roof of the cave.

"Who are they?" Elaine pointed to the statues.

Aya shrugged. "No clue. Purgatory is full of mysteries like them."

Ones Aya had little interest in unraveling. Their lives were in danger, and things were only going to get worse. If they had any chance of surviving the coming weeks, she prayed she still had some allies left in the place she swore never to return to.

The warm light beckoned them to enter, the same way as it had all those years ago to her; a teasing promise of wealth, of power to be claimed and danger to be courted. A poisonous lie if there was ever one.

"Aya?" Elaine's hand gently brushed her own.

All eyes were on her, though it was Sabra whose eyes bore the look of understanding. When they left years ago, it was under the hope they'd never have to return.

That she'd be able to escape her demons.

Once more, fate laughed in her face.

"Let's get this over and done with, shall we?"

At the bottom of a short slope, the Dusk Quarter appeared. Shop fronts dotted the main cave, clustered together in streets resembling rabbit warrens. Lanterns lit with glowing witchlights hung from ropes stretched between the buildings.

As Aya wandered ahead of the others, she realized that little had changed. It was almost as though she were stepping into her past. Familiar shops where she'd run jobs for owners, others that she'd robbed, some that offered her shelter in the early days.

It felt as if she'd never left.

Music and drunken laughter spilled from open windows and through doors as revelers stumbled out into the street. The stench of sour ale brushed her nose, pungent as they passed the first few taverns.

Several people shot looks her way as she walked past. At first, no one appeared to recognize her and a flicker of hope kindled in her chest. Then the first whisper brushed her ear.

"Is that her?"

"I think it is!"

"Bold, coming back, don't you think?"

Aya's jaw clenched. Home sweet home.

· · · · · · · · · ·

The club they were seeking was deep in the underground, nestled in the middle of a large cavern, pinched between two other inns. The porch was crammed with patrons, drinks in hand, leaning out, chatting animatedly together. As they approached, silence fell. At the first step, Aya paused, tension sharpening in her body. Elaine grabbed her hand with a firm squeeze. Instinctively, she threaded their fingers together.

"Whatever happens, don't leave my side," Aya muttered.

Sabra and Tobias offered their nods of support, the former slinging her arm over Aya.

"You think Nora is going to be pissed to see us?" Sabra mused.

"Me? Hard to say. You? Definitely."

"You think she's still holding that grudge?"

Aya snorted softly. "What do you think? You burned down her old club."

"*Accidentally.*"

Tobias moved in front, holding the door open as they went inside. Warm air washed over Aya, laden with the stench of sour ale, sweat, and ash. Wreaths of smoke eddied overhead, thickened from the small booths off to one side where people sat smoking. A young woman with catlike eyes inhaled deeply from a golden pipe, the end of which was connected to a tube that ran into a central metallic box.

Aya tore her attention away, examining her surroundings. Every inch was crammed with people, drinking, and smoking. Some were seated on tall chairs, gambling with cards, a pile of gold gleaming on the table in front of them. Musicians played from a nearby dais, a woman's voice drifting across the fray, rising and falling in a sultry song.

Elaine's grip on her loosened. Her gray eyes were glassy.

"First time hearing a Syren sing?" Aya murmured, brushing a hand across Elaine's cheek.

Gray eyes jolted to her, clearing. "That's a hell of a song."

"Focus on me and you'll be fine. It becomes easy to tune it out when you're aware of it."

The deeper they snaked their way into the club, the clearer the song became. At last, Aya got a clear view of the songstress. She was tall and willowy, with ethereal features and dark skin. Her black hair was braided intricately down her back, and every inch of her body was draped in jewels. Was she one of Nora's spies? Or one of her strays?

The Syren's gaze flicked to her, a coy smile teasing that roughed mouth. Spy, then.

Aya veered off to the rear of the club. Two burly men guarded a door, barring the way. Were they not expected, a snarling warning would've shooed them away. Nora might be still pissed with the way things had ended all those years ago, but she hadn't been in a hurry to deny a request for a meeting. No doubt the scandal chasing Aya was enough to pique Nora's interest and her opportunistic nature.

One of the guards pushed the door open, jerking his chin for them to head inside. Aya strode through first, leading the way up the narrow stairs. Witchlights flickered overhead, alighting on the myriad portraits adorning the wall. At the top of the stairs, one caught her attention. A painting of her with Sabra, their backs to each other, brandishing swords. She'd vaguely remembered the day Nora had drawn it.

Elaine stood with a look of awe on her face. "By the gods, is that *you?*"

"In another life," she replied tightly, heading to the first door down the hall.

Another burly man greeted them, opening the door with a curt nod.

A lump lodged in her throat as she passed through the doorway. It was years since she'd last spoken to Nora, and while she'd been surprised Nora even agreed to a meeting, her stomach still coiled into knots.

The familiar office, where she once whittled hours away long ago, greeted her with all its fine touches and warm lighting. A crackling fire lit the sprawling space, bathing the cluttered shelves and ornate furnishings in an intimate glow. It smelled of old books and honeyed wine and that lavender oil perfume she knew Nora liked.

Predictably, the woman in question was lounging by the fire, half-concealed by the tall back of a chair. One slender hand, deeply tanned and mottled with scars, held up a glass, idly swirling a golden liquid.

Aya lowered herself into the opposite chair, meeting a pair of piercing blue eyes and a heart-shaped face framed by a waterfall of black curls. "Nora."

Nora's smile split her cheeks. "Got yourself in a bit of a bind, I hear?"

"A little."

"No proclamations of innocence?"

Aya's brow lifted. "Do you really think I'd kill Calix?"

The woman stared at her with the same gaze that had cut Aya to the bone as a youth. "No. That's not who you are."

Because of their complicated relationship, Nora knew exactly who Aya was. She'd seen the uglier side of Aya's nature and survived. Few could say that.

"About why we—"

"Is that her? The Harvest Witch?" Nora cut her off, leaning forward in her chair to peer at where Elaine stood in the shadows.

Aya's grip tightened on the armrest. "If I said yes?"

"Well, bring her over."

As much as she'd rather keep Elaine as far from Nora as possible, it was unavoidable. She raised her hand, beckoning her to join them.

For a moment, she remained frozen at Tobias's side until he whispered something in her ear.

Aya didn't like how Nora studied Elaine; curious, assessing the girl for both a threat and an opportunity. If she believed Elaine was a risk to her little empire, their mission was over. And if she wanted her? Aya would destroy the one chance they had for solving the whole Calix mess.

And if that happened, no one else in the Dusk Quarter would help them.

"So, the rumors are true. A witch in the same room as Sabra and Aya." Interest laced Nora's words as she took a sip of her drink. "What's your name?"

Something flashed in Elaine's eyes and her head cocked. "You don't strike me as someone who would permit a meeting with someone whose name you didn't already know."

Nora tipped her head back and laughed. "What a delightful creature you are! No wonder Aya has kept you so close. She always had an eye for such *treasures.*"

The glance from Elaine at that statement had Aya wanting to throttle Nora.

Nora's teasing smile fell away. "May I have your hand, Elaine?"

Aya groaned inwardly. She'd known that Nora would want to do a reading.

Elaine nodded her assent and slipped her hand into Nora's. For a moment, there was silence. Nora peered closer and muttered something.

Aya couldn't breathe. She'd felt firsthand how intense Nora's prying could be. Surely Nora wasn't going to—

Elaine staggered back with a soundless cry and fell to the floor.

Aya was on her feet in a flash, the others striding across the room. "What did you do?" she snarled, kneeling at Elaine's side.

Nora's lips twitched. "I merely wanted to see if the rumors were true." Her gaze slid to Elaine, and Aya felt the twinge of unease as Nora spoke again. "This little witch is going to change everything in Purgatory. I can feel it."

Aya helped Elaine up. "Since when do you believe in destiny?"

"Things aren't like they once were, Aya." Nora reclined in her armchair, that unreadable gaze flickering to the fire. "Your request for refuge and aid is accepted."

CHAPTER 30

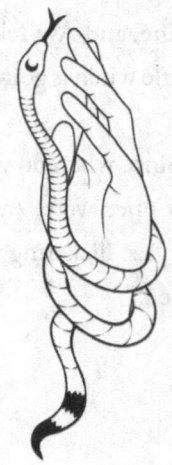

A s THE OTHERS WERE led away by one of Nora's attendants, Elaine cast Aya a final worried glance before she, too, was out of sight. Once the door shut, silence hung heavy in the room. Aya closed her eyes, savoring the notes of ash and charred wood. It reminded her of home, allowing her to imagine for a moment that not everything had gone to shit.

"So, let me get this straight. You're with a witch. You're accused of a murder you didn't *actually* commit, and you've pissed off the council," drawled Nora. "You've been busy since you left."

Aya slanted her an arch look. "So have you. This place is much nicer than the last club."

"Yes, well, had to do a little rebuilding after Sabra's little fire incident."

"Accidentally."

Nora snorted. "Accidentally drunk?" She waved a manicured hand. "Anyway, enough about that. Tell me what happened?"

"Didn't your spies tell you everything?"

"*Aya.*"

She grumbled beneath her breath and turned toward the fire, crossing her arms across her chest. The words spilled from her lips; from Elaine's arrival, the work with Calix, right up until she walked into the club. When she finished, only the crackling fire and distant music permeated the office. After what felt like an eternity, there was a rustle of movement and Nora appeared beside her, swathed in firelight. Those once vibrant, wild eyes with such youthful fire were dimmed by responsibility, and shadows crowded her face.

"Well, I'm glad I'm not the only one at odds with council," murmured Nora, a ghost of a smile pulling at her mouth.

Aya turned to her friend. "What happened?"

"Beyond the usual shit?" Nora laughed dryly; sobering, she stared deeply into the fire. "Started with a few disappearances; some excommunicated witches, a nymph, two of my people, and a wolf. Normally, folks vanish for a few days here, but it's the Dusk Quarter. No one really disappears into thin air. After a while, they started turning up dead, discarded in alleys."

"Signs of torture or...?"

"None. Their necks were snapped, but that's it. Any leads we had quickly dried up and...and I reached out to the one person who has a better spy network than me."

Aya's breath hitched. "Calix."

"I didn't expect him to help but he did. Had some of his contacts make inquiries, tracked down leads they found—all of which amounted to only one thing. A woman, can't pin down an exact description, was seen with *all* the victims. She was seen walking with them down one of the tunnels that runs off this cavern. After that, none of them were seen alive again."

"Were you able to find out anything else?"

Nora shook her head grimly. "No. The disappearances stopped right before the first assassination attempt on Calix. After that, he withdrew his men to focus on that. Not that I blame him for doing so." She raked a slender hand through her hair. "I'm sorry he died, though. He was one of the good ones. Helped keep tensions down between the Dusk Quarter and the Inner District. Won't be long until it goes back to being a shit show again."

"I'm sorry," said Aya. She didn't know what else to say, how to comfort a friend she badly hurt years ago. Back then, Nora was the sort to fight for those who couldn't defend themselves, and she was fiercely passionate. Every loss always struck her hard then and time, it seemed, hadn't diminished that trait.

"Some of them had family and I haven't been able to give any answers." Nora shook her head, as if clearing an errant thought away. "But you didn't come here to listen to my problems. Your situation...

It's interesting. I mean, I certainly never imagined I'd see you look at a witch the way you do."

Aya scowled. "I don't... It's not like that."

Nora snorted. "You have feelings for her. More than I've seen you show for anyone. Not that you don't care for Sabra or Tobias. Your bond with them is different."

Shifting uncomfortably in the chair, she sighed. "It's complicated."

"Because of what you are?"

Aya wasn't surprised that Nora knew what she was. If anyone was smart enough to figure it out, Nora was.

"You could've made yourself a rich woman, Nora." Aya frowned at the siren, wondering why her secret had never been revealed.

Nora rolled her eyes. "I *am* a rich woman. Just because I prefer this den of depravity for my sacred ground doesn't mean I'm poor, or desperate. Besides, why would I dare to risk Akaria's wrath? You're probably the last of her descendants. Any of the new arrivals we've had over the years spoke of the slaughter of the necromancers, how horrific it was. I'd like to think I have some standards."

"You have standards?"

"Some." Nora pushed away from the fire and stalked back to her chair. "I'll help you but I want something in return."

Aya returned to the other seat and sat down. Walking into the club, she knew there would be a price, but a little part of her was afraid of what Nora might want. Aya was a very different person when she lived in the Dusk Quarter—vicious, violent and utterly destructive. It served her well to *remove* folks when she was paid to do so, an act Nora even hired her for on occasion.

For a girl of sixteen, Aya already had a trail of bodies in her wake. Honoria's sister wasn't the first—or the last.

"What's the price?"

"A job of my choosing. Just one."

There was more to it but, for now, Nora was clearly inclined to omit the details. Were it not for her present circumstance, Aya might've dug her heels in. As it was, she was fresh out of options and allies, both of which she sorely needed. Nora was the second-best option to Calix; just as clever, nearly as resourceful, and for whatever reason, did care about Aya to some degree.

"You have a deal."

Nora leaned forward in her chair. "Good, now tell me what do you require?"

Before she uttered a single word, the door swung open. A hooded woman strode in and handed Nora a letter before bowing, then slipping out. All of it was over in a matter of seconds. Nora tore open the letter, her eyes flying across the word before they snapped up.

"What is it?" asked Aya, taking a step forward.

"It's Alexios. The council arrested him on charges of murder and treason."

CHAPTER 31

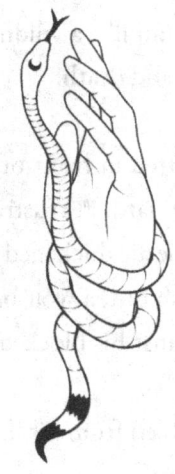

N O ONE SAID ANYTHING as Aya relayed Nora's words.

Sabra dropped her drink, the glass shattering across the floor. Fragments glittered with golden liqueur. A heavy silence reigned over the small room.

Tobias froze. All color drained from his face as he slumped against the wall. His eyes were wide, unseeing, as if he were in his own terrible nightmare they were not privy to. She knew that look of horror, the terrible darkness consuming him from within, and ached to comfort him.

She reached for him. "Tobias?"

He stared at her; his agony laid bare in those tortured, dark eyes. "Please tell me she's wrong, Aya."

"Tobias—"

At the gentleness in her voice, he surged off the wall and shoved past her. A new fire seized his eyes and understood exactly what thought burned through him like a wildfire. One that would only end in blood and madness and death.

"Tobias!"

In a blink, Sabra teleported in front of him, barring his escape. Tobias stopped, breathing hard. A frustrated growl tore from his throat, rippling through the air thickened with tension. Every inch of him was straining to lash out, a wolf barely contained. Yet even as he appeared to rage against his blocked path, he refrained from hurting Sabra.

Only a single word tumbled from his lips, as if it was all the wolf within would permit spoken.

"*Move.*"

Sabra didn't even flinch.

Aya drifted cautiously closer, stopping just out of reach.

All the suspicions that whispered to her for the past few months corralled in her chest, gathering momentum into a single question. One she'd dared not ask, if only to allow him time to tell her himself. For there was only one reason to compel a wolf—especially one such as Tobias, typically so calm and in control—to act that way.

"Tobias, is Alexios your mate?"

The fight rushed from Tobias's shoulders and he uttered in such a soft, broken voice, her soul cried out. "Yes."

Her breath caught in her throat, and a single word in her own mind was uttered by Sabra at the same time.

"Fuck."

"Are you bonded?" she asked next as the whisper of fear gnawed at her mind.

He managed a tiny shake of his head.

She repressed the relief flaring low in her belly, easing a fraction of the tension from her body. It was a selfish thought and she loathed every second of it. Before she could even offer a fraction of comfort, Elaine swept past and grabbed his hand.

Aya took a step forward by instinct.

Tobias softened at Elaine's touch and as the witch began to pull him from the door, he offered no protest. Aya remained poised where she was, watching them both with hawkish eyes. As much as she trusted her friend, he was a wolf in agony over his captured mate.

There were no guarantees.

Tobias moved first; slowly, his head bowed in defeat. For a man usually larger than life, he appeared frail and small as Elaine gently guided him from the door. A little of the tension eased within Aya as she released a shaky breath. The shadows retreated. Sabra's brow lifted in unison with her as they watched the other two move toward the fireplace.

He offered no fight either when Elaine encouraged him to sit, and she knelt before him. The crackling firelight danced across her pale skin, through the wild curls down her back, reminding Aya of a goddess. Her heart gave a traitorous flip.

"Can we keep her?" Sabra murmured.

"What?"

Sabra shrugged. "All I'm saying is that it's handy having someone who can calm him down." As Elaine murmured something to Tobias, Sabra whispered to Aya, "I knew he had someone on the side, but I didn't think it was a mate—let alone Alexios. Did you know?"

She frowned. "I had...suspicions but that doesn't mean much now. We'll have to save Alexios now. That much is decided."

Sabra sighed. "Of course, but it's probably going to get us all killed."

Aya smiled. "When did that ever stop us from doing anything?"

∗∗∗∗∗∗∗∗∗∗

A few minutes later, a young woman entered with some food. By this time, Tobias had calmed down. They had gotten him to eat a few mouthfuls, though he chewed with a distracted stare. He glanced out the window, silent. Aya knew that dark look in his eyes. They had to make a move fast before he did something foolish.

Sabra repeatedly attempted to lure him into a conversation, but after several minutes of trying, she shot an exasperated look at Aya. Tobias would not be distracted from whatever he was planning. And he had something in mind. Aya knew him for far too long to be fooled by his momentary obedience. He bore just as much cunning as the rest of them.

Aya tried to eat, but every mouthful felt as if she were chewing on leather. Not even the honeyed wine could ease the tension tangled in her stomach.

She eyed Elaine who was picking distractedly at her plate. Almost without thinking, she placed her hand on Elaine's. She flinched, glancing up with wide eyes.

"Yes?"

"Are you okay?" Aya asked gently.

Elaine's mouth tightened into a thin line, and her gaze slid to Tobias. "I'm worried about him."

She opened her mouth to respond when someone knocked at the door. Tobias was on his feet in a flash. The door opened and Nora stood in the doorway.

"Do you have news of Alexios?" Tobias asked a note of urgency in his voice.

Nora shook her head. "No, but I have something else that might interest you."

"What is it?" asked Aya.

"I found an old friend of mine who might be able to translate those books of yours. She'll come here tomorrow."

Aya's brow lifted. "Well, that's mysterious. Who is she?"

"Penelope Dava, a former witch of the Dianeran temple."

CHAPTER 32

THE GRIMOIRE, AS IT turned out, was a lesson in madness. Elaine curled up in the armchair by the fireplace, trying—and failing—to make sense of the mystery in her hands. Though she was fairly educated in a myriad of languages, allowing her to recognize a little of the text, she was still frustratingly lost.

She was so lost in her thoughts she didn't realize she was no longer alone until someone cleared their throat. A yelp tore from her lips and the book tumbled from her hands, hitting the floor with a muted thump. She quickly picked it up off the ground, shooting a withering look at the demon by the door.

Sabra's musical laugh spilled across the room. She leaned against the wall, half shrouded in shadow, with a glint of humor glittering in her dark eyes. One pale blue hand was pressed over her mouth, as attempting to stifle any further sound.

"My, you *are* jumpy. If I'd wanted to kill you, you'd already be dead," Sabra said serenely.

The smile did nothing to comfort her. Elaine bent down, keeping her eyes on Sabra as she grabbed the diary. "Couldn't sleep?"

"I don't sleep much," Sabra replied, studying her fingers as if they were the most interesting thing in the room. "What about you? Worried?"

"You will have to be more specific."

Sabra gave her an arch look. "Perhaps the fact the council is hunting us; that there appears to be some grand conspiracy threatening Purgatory, the first place you're considering calling home; or Tobias, who may or may not run off on some stupid mission to save his mate."

Elaine laughed. "You're forgetting the part where Honoria wants me for my power."

"Ah yes, that little delight." Sabra glided forward and dropped into the opposite chair. She reached out to the fire, rubbing her hands together before facing her palms to the flames. "Any luck with that grimoire of yours?"

"Nothing helpful. I just wish I could understand how Yrene plays into this—if she does, at all." Elaine closed the book with a frown. "Someone ensured that even in death, we couldn't learn her secrets. Why do that if she wasn't involved somehow?"

"A bargaining chip to ensure her lover's obedience?"

She slumped back in her chair with a heavy sigh. "Perhaps. She might have seen who manipulated him. Maybe that is all her connection to this is." After a beat, she shot Sabra a curious look. "You're being nice to me."

Something flickered in Sabra's eyes. The glittering humor vanished beneath a quiet air, and Sabra looked to the fire, as if searching for strength or answers. It was the first time, Elaine realized, she was in the room with Sabra without any concern. There was no niggling voice whispering this demon loathed her existence, nor wanted her dead.

"I wanted to say I'm sorry," whispered Sabra. "For how I treated you."

A lump lodged in Elaine's throat. "I... You had your reasons."

"Perhaps but that hardly excuses it."

Elaine never liked receiving apologies, mostly because she scarcely understood how to act afterward. She knew Sabra's story, at least enough to know why she struggled so much with witches—Aya included. But she still felt unworthy of Sabra's acceptance. All she'd done was heal her. It didn't feel like it was *enough*.

Before she could say anything, the door was flung open. Aya strode in with an expression of fury on her face.

Sabra jumped up. "What is it?"

Aya rubbed the back of her neck. "Have you seen Tobias?"

"Not since the dinner. Oh, fuck. He's gone, isn't he?"

Elaine's strength rushed from her. Tobias had run after Alexios. She'd hoped that Aya's words might've stopped any reckless actions.

Aya paced the room, cursing over and over. The anger yielded to panic; her face pale as death.

"He's going to get himself killed," she snarled.

Sabra grabbed Aya by the shoulders. "No, he's not, because we're going to go after him. Aren't we, Elaine?"

The pair turned to stare at her. She moved to join them. In the short time that she'd known them all, they'd become as dear to her as family. Tobias was the first one to show her kindness when she felt alone and confused.

"Sabra is right," she said, grabbing Aya's hand, "we're going to find him and bring him home."

CHAPTER 33

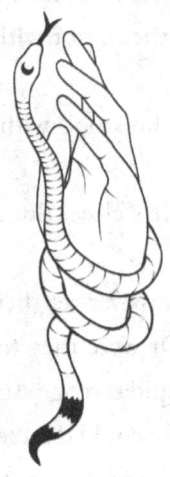

T HE SHADOWS BLED AWAY as they emerged at the edge of the
Inner District. The glittering lights strung between buildings
shone brightly in the dark. Carriages trundled along the cobblestone
streets and groups of people ambled along without a care at all.
Outwardly, it appeared as little had changed, and as though their
small, fragile world wasn't on the cusp of chaos.

As a creature of death, Aya felt the change stirring in the shadows.
Something out of sight was calling to her. A voice, soft and ancient,
bursting with unbridled power.

"Aya?" Elaine's voice brushed her mind.

She blinked. "I'm okay."

Elaine's brow lifted, as if to say, *I don't believe you one bit.* Mercifully, she offered no argument and let the lie be.

Their spot at the tree line kept them from view, but that didn't make her feel any less exposed. At least at the Dusk Quarter, the council could not touch them, not without starting a fight they weren't ready for.

Aya glanced at Sabra, who stood with her eyes shut. "Can you sense him?"

Sabra's eyes opened. "He's close. But Aya, I can sense wards all over the place."

Traps for them. Had whoever set them known about Tobias's connection to Alexios? Or were they for Aya, thinking that she might lash out in some stupid revenge attack?

"Elaine, do you think you could disable them?" Aya asked.

Elaine pushed back her hood, her eyes glowing gold in the dark. "Maybe. I can't make any promises. I won't know until I get closer."

It was better than nothing.

"Let's hope we can find him before he does anything stupid."

·········

They hung close to the trees as long as they could, following the forest along the outskirts of town until the council building appeared. It sat apart from the other larger buildings in the area. The pale cream stone, unblemished despite its age, and the windows reminded her of a ghostly face. Dark eyes that watched without feeling, passing judgment on all who passed through those fateful doors.

Outwardly, one might not know of the cells deep beneath the earth, harboring those convicted of heinous crimes and condemned to death. More than once, Aya met the ghosts that called that hell their home, indifferent to their pleas of innocence. They didn't know she could see within their broken souls, like recognizing like.

"Ah, *fuck*," said Sabra. As Aya glanced at her, Sabra pinched the bridge of her nose. "You're going to be pissed."

Aya sighed heavily. "He's already broken in, hasn't he?"

"He's tripped the wards, tore right through them. If they haven't realized he's inside, they're about to."

If they were caught, it was going to be a fight to get out. Blood would stain the walls tonight.

"Are you ready?" she whispered.

Elaine stared at the council building for a moment, then to her and nodded once. "Let's bring him home."

Something squeezed inside of her at Elaine mentioning *home*, as if she already considered herself part of it. It wasn't a conversation they'd had, but she found herself wanting to have it all the same. Later, she resolved. Maybe when not so many people wanted them dead.

Aya pulled away from the shadows first, cloak drawn low over her face, and the others followed close behind. Darkness flowed over them, masking their entrance into the council building. The dark hallway was cold, thick with shadows. Only a distant band of moonlight piercing a window at the end of the hall offered any light.

"This way," Sabra said, taking off.

Aya shot after her, sprinting hard along the hall. Their boots thumped softly on the tiles. Sabra powered ahead, tearing through the open doorway first.

"Aya—there!" Sabra whispered sharply.

A narrow path cut along down the side of the council building, the looming wall of the prison flanking the other side. Like a creature of the night, a lone figure dashed along the path, focused solely on the task at hand.

Sabra shot forward, vanishing in a burst of smoke, only to appear right behind him. She grabbed Tobias, slamming him into the wall. Aya and Elaine hurried over to join them. His eyes flew between Sabra and her, then shot to Elaine as she hurried over.

When it returned to Aya, she scowled. "What the fuck were you thinking?"

"I couldn't leave him here. They'll kill him!" Tobias snapped

She spun away with a string of curses. It took all her strength *not* to want to rip his throat out. "You weren't concerned you'd get us killed?"

"What?"

"You had to know we'd come after you." She threw him a frosty look, and his face crumpled beneath her fury. "We're *family*, Tobias, which means we have your back. I was planning to get your mate back. Do you honestly believe we were going to let him die?"

Wisely, he didn't respond, possibly sensing how close she was to shredding him.

"We've got company!" Elaine cried.

Aya pivoted to see a large group of soldiers had amassed down the path. The hairs on her neck lifted. She glanced down the other way, and that path was also blocked. They were trapped.

"Sab, can you get us out of here?" she asked softly.

A string of curses sounded behind her. "They've put up some kind of ward that's blocking my power."

"Aya, I'm—" Tobias tried to speak but she threw up a hand.

It wasn't the time for apologies.

She schooled her nerves and stepped forward. Elaine grabbed her wrist, stopping her.

"Elaine, cover the rear. Don't let anyone get too close."

"What are you going to do?" Elaine demanded.

Aya pulled her hand free. "I'm going to clear a path."

She reached over her shoulder, drawing her sword with a metallic hiss. A cold calm flooded her veins, steadying her racing heart. The men didn't flinch as she prowled toward them. Not even as the shadows stretched out, thickening around her. When the first man was close enough that she could see the white of his eyes, she raised her sword to him.

"You will be the first to die unless you let us pass."

The man, to her respect, tightened his grip on the blade. "Aya Sinclair, you are—"

He never finished. Aya exploded forward, darkness plunging over the soldiers. Their shouts filled her ears as she launched at the first man, sinking her sword through his throat. As he fell back, she ripped it free and plowed it into the rest. With no light, they had no chance, and she cut through them all without mercy.

Hot blood splashed her cheek, staining her lips. She pushed on. The last man dropped dead, his head rolling away. The shadows retreated, revealing the trail of carnage. No one could be left alive to bear witness to the power she just wielded.

There was no time to linger as the others joined her, Elaine holding up a shield of fire at the rear.

Aya set off, sprinting down the path, and throwing herself through the doorway they'd come through. Their boots drummed rapidly across the floor. The glow of Elaine's fire lit the way as they dashed along the path.

Heat burned through her veins, every breath searing her lips. By the gods, she needed to train more.

At the next corner, she drove her shoulder into the double doors, stumbling into the chamber hall. The tall, arched ceiling greeted her with the dominating presence of the council table. Moonlight spilled in from a circular window above, casting its silvery hue across the room.

The shouts inched closer.

"This way!" she cried, sprinting for the double doors at the far end of the room. Grabbing hold of the heavy handle, she dragged it open, calling for the others to hurry. As they passed through the doorway, the pursuing soldiers surged into the hall. The men were halfway across the space when Elaine slammed her palm onto the handle, sealing it shut.

A heavy force slammed into the door, but the seal held.

The main foyer was eerily quiet. Aya led the way to the main doors, dragging them open. Once more, the others rushed through, leaving her to come out last—right into Tobias's back.

"What the—?" The words died on her lips as she moved around him, freezing between him and Elaine.

A row of soldiers greeted her, along with dozens of witches, their hands raised. A glowing wall of light barred their escape. Honoria stood among them, smirking.

"Hello, Miss Sinclair. How kind of you to join us."

Aya took a deep breath, trying to slow her racing heart. They were outnumbered, though perhaps not completely outmatched.

"Do you think you could bring that shield down, Elaine?" she whispered.

"What?"

"Can you?"

Elaine muttered something, too soft for her to catch. After a beat, she sighed. "Maybe. I don't know. What are you going to do? That shadow thing again?"

Aya shook her head. "I can't. Honoria will know what I am."

Understanding dawned on Elaine's face. "Oh, I see."

Aya knew Honoria might have her suspicions about what she was, but she very much doubted the Grand Matron was sure. Even if she cleared her name of Calix's murder, Honoria would never give her any peace for being a necromancer. Plus, it would put any who aided her in her sights.

"Sab, remember the butcher job?"

Sabra snorted. "You want to try that here?"

It was probably the dumbest decision she could make, but the choice wasn't a luxury any of them had.

"Can you do it?"

There was a pause. "Do I have your consent?"

"Yes. Of course."

Aya turned to Elaine. "When I give the signal, I want you to throw all you have at that shield. The second it's down, grab hold of me. You, too, Tobias."

"What are you planning?" Tobias asked.

She glared at him over her shoulder. "Now you know what it feels like to be kept in the dark."

He shut up.

Tearing her gaze away, she moved to Sabra's side, standing with her back to her friend. Honoria stared at them, frowning. Good. The witch had no idea what they were about to do. Probably because it was stupid and, if it didn't leave her throwing up blood for the next two days, it was going to give her one hell of a headache.

"Ready Elaine?" she repeated.

"Yes. No. About as much as I can be. Just give me the signal."

Elaine was trying to sound confident, though the tremble in her voice betrayed her.

"You can do it, okay? You're a tough bitch and it's time for these losers to see that. Let them know they won't ever control you and that you will never yield to another." She glanced at Elaine, meeting those wide eyes, and smiled. "*Now.*"

Elaine threw up her hands, and the world exploded into light.

Something sharp plunged into Aya's neck, and within seconds, she felt nothing at all. A low voice slid into her mind.

Let's give them hell.

CHAPTER 34

ELAINE'S MAGIC COLLIDED WITH the shield in a thundering bang, shattering it into a thousand shards. The witches staggered back under the force of her attack, cursing and snarling. All of her muscles burned, her legs threatening to give out beneath her. Heavy breaths offered little in the way of relief and her vision swam, leaving her teetering for a moment. It took all she had to lower her arms and not pass out.

The courtyard was a mess of bodies and rubble. A few witches were sprawled out across the stone, bloodied and unconscious—or dead. Others rose shakily, battered but okay. And all eyes were on her,

The victory was short-lived as a figure shot past her. Aya. Shadowy wings exploded from her back, and wreaths of smoke spilled from her skin, trailing in her wake like the tail of a falling star. Aya surged into the sky, her wings powering up high above the soldiers.

"What the hell?" Elaine shrieked.

Aya's wings snapped in, and she dropped, slamming her fist into the ground. Stone exploded, tearing up in waves. Soldiers and witches went flying.

By the gods...

She shot Tobias a look when she discovered he'd already shifted, and took off, thundering across the courtyard. There was no sign of Sabra. So much for answers. She chased after him, digging in deep. Aya spun around, facing them with black, inhuman eyes.

Possession.

That's where Sabra had gone. Inside Aya.

"*Everyone, take my hand!*" Aya and Sabra's voices slid out at once, entangled.

Elaine nodded. She grabbed their hand and sank her fingers into Tobias's fur. The world tumbled away into darkness.

· · · • • · • • · ·

Wherever they'd ended up, it was far from the Grand Matron. Elaine exhaled shakily as the shadows fell away, yielding to an ancient forest. The fragrant notes perfumed the air, and a gentle breeze whispered through the trees, rustling the leaves. Darkness corralled around them, broken only by thin bands of moonlight piercing through the canopy.

Aya staggered forward with a cry, crashing into a tree. A second later, a shadow figure appeared to crawl from her back, crumpling onto the dirt. Shadows bled away, revealing Sabra's trembling body.

Aya collapsed to her knees, hurling blood onto the ground.

"Aya!" Elaine dashed over.

Tobias reached for Aya, but Elaine shoved his hand away. He jerked away with a shuttered expression, his face pinched, but offering no fight.

Fury made her voice bitter. "You've done enough," she snapped. "Why the hell didn't you trust us? Trust Aya?"

Tobias hung his head, saying nothing.

Aya's body shuddered violently, and she doubled over, retching until there was nothing left in her stomach. Wrenching her focus away from the wolf she wanted to throttle with her bare hands, she focused on Aya. Elaine's hand slid over her sweaty back, the damp fabric clinging to the skin.

"Aya, talk to me. What can I do?" she asked gently.

The only response was a tortured groan of agony as Aya stood, smearing blood across her cheek with the back of her hand. Before Aya could fight her, Elaine slid her hand down to Aya's belly, closing her eyes.

Warm energy rippled up from the depths of her soul, coursing from her hand into Aya's skin. She pictured the damage done to Aya's gut, the inside shredded to ribbons. A bead of sweat dripped from her brow as she focused on stemming the blood and repairing the torn muscles. At last, her hand fell away and Aya's breathing calmed.

"There, that should be—"

Lips crashed against hers. At first, she was frozen in response, but quickly answered the kiss. It burned with need, a hunger that burned like a raging storm, sparking across her skin. Arms surrounded her in a warm embrace, pulling her close. Even the taste of blood on her lips didn't stop her as she met the kiss with an urgency of her own.

Someone cleared their throat.

Aya buried her face in Elaine's hair. "Thank you for that."

"Oh, Aya. I—"

Sabra snorted. "All right, you two, that's enough. Some of us feel like absolute shit and haven't been healed. So, if you don't mind, I'd like to head back and sleep for the next week?"

Elaine untangled herself from Aya. Sabra had managed to stand but still swayed unsteadily on her feet.

"Do you want me to heal you?"

Sabra shook her head. "I'm okay. I think I'm up for doing another jump."

"I don't think that will be necessary," Tobias murmured.

When she turned to see what he was pointing at through the trees, she stilled. A faint light glowed through the thicket, carrying with it a familiar smell of booze and depravity.

The Dusk Quarter.

•••••••••

No one said a word as they entered the living room. A heaviness choked the air and Elaine swore if a pin dropped, it would echo like a clap of thunder. Even Sabra was quiet as she stumbled over to one of the armchairs, sinking in exhaustion. Tobias and Aya stood on opposite sides of the room, darting looks when the other's back was turned.

She hated the tension that thickened the air, pressing down on her shoulders. A part of her wanted to sympathize with Tobias, to offer a hand in support, but the sight of Aya throwing up blood stemmed those thoughts.

Tobias glanced her way, his eyes so shadowed with the misery that she almost cracked.

"I'm sorry," he murmured.

Aya glared at him with a look that could've frozen all of Purgatory.

"Why?" That single word carried with it wrath that could not be ignored.

"I didn't want you to get—"

"*Hurt?* I'm a goddamn necromancer that has survived the complete genocide of my people. I can *handle* the fucking council and their goons. Sabra was a fucking demon soldier once and Elaine has evaded being captured for almost a decade. None of us are weak, so *why?*" Aya thundered furiously.

"*Because I didn't want you to expose yourself!*" he exploded.

Something unreadable flashed in Aya's eyes, and they narrowed faintly. "That is *my* choice to make if I so choose."

"And if you are exposed, then Sabra *and* Elaine are in danger." He glanced away, rubbing the back of his neck. "I admit I was I fool to go by myself, but I thought I could do it. I could have—"

"Choose your next words carefully," Aya warned softly. "They should be framed as an apology to Sabra and Elaine, seeing as you nearly got them both killed. If you can manage that, we'll talk."

That was the end of the conversation. Tobias dropped his head, retreating from the room. Once the door shut behind him, Sabra whistled softly.

"Well, that was a fucking mess and a half. I would like to point out I said that it wasn't a great idea to have a werewolf around, what with the whole mate issue," she muttered.

Aya snorted the edge of her mouth curling into a tired smile. "You didn't say shit. You're just as angry at him as I am."

"I was thinking it, which still counts." Sabra eyed Elaine from across the room. "You've been awfully quiet. What's going on in that head of yours?"

She shifted on her feet. All eyes were on her. "I'm mad at him, of course. It was reckless, but I get it. I once saw a wolf take on a whole village of humans to get his wife back. It was... bloody." She gave Aya a searching look. "What will happen to him if Alexios is killed?"

Aya glanced away. "It depends if Tobias has cemented the bond or not. Best case, he's a shadow of himself for the rest of his life. Worst case? It kills him." A muscle in her jaw twitched as she paused, running a hand over her face. "He should've *told* us. I would've..."

The rush of the fight appeared to be taking its toll on her as she stood swaying. A yawn escaped her mouth when the door swung open, and a woman with pale blond hair swept in. Her heels clicked softly on the wood, peeking out beneath the full red skirt of a simple dress.

It seemed the outside world was not to leave them alone for long.

The newcomer stopped, smiling with a rouged mouth and brightly made-up eyes.

"Hello, my name is Penelope. Nora sent me, told me you had a rather interesting grimoire in your possession?"

CHAPTER 35

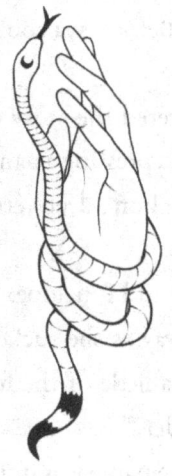

THE HOURS PROGRESSED IN relative silence. Elaine and Penelope worked diligently. Pen murmured the words on the page, translating slowly for Elaine to transcribe the words, neither stopping for break. Tobias appeared at some point with a pitcher of water and some glasses. He tried to offer Aya one but, still mad at his actions, she glowered until he shrank away. In time, she'd forgive him—none of them were without flaws—but she was damn well entitled to hold on to that anger for a little longer.

He left without a word after that.

Aya returned to her vigil in the shadows.

After what felt like an eternity, Penelope scrambled out of her chair. "Oh no..."

Aya was striding forward, the shadows stretching out, as if to pull her back. "What is it?"

"Where did you get this grimoire from?" Penelope's voice was scarcely above a whisper. Before Aya could speak, the witch turned to her, pale as death.

No sooner had she uttered the story of Yrene, Penelope's eyes widened. She stepped back, pressing a hand over her mouth, as if she was going to be sick. True bone-deep terror darkened those eyes, a fear Aya knew all too well.

Aya slid between Elaine and Penelope. "Speak."

Penelope's hand fell away as she sucked in a deep breath. Only once she exhaled deeply, a little of the fear bled away. "Have you heard of the Tyrenian Order?"

Aya shook her head. The name was unfamiliar. "Who are they?"

"Were they," corrected Penelope. "I didn't think there were any left. Witches. Long before I came to Purgatory, I heard rumors of a sect of witches who worshipped an unknown deity. That they were hunted and exterminated. I heard nothing more about them it until I arrived here...and heard the rumors start again."

Elaine appeared at Aya's side, their shoulders touching. A little of the tension eased from Aya.

"So why the fear?" murmured Elaine.

"I saw what happened to someone who was looking into those rumors." Penelope laughed shakily. "A spirit grabbed them a few streets away from here, dragged them into the dark. A few days later, they found the body; the throat was ripped out. After that, I didn't hear anymore rumors."

Elaine might not understand the significance of those words but Aya did. She'd lived and breathed and walked the Dusk Quarter after fleeing the refuge at twelve years old. For four years, she lived among monsters, embracing her own rage and darkness. She learned to listen to the never-ending stream of whispers that flowed from shuttered windows, locked doors, and the narrow alleys between the cramped buildings. Very little stopped the whispers but apparently, something had.

A spirit, no less.

"So how might a witch of this order—if that's what she is—be involved in threats against Calix?" Aya ventured.

Penelope shook her head. "I don't know. Whatever they were, whoever they worshipped, the spirits clearly don't want anyone talking or looking into them. I'm sorry, I can't help you. I'll...I'll speak to Nora."

· · · · • • • · · ·

They returned to their rooms in silence. Only the soft scrape of their boots across the floor echoed through the hall. It was so narrow, their shoulders brushed against each other, and even when it eventually widened, Aya made no move to widen the distance between them. With every step, the air thickened with unsaid words and promises.

The doors to their rooms appeared far too quickly. Elaine pulled away first, reaching for the door. Her hand paused on the handle.

"Why did they save me?" Five little words carried the weight of so many years on the run, alone and afraid, untrusting of any act of kindness.

Aya ached to close the distance but she refrained. "I don't know."

There was no point for lies, no kindness to be given in the uncertainty of the situation that threatened to consume them.

Elaine's eyes fluttered shut as she leaned forward, pressing her forehead against the door. "I don't understand any of this."

"It is certainly a mess."

"I don't know how you're so calm." Elaine shook her head. "I need to get some sleep."

As Elaine opened the door, slipping inside, something inside of Aya snapped to life and she stopped by the door—frozen. It was madness. She shouldn't have followed.

"Stay."

One word bound her to the spot.

"Elaine..." she whispered hoarsely.

"This whole situation is a mess I can't make sense of. A witch of a mysterious order, pretending to be human; two seemingly innocent folks forged into assassins; a plan to kill one of the most important people in Purgatory; a murder you've been accused of! It feels like a spider web and we're still only seeing a part of it."

Aya finally turned. "We will figure it out."

Their eyes met across the room.

"Aya—"

"Elaine—"

They laughed. Even as wrung out as she was, something about Elaine's presence helped her breathe a little easier.

Elaine tugged restlessly at her sleeve. "I should, uh, sleep. Yes. Try, anyway."

"Of course." Aya dragged herself to the door and started to pull it open when a hand landed on her upper arm. Her breath caught. Blood roared in her ears as she turned her head slowly, meeting those jeweled depths. "Elaine?"

"Stay."

Aya's hand fell away from the door, all sense abandoned as she fully turned to Elaine. Their chests nearly touched, breaths tangling together as neither spoke. A tremulous breath skittered from her lips. One word rose from the depths of her broken soul, clawing up her throat and prying out of her mouth.

Aya leaned in close, lips nearly touching as she spoke again. "Say it again."

Elaine finally smiled; blindingly brilliant, the nerves tumbling away. "*Stay.*"

Aya kissed her.

At first, Elaine was frozen beneath her lips. Aya pulled away when hands seized her waist, hauling her back in. Their lips collided in a frantic kiss, fire sparking through her veins. Breaths became one, their souls reaching out in the darkness of that room. Hands moved desperately, blindly, pulling at cloth and string ties.

She stumbled back, pulling Elaine with her. Her legs hit the bed and she fell back. Their mouths parted for scarcely a moment before Elaine was on her, straddling her hips. Aya reached for her, pushing up Elaine's shirt. The second it lifted, exposing the gentle slope of her stomach, soft and streaked with white lines, her breath hitched.

Inch by agonizing inch, more skin was exposed. Then her breasts. Aya's core clenched. Elaine sat, naked from the waist up, a goddess laid bare. She'd never seen anything so damn beautiful. Reverently, she ran her hand over that skin, as if she might never have enough of it. Elaine shuddered beneath her touch, surrendering with a low groan.

"You are far too dressed for my liking," Aya muttered.

Elaine chuckled. "Care to rectify it?"

"Is that a command?"

"Like you'd be so obedient."

Aya settled her hand on Elaine's hip and flipped over, pinning her down. She kissed her, drowning in Elaine. By the gods, it was heaven. She pulled back, wasting no time as she peeled each layer of clothing from her skin until every scar and blemish was revealed.

Elaine's eyes widened, drinking it in. Aya had never felt more exposed in her whole life. She held her breath as Elaine moved from the bed, peeling off the rest of her things. Then, she too was naked. The mattress dipped as she joined Aya, reaching out nervously.

"May I?" Aya could barely manage a nod before Elaine touched her lingering over each scar; adoration in her eyes.

She shuddered as Elaine's arms encircled her.

"So much violence and pain."

Aya felt lips pressed along her back, each one trailing fire across her skin. She shivered, helpless to Elaine's delicate touch, thinking that if she died at that moment, it'd be a blissful end.

"Elaine." She dragged the name over her lips, whimpering as kisses burned along her neck and across her jaw. She twisted sharply, pushing Elaine back onto the bed. "Tell me to stop now, please."

As Elaine stared up at her, full of trust and warmth, the air crackled with a newfound light. It was as though something had sparked deep in her soul, and was flaring outwards, filling her. Elaine reached up, cupping her cheek once more.

"No. I want this, Aya. I want *you*, scars and all. Now, shut up and kiss me."

"As you command."

Aya crushed her mouth to Elaine's, savoring the sweet taste that she surrendered herself to. Her hands trailed low across the slope of her chest, plunging down her belly to the thatch of curls between Elaine's legs. That wondrous heat met her, and Elaine wrenched her mouth away with a moan, writhing at her touch. Every breathless cry spurred her on, those pleas music to her ears. And as that sound rose, the end nearing in the blissful light in Elaine's eyes, Aya yanked her hand away. A tortured groan came from Elaine's lips. Aya ignored it, trailing kisses, to where Elaine was already shifting her hips up to meet her mouth.

Aya found Elaine's slick heat, hot and welcoming. The salty-sweet taste slid over her tongue, drawing her deeper into the warmth. Hands dug tight in her hair, pushing her on with her attack. The sting on her scalp spurred her on. She licked, teased, and sucked, savoring every delirious plea that answered her ministrations. Heave was in that room, and every gentle touch had Elaine crumbling in her bed.

Elaine jolted hard beneath her. *"Aya!"*

The sound of her name, a hoarse scream echoing off the walls, made her pull away and seek Elaine's hungry mouth. They lost each other in a tangle of limbs, of drunken kisses. Sweat glistened off bare skin, shining in the candlelight. The flickering light was dying slowly beside her bed, plunging the room into darkness, as Elaine's mouth found her aching core.

Aya threw her head back in a string of pleas, tumbling over the edge into glorious oblivion.

•••••••••

She woke the next morning, a warm body draped over her. Rubbing her eyes, she blinked and realized Elaine was still in her bed. The memories of night crashed back in. Every kiss and touch, the fire that had blazed between them. Before, when she'd pictured that moment, she'd imagined waking up with regret. Yet as she lay there, deliciously relaxed, her body molten in the witch's arms, she discovered no lingering regrets. Satisfaction hummed through her veins.

Elaine's face was pressed against her chest, her hair splayed out across the pillow. Aya fought the urge to run her hand down Elaine's face. She didn't want to wake her and break the moment. If that happened, that was an invitation to the world outside, and she wanted to cling selfishly to the peace in the room and keep it close to her chest.

"Will you stay?" she murmured.

A soft yawn escaped Elaine's lips as her head lifted, gazing at her. "What do you mean?"

"At the house," Aya clarified. *With me,* she wanted to add, but old wounds had her hesitating.

Elaine was hunted for years—a sentiment Aya knew all too well—and the last thing she wanted to do was have Elaine feel trapped. Even if letting go would tear her heart in two.

A heavy silence filled the room, and though their bodies touched, an ocean seemed to stretch between them. Elaine's eyes were fathomless pools she could glean no answers from, and her heart pounded, awaiting a reply.

"Do you want me to stay?" Elaine countered, her voice soft and unreadable.

A carefully measured reply if ever there was one.

Her heart was a restless bird beating its wings against the bars of its cage, and a single word rose to her lips. It was all she could manage.

"Yes."

That unreadable mask slipped from Elaine's face, and a gentle smile curled her lips. No words passed between them, yet Aya felt the tension bleed away all the same. She grinned as she reached out, running a hand down Elaine's face, tucking a stray strand of hair behind her ear.

"After so many years on the run, I stopped believing I'd ever find somewhere like this, like you," Elaine murmured.

Aya's chest filled with a warmth and happiness that took her breath away. "You've never talked of your time at your first temple. Did you always know you were a Harvest Witch?"

When shadows flittered into Elaine's gaze, Aya began to regret her words. Though she hated to cause pain and dig up an ugly past, she ached to know more about this witch who enraptured her.

Elaine sat up, her tawny curls tumbling loosely over her tattooed skin. The marks of the gods who had branded her had Aya itching to trace them.

"I always knew I was different. Witches are usually given their tattoos when they take the oath of their temple, which is never younger than sixteen. They learn their magic from then on, but I was born with my tattoos. I hadn't known *what* it meant at first, only that I was different." One of Elaine's hands traced the swirling mark of Arcan that coiled on the inside of her forearm. "They later told me that being a Harvest Witch meant I was destined for a noble position in the royal family. The Grand Matron said it was an honor only I could experience. I felt special and loved, but it was all a lie."

Aya shifted closer, reaching out to cover Elaine's hand with her own, stopping its idle wander over the tattoos. "How did you find out?"

"I overheard a young witch remark I was nothing more than a sacrifice, that I would be dead soon enough. I got curious, sneaked around old records and after a few weeks, I found out the truth."

"And then?" Aya's gut filled with poison, and she knew even before the words were uttered that the story of how Elaine went on the run began with betrayal.

Elaine twisted on the bed, leveling a somber look that broke her heart all over again. "I planned to escape, naturally, and I placed my trust in people that went straight to the Grand Matron. After that, I was imprisoned, starved, and beaten. They thought they broke me, but something in me hardened after that. I planned another escape, though I told no one. One day I took a chance again, and I escaped. The rest is history."

The finality of those final words held back any further questions Aya had. There would be time to dissect those long years on the run, just as Aya would speak of her ugly history in the Dusk Quarter.

But the time had come, however, to reopen some of her wounds. It was only fair.

"I was five when I watched as my father and my young brothers were hung in the market square of our village. We'd walked in from our home in the woods to trade, and it was a normal, sunny day. I got distracted by a cat and ran into the crowd. The next thing I remember is my father shouting for my brothers, screaming, and then soldiers yelling. I rushed back through the crowd, but it was hard and I was small. By the time I got to a place I could see, it was too late. I watched them die. Terrified, I ran all the way home. My mother opened the door, took one look at me, and somehow she knew. Bundled my sister, myself, some supplies, and herself onto a horse, and we ran."

Elaine's breath hitched. "By the gods..."

A bitter laugh broke from Aya. "The gods don't care. Akaria ignored my mother's prayers for a rescue. Four years later, we were living in another village...and the soldiers found us again. My mother didn't have time to warn my sister. She grabbed me and hid me in a storage space beneath the floor. I could see through a gap in the floorboards when they came for her. When the soldier drove a sword through her chest, I bit my lip so hard to stop myself from screaming that I tasted blood. I hid there for days, and the whole time I knew my sister was dead, even without seeing her die. I just *knew*. When I eventually crawled out, I found they had decapitated my sister outside the front door and left her body to rot."

A long, heavy silence consumed the room once more. Aya had to close her eyes and force those terrible memories down to the far reaches of her mind. Blood pounded in her ears until, finally, her mind grew quiet, and she realized a warmth had settled on her hand.

"And the witches of the Arcan temple helped hunt your kind."

Aya laughed bitterly. "Not simply that, but it is quite a lot why. They made their choice to involve themselves, but it was the royal family of Vesmir that decreed the massacre. The king wanted us dead, or so the parchments ordering it said." She paused for a moment, remembering her time as a child after everyone was slaughtered when she found one of those letters. It was burned into her mind. "It said we were monsters that were to be destroyed, a threat to the kingdom."

"Is that why you hide what you are?" Elaine inquired.

"I know that being the last necromancer makes me valuable. I wouldn't want to bring that attention to those close to me, and I rather like the mystery I present." Aya fell silent for a moment before she continued. "I'd like to reveal myself someday, but it's not time."

She didn't know if she'd be ever ready for that, however. After burying that truth for so long, the idea of shouting what she was to the world made her feel more exposed than ever before. Because at that moment, everyone would know not only her nature but also the blood-soaked tragedy that stalked her past.

"If I could, I'd murder every soldier who harmed a necromancer," Elaine whispered fervently. "I'd make them all pay."

It should've sounded like bravado, a false promise, but from Elaine, it carried with it the weight of an oath. Just as Aya would swear to any she found who had brought Elaine pain or sought to sacrifice her.

Aya leaned in close, wrapping her arms around Elaine until their foreheads touched and their breaths tangled together. "I do not deserve you."

"Yes, you do."

· · · • • • • • · ·

Before the Dusk Quarter awoke from its slumber, the streets were quiet. Aya lay in bed wide awake with Elaine, curled at her side, sleeping soundly. Never had she imagined a witch in her bed, or that the shame she expected was silent. An easy contentment settled into her bones as she idly toyed with Elaine's wild curls.

The hazy whisper of sleep started to pull at her when a knock rattled the door. At once, the tension ratcheted through her body and she stilled. The knock came again. Elaine stirred in her arms, grumbling something into her chest.

"I'll see who it is," she murmured and climbed out of bed.

Halfway across the room, she scooped up her shirt and slipped it on. The blanket was draped precariously over Elaine, but offered enough modesty. Aya dragged her gaze away with a reluctant groan and opened the door.

Nora thrusted a letter into her hands. "I'm sorry Penelope couldn't help you."

Aya opened up the letter. A messily written address stared back. "What's this?" When there was no reply, she glanced up. Those hard, dark eyes were soft, catching her off guard for a moment, and that understanding bloomed in her chest. "You really need my help, don't you?"

"With Calix dead, things are already becoming difficult for the Dusk Quarter. Handing you over to the council won't fix that, either." Nora rubbed the back of her neck, closing her eyes for a moment. "I thought about it, you know?"

"I know."

Nora's eyes flickered open. "Damn you. I wish I could have. Regardless, since I wasn't much help with the witch situation, I looked into your assassins. There wasn't much, but both were seen visiting a local apothecary accompanied by a woman wearing a green and gold cloak."

"Did you find out who the woman is?"

"Whoever she is, she's a mystery."

CHAPTER 36

T HE LITTLE APOTHECARY WAS at the end of a dingy little alley in the Dusk Quarter. Dying witchlights hovered overhead, lighting the way in a powdery blue light. The air was strangely quiet, broken only by the distant shouts from the livelier streets and music from an unseen tavern. The thick shadows pressing around them, and the stale air reeking of something dying close by. It reminded Elaine of being back in the capital.

The first few months after her flight from the temple had been hard. The city walls had slammed shut barely an hour after her escape, he'd been trapped for months before she found a way out. The whole time she'd lived on the streets, barely scraping by and avoiding detection. She still had no idea how she'd managed to stay alive. Not when some nights when she'd slept in some dingy building with nothing but rats and spiders for company. She was so sure she was going to die.

A hand brushed hers, pulling her from the memory. Aya's voice brushed her ear. "Elaine?"

"Hmm?" She looked up and met Aya's piercing gaze.

"What's wrong?" Aya asked, one hand lingering on her waist.

The past beat inside her chest like a restless bird. What might Aya say if she knew all that Elaine had done? The carnage she'd wrought, the lies and the betrayal and the pain. Perhaps she might understand the most monstrous parts of herself. What if, however, she began to see her like the witches who had massacred the necromancers? The same Arcan power, the very magic that had helped hunt her people down, flowed through her veins.

"I'm fine," she said distractedly.

Aya's brow dipped, her mouth twisting into a frown. "Elaine—"

"It's okay. Really. We should focus on the mission."

So many lies tangled within her chest, a knot that scared her if it ever unraveled. After all, what would Aya say about Honoria's pin that Elaine had discovered at Lilibet's? She knew she should tell her. The truth burned on her lips, demanding release but try as she might, it never came out, and she bit back a sigh, frustrated. It was cowardice, pure and simple, and she loathed that weakness. That old terror of being alone again rendered her silent.

They had arrived at the front door, which was slightly ajar. Two small windows sat on either side, like the empty eyes of the house, staring back at them. Tattered curtains were drawn over the panes, concealing whatever lay within.

Tobias pushed ahead, sniffing the air.

"It's not good, is it?" Aya muttered.

"I smell blood. A lot. I can't hear anyone, though. Sab, can you sense anything?" Tobias asked, lingering by the front steps.

Sabra shook her head. Whatever horrible thing had happened inside was over. The culprit was long gone.

"Come on, let's see if there is anything left. We might get lucky," Aya said, following Tobias inside.

Sabra chuckled. "You're sure we'll have any luck given how things have been of late?"

"I'm an eternal optimist."

"And I'm a fucking unicorn," Sabra retorted.

The second Elaine crossed the threshold, the stench of blood and rotting flesh hit her like a wave. Bile rushed up her throat, burning her mouth as she fought to hold it back. Almost gagging, she pressed a hand to her mouth and followed Aya into the shop. The front section was a sprawling arrangement of shelves with hundreds of shattered jars strewn across the floor, spilling their liquid contents across the wood.

"Back here!" Tobias shouted from down the hall.

Elaine headed toward his voice. At an open doorway, she froze. A man hung from the ceiling, his stomach sliced open. His innards hung from his body like rotting ribbons. A pool of dried blood stained the floor.

She spun sharply on her heel, spewing the contents of her stomach onto the floor.

Aya moved by, stepping into the room with Sabra at her side.

"Well, he was certainly hung up to dry." Sabra sniggered.

Tobias groaned. "By the gods, *Sab*. The man was tortured."

Elaine's gut stopped clenching. She straightened up, wiping her mouth with the back of her hand. Aya brushed her hair out of the way and gave her a rueful smile.

"I thought you had seen death before," she murmured gently.

Elaine peered at the body. "Not like that."

"Do you want to step out? You don't have to stay inside. We can handle this."

She forced herself to shake her head. "I'll be okay."

Aya's brow dipped, unconvinced, but thankfully said nothing. Elaine quickly slipped past her, steeling her spine as the foul odor filled her lungs. Her stomach rolled, threatening to empty once more. She focused on the room, trying to make sense of what happened when Sabra cleared her throat.

"Aya, can you do your thing? See if he'll talk?"

Something unreadable flashed in Aya's eyes. "His ghost is long gone."

"I thought spirits hung around the body if they died violently," said Sabra.

"It would seem, like Yrene, whoever did this didn't want there to be any chance he would spill his secrets, even in death."

Aya led the way back into the main shop section. Glass crunched underfoot, making Elaine glad for her thick boots. Picking shards out of her feet wasn't an experience she was keen to repeat.

Her gaze caught on the shop's ledger cast aside on the ground. It was wide open and several sheets had been ripped out. Curious to know what was written in the remaining ones, she picked it up and started to read.

Elaine leafed through the ledger, skimming over the names and orders made over the last few weeks. Nothing stood out to her. None of the ingredients sold were key in potions for making one susceptible to compulsion, or to lower any sort of inhibition. The longer she pored over the ledger, the deeper her frown became. Something was staring her in the face but what?

"Anything?" Aya's voice brushed her, startling her out of her musing.

She jumped. "By the gods, Aya, a little warning."

The corner of Aya's mouth tipped up. "I called your name several times."

Elaine pursed her lips and glanced around the store. "Why would the assassins be brought here? Were they under duress, enchanted or just plain desperate?"

"There are some potions that must be consumed very quickly once mixed. Perhaps that's why they had to come here." Aya inched closer, their shoulders brushing together. "Anything in the ledger?"

Elaine frowned at the ledger. "Nothing much that I can make sense of."

"May I?" Aya gestured to the ledger, and when Elaine handed it over, she smiled, saying, "Thank you."

"Why, is that manners I hear?" Elaine teased.

Leaving Aya to study the ledger, Elaine wandered away. She lifted a hand, closing her eyes, probing for traces of magic. The air remained cold, dead to her touch. Either someone had covered their tracks exceptionally well, or the attacker had been without powers.

"*No,*" Aya breathed.

Elaine spun on her heel. "What is it?"

Color drained from Aya's cheeks as the ledger tumbled from her hands, forgotten on the floor. Elaine tried to reach out but Aya jerked away. Her gaze met Elaine's a look of anguish on her face.

"You were right..."

"About?"

"Lilibet. She...*oh gods.*"

Elaine stilled.

Aya opened her mouth again, as if to say more, but shadows darkened her face and she pushed past Elaine. "I need some air."

She was out the door in a flash. Elaine followed in pursuit, but a force slammed into her, sending her crashing into the wall. Stars flashed across her vision and she hit the ground, hard, pain shooting up her hands and arms. For a moment, the world doubled and swayed. Someone was calling her name, but as she tried to stand, her legs gave out.

A moment passed until she could stand. A few feet away, in the middle of that shadowy alley, Honoria stood over Aya's crumpled body. Several hooded witches encircled them, their hands interlocked, and a low chant spilled from their lips.

Elaine knew the spell well.

She launched to her feet, a scream ripping from her throat as if torn from the depths of her soul. The great light blazing within her sparked. All the primal magic from Dianera flooded down her arms. She lifted her hands—

The ground shuddered and the world exploded into darkness and noise. Elaine fell to the ground. Someone screamed her name. Sabra, she thought. But it was too late as the abyss consumed her whole and she felt no more.

CHAPTER 37

"*A*YA!*" ELAINE CRIED OUT, jerking awake. A hand fell to her shoulder, and she twisted sharply, grabbing at the first thing she could—a neck. Tobias stared back at her, eyes wide, his hands on her shoulder.

"It's okay, it's okay," he whispered hoarsely.

She released him and glanced around wildly. Ragged breaths shuddered through her body, leaving her heart slamming viciously against her ribs. They were back in the forest, the glittering night sky overhead. Sabra emerged from the shadows with a cut above her eye, and a trail of blood dried down the side of her face. Dark bruises mottled her blue skin.

Sabra kneeled. "How are you feeling?"

"Fine," she said automatically. The memories of what happened crashed into her. "Aya! What happened to Aya? Where is she?"

Sabra and Tobias shared an unreadable look before the former turned to meet her gaze.

"Honoria has her. Not sure how they found us, let alone launched an attack in the middle of the Dusk Quarter." Sabra rubbed the back of her neck with a wince. "They brought the house down on us. I barely got to Tobias and you before it was too late. Are you sure you're okay? You were thrown into that wall pretty hard. Tobias, can you look at her? She could be—"

"I'm *fine*," Elaine snapped as she hauled herself to her feet. "Can you sense Aya? Is she okay?"

Something unreadable flashed in Sabra's eyes. "She's alive, but that's about all I can sense. Whatever they've done to her, I can't get a message through. I'll keep trying. They won't be able to keep me out for long."

"And if you can't?"

Sabra hesitated, looking away.

All that happened flashed through Elaine's mind.

"By the gods," she gasped.

"What is it? Is something wrong?" Tobias touched her arm.

When she lifted her gaze, Sabra and Tobias watched her with concern, their faces pinched. For the first time in so long, she realized that the family she'd always wanted, she'd found it—and she was about to destroy it.

"I need to tell you something," she said quietly. The words spilled from her lips, slowly at first, then all in a rush; the pin she'd seen under the couch at Lilibet's and Aya's reaction to the name in the ledger. She shuddered and looked up. "I tried to ask Aya about it but she told me Lilibet wouldn't have betrayed us... and that I wasn't to ask anymore. I should've pushed. I *knew* something wasn't right!"

Tobias stepped closer; his eyes gentle. "You didn't exactly have a mountain of proof Lilibet was up to something. We should have been more vigilant."

"You're wrong. Lilibet wouldn't have been involved in this," said Sabra insistently.

Elaine swallowed back the lump in her throat. "Aya found proof in the ledger that Lilibet had been visiting that shop in the Dusk Quarter for months. The same one the assassins were last seen in before their attacks."

Tobias's hand fell away, and he inched back, sharing a look with Sabra. At that moment, Elaine felt once more like an outsider, and aching loneliness stirred once more within her soul.

"Lilibet is innocent! She's Aya's friend," Sabra said, though Elaine didn't miss the lack of conviction in those words.

Tobias frowned. "I always thought it was odd that Honoria had been there that day, though I cast it away under council business. Lilibet was an in-demand fairy..." The color drained from his face. "Oh gods, the Hell Fire...I always wondered who could've done that but maybe a witch and a fairy working together might be enough to create it? The right witch to summon it, and a fire fairy like her could stabilize it for it to work the way it did."

Sabra shook her head fiercely. "It's not possible."

As Tobias rose, Elaine didn't dare to move a muscle, and could only watch in terrified silence.

"If Honoria didn't want a witch to be suspected, a fairy *might* be an option. One could employ a Syren, but those are loyal to Councillor Yuriel, or Nora in the Dusk Quarter. Lilibet is adept in ancient magic."

Sabra's face paled to a frosty blue. "And Aya never would've looked for the signs of fairy magic because she would have never suspected Lilibet." Those cold, horrified eyes darkened to fathomless black pools that sent chills down Elaine's spine as they were leveled at her. "Why didn't Aya say anything? Why didn't *you?*"

Elaine flinched. "I'm sorry. I'm so gods damned sorry."

"You will be," Sabra snarled, and any warmth that she'd earned was snuffed out. "Right after I rip Aya's gods damned throat out myself. Why didn't even say you'd spoken to her? We might have secrets but not about shit like this."

"*That's enough, Sabra.*" Tobias's voice cut the air like a dagger. Before Elaine could muster a reply that Sabra was right in her fury, Tobias spoke once more. "She didn't know, and honestly that lack of trust I cannot blame. We're *all* guilty of that. As for Aya, that is—"

"Oh yes, your affair with Alexios," Sabra spat. "Aya nearly exposed herself to save your neck with that!"

"I'm *aware* of that," Tobias ground out. "But let's not throw stones. Your lies have caused trouble in the past, and if we continue to tear each other apart over our sins, Aya *will* die, and so will Alexios. And I, for one, have no intention of letting Honoria or Lilibet get away with their crimes."

Elaine dared to peek past Tobias, only to shrink away from Sabra's near-murderous gaze.

"*Fine,* but we need to rest and gather supplies. Since everyone thinks we're dead for the moment, we can probably return to the house," Sabra muttered.

•••••••••

The house stood undisturbed in the ancient woods. Even Sabra's wards remained intact. That bothered Elaine as they wandered to the front door. After their flight to the Dusk Quarter, no one had come to the house looking for them.

As if they'd known where they were the whole time.

Perhaps it was easier to grab them in the Quarter. No pesky wards to deal with and Elaine had a distinct feeling there were probably traps in the woods.

The other two strode inside first, but Elaine stopped at the door. The silence greeted her like an old friend. A sweet, faintly earthy scent washed over her, and she realized what it was—Aya's smell. The one that mere hours before, she'd been wrapped in, inhaling with kisses and deep, savoring breaths.

How had it all gone so wrong?

"Elaine?" Tobias called from inside.

"Coming!" She forced herself to go inside.

Sabra was already striding upstairs, leaving Elaine to mourn the damage she'd wrought with her lies. Sabra had trusted her, she had burned it all to ash.

It is *what you do best,* her inner voice sneered.

With a sigh, she headed upstairs to her room. She changed numbly, casting the tattered clothes aside. By the time she returned downstairs, Sabra was strapping a sword to her hip. The jeweled hint gleamed in the moonlight, the blood-red rubies glowing like burning coals. From far across the room, Elaine sensed the demonic magic from the blade. Ice flooded her veins. That was a weapon stained with death.

Sabra's head lifted, as if she sensed Elaine's interest, and smiled. The cold flash of her teeth was pure predatory. It reminded her that though this demon had become her friend—family, even—that she was no less dangerous than Aya.

It was then that Tobias strode out from his office in a black tunic that hugged his muscles and towering frame. She was so used to him in his loose shirts and scholarly attire that it struck for a moment. This was not a healer that stood before her, nor the friend that had comforted her. Like Sabra, this was someone ready for war.

Sabra cleared her throat. "Now, let us go have a little chat with dear Lilibet, shall we?"

· · · · · ● · · · · ·

The glittering lights of Purgatory's Inner District stretched out beneath a blanket of stars. The streets bustled with carriages and folks out for an evening stroll. Lanterns lit along the road, casting everything in a bright, buttery glow.

Elaine hated it. She felt exposed like at any moment the witches would appear from the shadows and attack.

Even with Sabra teleporting them so close to Lilibet's home, she kept glancing over her shoulder. No one on the street paid them any mind. Sabra was probably right. They were all assumed dead. Once they spoke to Lilibet, however, that illusion would be up...

"Maybe we shouldn't do this. We could use the fact they all think we're dead to our advantage," she murmured.

Sabra reached for the handle, pausing. "Frankly, it's clear they've been one step ahead of us in that respect. We need answers and we need to change the game."

It was an impossible situation. Everywhere she looked, their deaths loomed like coming storms they couldn't run from.

A flash of darkness came from Sabra's hand and with a clink, the door swung open. Elaine hurried in after them. Voices came from the rear drawing room, but it appeared their arrival had not yet been detected.

Sabra vanished from the hall in a plume of smoke. Seconds later, porcelain shattered, and someone yelped in terror. Elaine sprinted to the source, shadowed by Tobias. When they entered the drawing room, a young girl lay unconscious on the floor. Lilibet was on her knees, Sabra at her back with a knife to her throat. Tendrils of flames danced in the fairy's hands.

"Move an inch and I will slit your throat," Sabra sneered.

Lilibet's eyes flickered to where Elaine and Tobias stood in the doorway. Something in her seemed to darken. "So, you know."

Sabra shuddered with barely suppressed rage. "Traitorous bitch! You were her *friend*. Aya trusted you, but you sold her to the bloody witches, to *Honoria*."

Lilibet's eyes widened. "What?"

"Don't play coy. We know you're involved in this whole damn mess with Calix and the assassins. You were the one who enchanted them, weren't you? Guess by that point, selling out Aya wasn't that hard, was it?"

"I didn't know they'd blame Aya," Lilibet argued. Her hand dropped, and the flames snuffed out. "As for the others... Yes, that was me."

Elaine took a step forward. "And Calix? Did you murder him too?"

Lilibet nodded something almost like shame flashing momentarily in her eyes. "Yes."

Sabra wrenched her arm upward, the blade poised in her hand.

"Wait!" cried Elaine. "We need her alive for now."

She kneeled in front of Lilibet, staring into those wary eyes. "Tell us how you were involved in all of this and I might be able to persuade her not to kill you. It'll have to be good, though, because frankly, I'm in the mood to let her."

Lilibet's gaze dropped to the floor. "Honoria approached me several months ago with a proposition, to gather ingredients for this spell. She wanted me to enchant some assassins to go after Calix. The kind that couldn't be detected on bodies after death. Before you ask, I didn't ask why and she didn't tell me. I did as she asked and *that was it*. I knew nothing about her implicating Aya in Calix's death."

Every word was a knife to Elaine's gut. Lilibet had condemned three people to death and she didn't even give a damn. She sat back on her haunches, stifling the urge to make her pay. It'd be so *easy*. Her fingers twitched.

Tobias cleared his throat. "But *why* did you do it? What did you get out of all of this? Did she make you do it?"

A bitter smile curled at Lilibet's mouth. "No. I did it all voluntarily."

"*Why?*" Tobias pressed.

"Because I want to go home! To my *real* home. A hundred years ago I fell in love with someone I thought was my mate—I was wrong. When my people returned to their realms, I chose him. I stayed and the borders shut." Lilibet's mask slipped, exposing the rage and bitterness and grief. "He threw me aside the first chance he had. I made him pay. Made little difference in the end, though. I was stuck in this awful place. Then one day, Honoria comes, offering the one thing I've always wanted—to go *home.* Can you truly begrudge me that?"

Elaine stood. She needed space before she stabbed her. "You had people here who *cared* for you, friends who would fight for you. Instead, you threw it all aside and now Aya is facing death. Someone who would've walked through *hell* for you. Do you even care about her? Or was she disposable, like those kids you made killers? Did you even know one of them had a pregnant wife? I mean, it was *her* diary you had, which I'm assuming Honoria gave you."

"I didn't *know*—"

She never finished as Elaine drove her fist into Lilibet's cheek. "Tell me *one* good reason I shouldn't kill you. Give me *something*."

Whatever fight was left in Lilibet drained away. Her shoulders dropped. "It isn't just Aya she wants. She needs you too. Said you both were the key to getting what we wanted—me to go home and whatever her ambition was."

Elaine rolled her eyes. "You're wrong. If she wanted me, she wouldn't have dropped a house on me."

"And yet here you stand—alive and whole."

"To what end?"

Lilibet was silent for a moment. "All I know is that she was looking for something—or someone—and that it would change Purgatory forever. She wouldn't tell me any more than that, however. Trust me, I tried."

Elaine's breath hitched. "How did Yrene play into this? She was never an assassin, but she... Oh god, did you kill her too?"

Lilibet shook her head fiercely. "NO! I would *never* harm a mother and child. Never. As for what her role in all of this was... I'm not precisely sure. When I first met with Honoria, it was at the temple. I came as requested, and when I got there, Yrene was talking with Honoria in a language I'd never heard. Which was odd because I speak hundreds of tongues. When they noticed me, Yrene grabbed a book from Honoria's desk—that's right, it was a grimoire. Had all those symbols on the front and I sensed old magic about it."

Elaine glanced sharply at the others. They'd all assumed that Yrene had been innocent in all of this, somehow compelled into whatever scheme Honoria was up to. She pulled her gaze away, studying every inch of Lilibet's face for a lie. Yrene, part of a mysterious order, had been helping Honoria but why? To what end?

"So, they were allies?"

Lilibet frowned. "I think so. I only saw her a few times after; the last time was a few days before you came to me. I heard them arguing—I mean, it certainly sounded heated—and before I could enter the office, the door slammed open. Yrene rushed out, clutching at that grimoire, and I never saw her again."

If Elaine did the math's correctly, Yrene died in childbirth a few days later. Whatever secrets the girl had, they went to her grave, and measures had been taken to ensure that her spirit couldn't be spoken to...

Which meant Honoria had likely known the whole damn time Aya was a necromancer.

"We're done here, Sabra," said Elaine.

Lilibet opened her mouth to say something as Sabra slammed her fist into the back of her head, and the fairy dropped like a stone.

"Are we sure we should leave her?" she murmured.

The rest remained unsaid.

Alive, that is?

Sabra straightened up, dusting her pants off. "Aya will deal with her. Besides, when we're done, we're going to need her to clear our names."

Sabra tied Lilibet up using magical bonds she wouldn't be able to break. Elaine sank into a chair overcome with weariness.

"So, Honoria is behind all of this—no true surprise there. Doesn't clear up what exactly she is after." Tobias leaned against the wall, picking the invisible lint from his sleeve. "If Calix suspected Honoria was up to something, why not say anything to Aya about it?"

Elaine's brow dipped. "Maybe we're looking at that in the wrong order. Calix is a powerful figure in Purgatory. Perhaps his role in all of this was removing him; and the attempts weren't initially designed to be successful. My guess is that she used them to have Calix hire Aya—the one person she knew he would trust over council aid—which brought her into the fold."

A chill snaked down her spine. It made her wonder if events, since she'd arrived, were also orchestrated by Honoria...but if that was the case, why had the spirits called in the debt? Were they not also the ones who stole away the witches who were looking into the Tyrenian order, the same thing it appeared Honoria was doing?

"Well, now what do we do?" Sabra ventured.

Elaine realized they were staring at her, awaiting her decision. Were it not for the debt Aya had with the spirits, the witches would have laid their claim to her. Honoria would have had her blood and her powers.

She knew what she had to do next. "We need to speak to Nora. She might be our only chance to help Aya."

CHAPTER 38

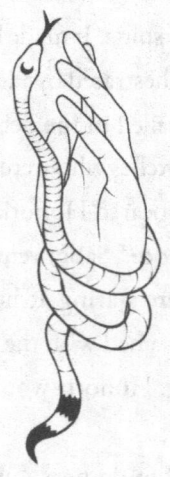

A YA'S CELL REEKED OF death.

It was stained deep into the stones and cracks, the lingering echoes of ghosts long gone. Old blood marked the walls with gouge marks from nails of those who in desperation had tried to claw their way free. The chains securing Aya to the floor showed signs of where someone had tried to break them. She might've attempted it herself, but the collar fastened around her neck rendered her powerless. It was blessed with an enchantment to sever her link to Akaria, drastically reducing what options she had for escape.

All she could do was sit and wait and think about her friend's betrayal. Why Lilibet had lied and worked with Honoria, she didn't know, and was terrified to ask. When she closed her eyes, she could see the dates going back months and her stomach turned. She didn't want to even consider that Lilibet had a part in her capture but, as she sat there alone in the dark, cold and confused, those dark thoughts whispered anyway.

She'd whittled away the hours, waiting for the click of those familiar shoes on the stone. It never came. She was alone in her cell, staring out through the bars and into the empty cell opposite. What were they waiting for?

No water or food had been left. Not even a bucket to relieve herself. A pile of filthy straw lay heaped in one corner. The only light came from a flickering witchlight beyond the bars, giving the faintest glow.

Escape would have to wait until the collar came off. They might be determined to kill her, but she hadn't survived hell merely to die in a dingy little cell

··········

It was hard to say how much time had elapsed since she'd woken up chained and collared. Nor how long she sat there, mulling over all she'd learned in the mission and what was going on.

The sound of footfalls broke the silence. Moments later, two guards arrived dragging a body, and threw it into the cell next to hers. The door was slammed shut with a rattling thump, and the guards departed without word.

She waited until they were gone and shuffled forward. The metal rattled and scraped along the floor. The chain meant she wasn't able to touch the bars, but she got close.

"Hello?" she called into the dark.

The lean figure groaned, cursing softly as they sat up, and the side of their face caught the witchlights' glow—Alexios.

"Aya? My god, I must be weaker than I thought," he muttered.

"You're not delusional." She rattled her chains for effect, grinning in the gloom. "See? I'm stuck here, like you."

Alexios stared at her. His pale skin was sunken in and mottled with bruises. She knew the look of a starved vampire when she saw one. In silence, he leaned back against the wall of his cell and stretched his legs. A low groan rumbled from his chest as he shut his eyes.

"Why haven't you asked if I killed Calix?" she asked.

One eye cracked open. "Did you?"

"No." She shuffled over to the side of the cell, resting as comfortably as the chains might permit. "Tobias is worried about you."

The other eye opened and he sat forward. "He told you?"

"That you are mates? Yes." Aya studied her hands, idly picking at the dirt gathered beneath her nails. "How long has this been going on between the pair of you?"

Alexios sighed. "It's complicated...but we met years ago, before he even left his pack. Things happened and we had to remain parted until recently."

"He never said anything."

She glanced up.

A shadow of a pained smile touched Alexios. "It didn't end well the last time."

"And yet, you're still together."

Alexios cocked his head. "Is this where you threaten me if I hurt him?"

Aya rolled her eyes. "I don't believe I am in *any* position to threaten anyone. Remind me to do it when we get out of here."

Alexios snorted. "Do you have a plan?"

"Do you?"

"Given they've not fed me for days and I can barely stand, *no*."

She laughed softly. "Well, I guess I'll have to play the hero."

But first, she needed to sleep.

· · · • · • · · · ·

Aya was ripped from her nightmares by rough hands and snarling voices. Her eyes flew open. Two guards were hauling her from the cell, not caring if she walked or not. She scrambled to her feet. At the base of a long set of stairs, she stilled. There might be more guards at the top of the stairs, more than she could fight in her current condition.

It was now or never.

"Sorry about this," she muttered, throwing herself back.

One of them grabbed her and threw a punch at her face. She raised her hands to block the blow when someone grabbed her from behind. But even with the shackles, she lunged for her attacker's face, gouging her nails across his cheeks. The man screamed, blood streaming down his face as he pressed his hands to his face, trying to stem the flow of blood.

"You fucking bitch!" he roared.

Several more guards rushed down the stairs and under their blows. She was forced to the ground. A man loomed over her, scowling and menacing, and drove his fist into the side of her face. Fiery heat bloomed across her cheek, blood pooling her mouth.

She was stuck, still chained, and now vastly outnumbered. Aya released a shuddering breath and spat blood onto the stone.

"What did that little display achieve? You're still chained," he sneered.

She flashed a bloody grin. "Felt pretty damn good, though."

There was no time to prepare as he drove his fist into her stomach, ripping the air from her lungs. Aya gasped, doubling over. Her lungs burned, and tears threatened to spill. She held back, refusing to break, to yield to weakness.

"You won't be so damn cocky soon enough," he said frostily.

She offered a bloody smile. "Care to make a bet on that?"

He didn't bother replying and snarled at his men to take her away. As she was dragged up the stairs, the man's pained curses fading behind her, the top door was thrown open. Sunlight burst in, blinding her for a moment. She slammed her eyes shut and stumbled forward. The men didn't even wait as they dragged her forward. A string of curses tumbled from her lips as she forced herself up again.

After a few moments, her eyes adjusted, and she could take in her surroundings. It wasn't the council prison as she'd expected, nor the witch temple. The ruins of an ancient stone village were spread out around her, half consumed by the wild woods. She'd ventured all over Purgatory, but she'd found no such place before. A glance down at her mark peeking through her tattered shirt told her she hadn't left.

The confusion deepened as she was led through the ruins and an old temple emerged in the darkness. Lanterns lit the polished pillar entrance. Two hooded witches greeted the guards, then pushed open the doors, holding them open.

Inside, the space was one long hall with a dais at the end. A stone table dominated it. Aya's blood cooled. Honoria awaited her... and beside her, Marisol.

CHAPTER 39

A<small>S THE SHADOWS FELL</small> away to reveal Nora's office, a blade
appeared at Elaine's throat. A slender hand gripped the leathery hilt, connected to a slender arm. Nora stared at her, eyes dark
with the promise of death, unyielding. No one uttered a word, nor
dared to move for what felt like an eternity. It was Nora who stepped
back first, quickly sheathing the dagger at her thigh.

"Where's Aya?"

"Honoria took her," said Elaine. "We need your help to get her
and Alexios back."

Nora snorted. "I can't join this fight."

A flicker of disappointment wormed its way through her belly.
Elaine stamped it back down. For Aya, she had to be strong. "I'm not

asking you to do that. We just need to know where Aya and Alexios are. You're their only hope."

Something unreadable flashed in those fathomless pools. Perhaps a glimmer of something softer, human even. As Nora turned away and walked to the desk at the end of the room, the air filled with such a pregnant silence, that the pressure bore down on Elaine. It propelled her toward Nora, even as her own heart thundered, fighting against the tiny flicker of hope deep in her heart.

Nora closed her eyes for a moment, leaning against the desk. A second later, her eyes opened. All the white was gone from her eyes, and two black pools stared back. Tiny black veins spider-webbed out along her cheek and forehead, turning the once strikingly beautiful woman into something utterly terrifying.

"I've made some inquiries. I should have some information back shortly...but you owe me a debt."

Sabra appeared at Elaine's side, her gaze dark. "A debt? Really?"

Nora cocked her head to the side as her eyes bled to normal. "I made inquiries with Yuriel. I now owe her debt, so now you owe one to me. A debt is a debt. One I expect you to honor and understand. Aya knows that."

Elaine gently touched Sabra's eyes, drawing the demon's gaze for a moment. The worry for Aya was clear as day in her face, pinched in the tight lines on her face. A small smile was all she could offer, and even that felt paltry for the situation they found themselves in.

"It's okay. I'll pay the debt." As Sabra opened her mouth in protest, Elaine turned to Nora. "I'll do it. Will that suffice?"

Nora inclined her head. "Careful, witch. I am not one to take betrayal lightly if you refuse to pay the debt when called. Do you understand?"

Elaine closed the distance and thrust her hand out over the desk. "I keep my word."

Something faintly amused glimmered in those inhuman depths, and a feline smile curled her lips. A shiver rippled across Elaine's skin, lifting the hairs. Every instinct warned her that she was treading in dangerous waters, urging her to reconsider. Run, flee. The smart move. As Nora's hand slid into hers, squeezing firmly, Elaine hardened her resolve. This was for Aya.

••••••••••

It wasn't safe for them to venture beyond Nora's office, so they remained safely contained there whilst Nora slipped out. Tobias prowled by the fire, pausing only to glance up on occasion, as if a new apology danced on his lips. Sabra stood in the shadows, glowering restlessly at the door, with her arms folded across her chest.

Elaine wished to fill the void that filled the room but nothing arose. What might she say to ease their nerves when Aya and Alexios's fate was unknown? The only thing they knew for sure was the pair was alive, a poor comfort to their rattled nerves. Elaine closed her eyes, pausing her own pacing in the middle of the room. What she'd give to sense Aya, to have the kind of connection that Sabra had to her, or even the one like Tobias and Alexios shared. All she had was her connection to the gods and that, as always, was silent of conversation and comfort.

When the door finally swung open, Nora strode in wearing a sodden green cloak. She shed it quickly, hanging it up. At once, Elaine strode over, shadowed by Sabra and Tobias. Her heart fluttered like a frantic bird in her chest, beating its wings against the bars of a tiny cage, desperate for escape. She barely trusted herself to speak as Nora finally turned to her.

"Aya isn't at the temple. Nor is Alexios. It would seem both were transported in the night from the temple into the forest." Nora swept past them, continuing toward her desk. She dug out a scroll from the shelves behind it and unfurled it, revealing a sprawling map of Purgatory. No one spoke as she ran a finger from the Inner District, deep into the ancient woods surrounding it. "Ah, that would be it."

Elaine neared the desk and squinted where Nora's hand fell. "I don't see anything. What is meant to be there?"

Sabra sucked in a sharp breath. "*That's* where she took them?"

"What is it?" Elaine spun to Sabra, grabbing her arm.

A look of unease alighted Sabra's eyes as she stepped back from the desk. "I came across it one day and... and I took Aya there. She liked exploring ruins back then, you see? But something happened to her there as soon as we arrived and she began to cry. She couldn't even talk until I got her away. When I got her home, all she said was that place was soaked with death. We never spoke of it again."

Elaine looked to the map again, wondering why Honoria chose to take Aya and Alexios there. Was this to do with whatever—or whoever—she was looking for? Perhaps this was the ruins of this mysterious order that even the spirits seemed determined to bury.

She bit her lip. There was something else she was missing but what? It danced just out of her reach, whispering that she still didn't hold all the pieces.

A curse burst from her lips as she wrenched away from the desk and raked her fingers through her curls. "I don't like this."

"We have where she's being held. That's good," said Sabra.

Elaine's hand fell to her side. "It is but why does it feel like we're walking into a trap? At the temple, it was going to be a hard fight in. Why take them to the ruins? To what end?"

Tobias made a hum of agreement. "A trap, if I had to hazard a guess. One we're probably going to walk right into. Nora, can we get any aid?"

Nora shook her head. "If Penelope is right, and this has anything to do with what I think it does, I can't. With Calix dead, I need to focus on my people here. Food supplies are already becoming tricky. The wolves have upped their prices and increased tension is already causing fights in the Dusk Quarter. This whole place is ready to explode. I can't afford to get entangled with this mess any further."

It was hardly surprising. Elaine suspected they were going into this rescue painfully undermanned. At least she had her magic, but she wondered if what she had was enough.

She shook off the thoughts and returned to the map. "Then we make a plan and we get Aya and Alexios back. Anyone have any ideas?"

CHAPTER 40

T HE TINIEST SLIVER OF moonlight presided over the ruins, casting wisps of silver over the crumbled stone and tangled ivy. What remained of a central temple was crouched among the towering thicket of ancient trees, and it peered over what was once a series of smaller stone buildings, half destroyed by time and nature. A few makeshift tents were scattered throughout, with a dozen or so witches drifting between, their hoods lowered. None spoke, moving hurriedly, glancing up occasionally toward the distant shadows of the surrounding forest. Once or twice, one would pause, stiff as a statue, as if ready for something to burst from the dark.

Elaine wondered if it was the spirits they were waiting for, ready to strike them down for whatever mission they were undertaking.

She wished Sabra was with her, Tobias too, but the pair broke off an hour before to make separate entries. They all had their roles. She just had to keep her nerve for the one she was to play. Taking one moment to herself, she closed her eyes, took a deep breath and exhaled, opening her eyes once more. Like a predator ready for the hunt, she rose up and glided from the shadows.

At first, no one paid her any mind. Only once she passed into the heart of the ruins did the first witch see her. Startled eyes snapped at her with predatory focus. A second later, the witch cried out, and the alarm spread across the ruins. Witchlights gathered in a blue wave as the witches scrambled to her arrival.

They encircled her, ribbons of light swirling about their hands. At any moment, they were ready to fight.

"I have come for Aya Sinclair," she announced.

The witches whispered among themselves, none deigning to answer her. She shifted restlessly, half considering how many she might take down before Honoria came out. The last thing she wanted to do was to be weakened by the time the matron arrived. She'd need every scrap of power she might summon.

Unless you accept the other god's blessings, her inner voice whispered.

But if she did that, she knew risked losing herself. No one was meant to wield that much power for long. And there was every chance that if she died, Honoria might steal *all* of her power. No, the Grand Matron would not have her power, not for whatever plan she had in mind. At least if she clung onto what she had, she stopped the woman from gaining anything else if she lost the fight. It wasn't ideal, but what choice did she have?

The witches parted like a hairline, bowing their heads. Elaine heard the soft footfalls and felt the crackle of magic in the air before she saw the approaching figure. Slender hands pushed back the hood. Honoria's burning gaze bore through her, plunging right down to the depths of her soul.

Her arrival had been expected.

Elaine's stomach flipped.

Buy Sabra and Tobias time, she chanted repeatedly in her head as Honoria drew closer.

"Ah, right on time," Honoria crooned.

Elaine pictured Aya beside her, imbuing all that snarky attitude on her face. When she spoke, she imagined it was Aya who was speaking through her. "Release Aya and Alexios and you might walk out of this alive."

Honoria cocked her head. "Why would I do that? I now have everything I need."

"Ah, yes, for your plan. Dangerous business I hear digging around the Tyrenian order. I didn't think the spirits would approve of that."

The smile on Honoria's withered mouth faltered for a split second. It regained quickly, but didn't quite touch her eyes. "Perhaps not but it won't matter soon enough. For your boldness, though, in coming here alone, I will offer you one thing. If you can beat me, I will release Aya and Alexios."

A trap, obviously. Elaine had heard those honeyed promises before, knowing full well the poisoned chalice they concealed. Honoria *knew* Elaine would come, likely knew the others were in on the rescue as well, and acted entirely unconcerned.

Elaine steeled her spine. "You truly think you can beat a Harvest Witch?"

"One who hasn't embraced all that she is blessed with? Yes."

She raised her hands, summoning the light of Dianera, the fire of Arcan, and the frost of Vikria until all three powers swirled around her. The witches shrank away, but Honoria held her ground, her smile only deepening.

"You're going to die here Honoria."

Honoria laughed. "Not before your friends. Now, come on little witch, *beat me.*"

Elaine exploded forward, the world erupting into a blaze of light.

CHAPTER 41

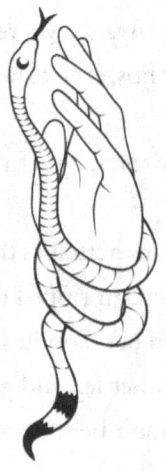

A PUDDLE OF AYA'S blood stained the stones below where she hung. A steady drip ran from the myriad of cuts that marred her skin. Everywhere, her body ached and throbbed. The dark nudged her vision, the cold hand of death pulling her into Akaria's embrace. If she closed her eyes, she swore she heard the distant melody of a song. A lullaby her mother used to sing to her when she was a child.

A song of death, a necromancer melody.

The cold abyss pulled her under.

Something sharp plunged into her thigh. Her eyes flew wide as she choked back a scream. Clenching her teeth hard, her jaw throbbing, she blinked away the tears.

"Now, now, it's not the time to rest Aya. I'm not done with you yet."

When the dagger was yanked out, a new stream of blood welled and trickled down her leg. Aya slowly released her jaw and forced steady breaths through her lips, even as her body begged for the pain to end.

She smiled bloodily. "I'm sorry. I was tired. Sleep *is* important, you know?"

There was no time to brace herself as the dagger plunged into her other leg and twisted. A scream ripped from her. The tears finally escaped, running free down her bloodied and bruised cheeks.

Marisol left the blade in her leg and grabbed her cheek, forcing Aya to look at her. "You won't be so damn smug after I'm finished with you."

"Bold words for a human. You think you're a monster? One truly capable of darkness? I am not afraid. I *live* and *breathe* the dark, a creature of death."

Marisol's hand fell away. "I'm counting on it."

As her old lover turned away, gliding over to the array of bloodied tools, one hand trailed over them. Marisol appeared in another world, Aya temporarily forgotten. She wondered if this side of Marisol had always been there, lurking just beneath the surface. Perhaps Honoria lured it forth with whispers of power.

"So, why *are* you doing all this? You're the most influential human in Purgatory and generally well-liked. Isn't that enough?"

Marisol's hand stilled over the knife, and she laughed softly. "After all your digging since Calix hired you, is that what you still think?"

"I know you and Honoria are digging into the Tyrenian order."

In a flash, Marisol was facing her again. Something akin to fear flashed in her eyes. "I'd be careful with that name."

"Tyren—"

The knife was ripped from her thigh. Aya snarled a string of curses as the fiery burn consumed her leg. Marisol lifted the dagger to her throat, staring her down. For a moment, Aya swore she glimpsed a war of emotions in those fathomless depths. The delicate hand gripping the dagger trembled for a moment, as if Marisol's resolve faltered.

Marisol stepped back. "This isn't about advancing my power."

"Then what *is* this all about?"

A sad smile pulled at Marisol's lips. "Righting an old wrong. One you will understand soon enough."

All the years of questions and rage and confusion bubbled to the surface; a wave of fiery wrath no longer contained. "That's why you left?"

"It's complicated."

Aya laughed harshly. "Fuck complicated. If I'm going to die, you owe me the truth. Can't I at least have that if you're not even going to tell me whatever mess you're supposedly righting?"

To her surprise, Marisol glanced around once more, as if in fear of someone unwanted overhearing. "I can't."

"Can't or won't?"

"Things are happening that are much bigger than either of us." Marisol's eyes hardened and whatever chance there had been for connecting burned to ashes. "I have a gift for you—well, two gifts, actually. Would you like to see them?"

Aya stared back, unflinching. "Do your worst. I'm not afraid."

Marisol returned that gaze, unflinching. "Very well."

She swept off to the door, knocking once. It opened with a low groan and two witches came through dragging something—no, *someone.* The stench of death washed over her, and the cold whisper of it brushed over her skin, lifting the hairs. She knew who it was even before the body dropped, and those empty eyes, once so full of life and humor, stared at her.

Even as the witches departed, she couldn't look away.

A pained, barely human sound tore from her throat. "*No...*"

Marisol stepped over Tobias's corpse as if he meant nothing anymore. "He tried to save you, the fool but he isn't part of the plan. We couldn't have him in the way."

Blood roared in her ears. She stared at the body of her friend as her soul split wide open. It was as though she were a child once more, seeing all that she loved ripped apart before her eyes.

"*Why?*" she croaked, scarcely able to utter anything more.

Fire flashed in Marisol's eyes. "Because it must be done. You will understand soon enough."

Aya's chest shuddered through a sob as she wrenched her gaze up. "What does that even *mean?*"

Marisol whistled in response, the sound cleaving the silence like a blade. A breath lodged in Aya's throat as the doors opened once more.

Two witches appeared, hauling a second bleeding figure. Aya froze.

Sabra was thrown to the ground in front of her, barely breathing. Her blue skin was now a pale hue. The rage built low in her belly, erupting in a flash of power, surging through her limbs like a bolt of lightning.

Sabra was alive—just—and something inside of her broke.

"I'm going to kill you slowly. I'm going to make you *beg* and scream as you die alone," Aya seethed.

Marisol kneeled and grabbed Sabra by the throat, jerking her up. Sabra's eyes flickered weakly, slowly opening with a groggy frown. The stab wounds to her torso left her shirt stained with blood. Aya's heart shattered in her chest. Tears flowed freely, and life was leeching out of Sabra. The thread that had bound them for nearly a decade was fraying, barely holding them together.

"Look at me," Marisol hissed.

Aya choked back a sob and did as she was asked. Those eyes, once so full of warmth and light and love, were hardened and bitter. No trace of the girl she had cared for remained.

"Please kill me. Not her. Please, not her," Aya pleaded softly. She hadn't begged in years, not since she'd been the child who'd asked her mother not to leave her. That same soul-shattering ache cleaved her soul in two. She couldn't go through that agony again.

Marisol stared as if she felt nothing for the tears that flowed down Aya's cheeks or the agony that choked every word from her lips. "Know I take no pleasure in this. This must be done to prepare you."

"*Please,* Marisol." Sobs racked Aya's body. At any moment, she'd become shattered glass, irrevocably broken. After the murder of her family, Sabra had been the first person to see her as something other than broken and monstrous.

"Say goodbye, Aya."

The scream tore from her lips as Marisol slashed the blade across Sabra's throat. Her soul ripped apart, the roaring cry filling the room. Tears blinded her as Sabra was dropped to the ground, the blood pooling around her. Aya screamed and thrashed and raged.

She never saw the blade coming, only felt the sharp burn of metal as it plunged into her heart. She slumped forward, glimpsing the flow of blood as it spilled onto the stone. A cold embrace wrapped around her and a single face bloomed in her mind, smiling and warm. So full of life.

"*Elaine...*"

CHAPTER 42

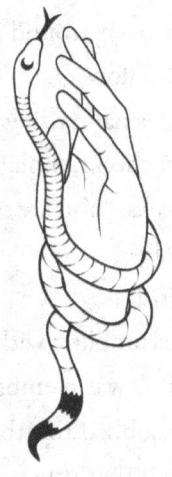

D EATH WAS WARMER THAN Aya expected.

As her eyes flickered open to a bright blue sky, cloudless and warm, she sat up slowly. There was pain, no hint of the wounds that riddled her body. Even her cheeks were dry and no rasp in her throat from the screams. When she looked down, she swore at a simple black dress. The skirt was embroidered with Akaria's emblem, thorns, and roses.

"Hello, who are you?" Aya froze at the voice drawn from the depths of her memories.

No, it can't be...

She scrambled to her feet, the air fleeing her. Standing a few feet away, as if death had never separated them, was her sister.

Her sister's name danced breathlessly upon her lips. "Una?"

It was like staring in a mirror. They had the same sloped nose, cynical smile, and amber eyes. Long brown hair flowed freely down Una's back, with flowers woven around the top like a crown. Aya had forgotten her sister liked flowers.

Her sister's eyes widened, a hand rising to cover her mouth. Tears welled and spilled down her cheeks, sunlight turning every drop into glittering jewels on her cheeks. "You are so grown up. If you didn't look so much like mother, I—"

Una's voice choked off in a sob.

Aya stumbled forward, crumbling with every step and as she fell into Una's arms, she cried. A warm embrace wrapped around her, holding on so tight. They sobbed together, bodies trembling. Aya finally pulled back, realizing that others had appeared behind her sister.

Others emerged from a nearby tree line, and she knew at that moment, it was no mere delusion of death or final tease of madness. This was the afterlife of the necromancers—the Endless Woods—and a place that if she were trained in the ways of her people, she would've been able to visit on command. It was how she knew her people used to commune with the dead, and that lack of connection pained her more deeply in the moment as her family appeared.

She pulled away, a lump catching in her throat. "Mother? Father?"

Her parents stared, their wide eyes and parted lips that made no sound, remaining where they stood. Aya was the first to move. Slow steps at first, shy in fear of it all ending without warning. As she neared them, her courage welled and her steps stretched out, quickening to a stumbling run. Aya threw herself into her mother, clinging on tight, as she had the last time they'd spoken. Her mother's warm, floral scent perfumed the air, filling every breath. The tears continued to run down her face as if years of grief had finally crashed through the walls she built.

She was undone, a child once more.

Her father's choking sobs filled her ears as he hugged her as well, and soon her sister joined. Soon, other voices brushed her ear.

"Wait, Aya? Aya?"

"Aya, is that you?"

A pair of young, boyish voices had her pulling away. Two young boys, frozen at the end of childhood, stumbled through the crowd.

"*Soren, Kai!*" Aya screamed her brothers' names, rushing forward and dropping to her knees. She hauled them into her arms. They chanted her name like a prayer to Akaria, laughing and crying. The twinkling sound that once haunted her nightmares suddenly made her smile. She joined in with them, overflowing with joy. A smile split her cheeks. "I've missed you both so terribly."

"Mother said you'd come home," Soren said.

Aya cupped his cheek, mourning for the man he would never become, for the loss that had scarred her soul. "Mother never lies. You should know that."

Excited whispers eddied around her but she didn't give a damn. It was only upon the silencing claiming the world once more did she still. A chill brushed the nape of her neck. She reluctantly pulled away, rising slowly. The old instinct to fight curled tightly through her limbs, poising her into position.

The crowd parted, bowing deeply, as a spirit appeared. The very same she struck the fated deal with, and the bane of her existence.

Those dark, fathomless pits landed on Aya. She tried to move her lips, but her body was frozen, her lips sealed shut. Why was the spirit who she bargained with all those years ago here?

"Hello, my child."

Finally, her lips moved. "What's going on?"

"A plan long in the making."

Aya jerked back. "You're working with them? Honoria and Marisol?"

The spirit shook her head. "Once, yes, but they have strayed far from the original plan. I believed they understood the path, which is why I brought Elaine Tormelin to Purgatory—to you—but they deceived me. The Grand Matron does not believe your witch can do what must be done, and so will take her power for herself. Then she will use your blood and the plan will be complete."

"And what exactly is this grand scheme of yours? The one that has gotten my friends killed?"

The spirit waved her hands, and Aya's people vanished. A startled cry rose to her lips, followed by a demand for where the hell they'd gone, but the spirit spoke again. "They are well but this is not for their ears. I can only shield us from unwelcome eyes for so long.

As for the plan, it is simple. Purgatory was never intended to be a haven—it is a prison. Not for you or the residents you know but for a goddess. The marks you all bear? They are the chains that provide the very power sustaining the barrier. It is why the residents are permitted to stay."

The air rushed from Aya. Her gaze flew to the brand on her upper arm. Instinctively, she touched it and as her hand fell away, she swallowed a lump lodged in her throat. Not for the first time in her life, all she knew was uprooted and she was left drowning.

"What does this have to do with me?"

"Honoria doesn't believe there is a way to free the goddess without fully bringing the barrier down."

Ice flooded Aya's veins. The barrier was the very thing keeping those who wanted her dead out. If it fell...She shook her head. No, she wasn't going back to that life.

"But you think otherwise?"

"I do."

"How?"

"If Elaine can embrace *all* of her powers and you the same, perhaps there is a chance you can stop the barrier from collapsing."

Aya fell silent again, mulling over the words for a moment.

She straightened up, wishing nothing more at the moment than to have a friend with her. The decision loomed before her, leaving her with the distinct impression that whatever she decided, her life would be forever changed. That it wouldn't be her own life to be affected but of everyone within Purgatory. The weight of the responsibility pressed heavily upon her shoulders.

"Who is this goddess? You haven't said her name." When the answer didn't arise, she glanced up and witnessed the shadows in the spirit's eyes. "You don't *know* her name?"

"It was struck from memory."

Aya sucked in a sharp breath. "So, you could be unleashing a monster?"

"This goddess was imprisoned and the consequence was an immediate imbalance of magic, of the veil between realms being weakened. The gods hungered for her power and after they trapped her, they removed any trace she existed." The spirit paused for a moment, then stepped forward and opened her palm to the sky. A tiny amulet was cradled there. "This is the last remnant of her order."

Aya reached for it, lifting it with delicate hands. On one side of the golden amulet was the sigil from the grimoire...and on the other, the mark of Akaria. Her gaze snapped up. "What is this?"

"Life and death have always been bound together; when the followers of one was struck from the world, the other was to follow."

She staggered back, her stomach twisting viciously into knots. "Don't tell me that's why my people were *butchered*." The spirit stared at her with gentle eyes. Aya choked back a bitter laugh. "Then why was I spared?"

"Because you were powerless. A child no threat to them."

Aya rolled her eyes. "I'm not powerless anymore."

"But by then, you were here and the prison they designed oh so well? It kept you from them."

A bitter laugh welled up from the pit of her broken and angry soul, spilling from her lips like shattered glass. She'd believed for *years* she survived by her strength, rage and luck; now, it appeared all her survival boiled down to in the end was the gods seeing her as unimportant and lucky enough to avoid the soldiers.

"Why tell me this? I'm dead."

"And if I could change that?" The spirit stared back, unflinching, those cold depths revealing nothing.

Aya released a shaky breath. "*Why* would you?"

"Because I believe my plan can work, but for that to happen, you must live, Aya Sinclair. As for bringing you back? I might not have much magic after all my years of meddling, but that I could do."

The truth of those very words settled in Aya, and she straightened up, squaring her shoulders in response. "It would kill you."

The spirit merely smiled; but it was a sad, resigned smile that bore the years of struggle and loneliness. "We must all make sacrifices. One way or another, the goddess will awaken...but only you can determine how that outcome occurs. The choice is yours. Now, what will it be?"

CHAPTER 43

DARK THUNDERCLOUDS ROLLED ACROSS the sky, and lightning burst across the clouds as if tearing them apart at the
seams. The shadows thickened around the temple. Leaves rustled
a rising cacophony, drowning out the blood thundering in Elaine's
ears.

Time slowed, raking over her skin as she fought a battle within.
Every muscle whimpered and ached. The pool of her magic deep
within raged like a storm churning across a vast ocean. She tried to
reach for it but the endless stretch of it refused any command. But
she would not yield.

Her legs wobbled, threatening to give out. Every inch of her body was bloodied and bruised. Thin reeds of light flickered precariously in her hands as she stood facing Honoria.

"Do you think you can beat me?" Honoria taunted, stepping forward. Wreaths of light swirled around her billowing robes. "The end result is inevitable. She will be freed."

"At what cost?" Elaine spat. "You would damn us all!"

"Damn us? I would *free* us. Purgatory is a prison and we're nothing more than a gods damned power supply to keep the barrier up."

Elaine thought of those like Aya who the barrier kept safe, far from those who would seek them harm. Of the generations who knew Purgatory as the safe haven it was and, finally, of those who lay beyond the barrier. The ones that would march on Purgatory and claim its vast territory, full of magic and resources

She lifted her trembling hands. Channeling the deep pools of magic in her blood was proving impossible. Each time she tried to summon more of it, her control slipped and the power threatened to overwhelm her senses.

"We shall see," Elaine said as she burst forward.

The distance closed rapidly, and she dropped low at the last second, pivoting out of the way of Honoria's attacks. She barely dodged out of the way as the Grand Matron rushed at her in a dizzying blur. Desperately, she sought an opening.

She would not fail—

Light exploded in her face, blinding her. A cry ripped free as she staggered back, blinking rapidly. As the world focused, something crashed into her from behind, driving her to her knees. A hand curled around her throat, warm breath brushing the shell of her ear. Tendrils of magic tumbled over her shoulder, sparking over her skin, lifting the hairs in its wake.

The temple doors were flung open.

Elaine gasped as Marisol swept out, splattered in blood. A single dagger dripped with glossy red blood, trailing droplets across the steps and down onto the grass. She stilled, watching the advancing council figure. Ice flooded her veins.

"Is it done?" Honoria asked.

Marisol flashed a predatory smile. "Aya, Sabra and Tobias are dead. Everything is continuing as planned."

"Good. You best inside. It won't be long now."

With a bow, Marisol departed.

A tangle of thoughts rushed through Elaine. Her family was dead. She had failed. Once more, death claimed those who had gotten too close. Her soul screamed out, the grief tearing her apart at the seam. She felt something inside of her ripped tight—

And snapped.

She slumped forward.

"*There* it is," Honoria crooned.

Something cold and sharp pressed against her neck, biting into her skin. What was the point of fighting anymore when everyone she ever loved died?

"I..." The words died on her lips.

Chilling magic flooded in from the blade's edge, shooting to her heart. It flared outwards, splintering like a spiderweb across her bones, freezing her rigid. All control vanished, rendering her a prisoner in her own body.

"Take heart, Elaine, you have a noble soul. You *like* helping people...and this is doing just that."

The fight in her sputtered out, a dying candle in the dark, and she slumped forward, yielding to whatever fate awaited her.

CHAPTER 44

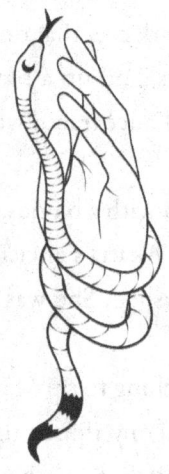

THE FIRST BREATH OF life flowed into Aya's lungs like liquid fire. She roared back into the waking realm. All light and dizzying sounds crashed through her like a winter storm, pulling her in every direction simultaneously. She shuddered, and finally, the world took shape in shadows and blood-stained stone.

Chains shattered around her wrists and she dropped to the floor. Her knees hit the ground first, burning pain bursting up her leg. The collar around her neck crumbled away, the shards of metal falling like silver snow.

A heavy bang broke across the fray, silence crashing down in its wake.

"Welcome back."

It was a voice Aya knew, one that had been burned into her soul at her death. A blazing fire lashed her chest as she lifted her gaze from the floor. Across the stones stained with her blood, and over Sabra's corpse and those dark eyes that once held such life. Her eyes landed on fine black boots, and up a blood-splattered dress, until they reached a face she had once traced with tenderness.

Marisol.

"Hello," Aya murmured with a bloody smile.

She pushed to her feet, Akaria's ancient power roaring through her veins as a storm unleashed. She was a goddess. Untouchable. Unyielding. *Unstoppable.*

Her fingers twitched, itching to rip Marisol apart. As she stepped forward, sharp talons of agony ripped up her back. She staggered forward, crying out soundlessly. Something heavy dragged her down from her shoulder blades, throwing her off balance.

Throbbing waves of white-hot molten pain rolled down her spine, blinding her to all else for several breaths. Aya turned her head to peer over her shoulder. Her breath hitched. A pair of leathery black wings stretched wide from her back.

"It *worked.*" Marisol's voice came from the other side of the room.

Aya dragged her gaze back. "What did you say?"

Marisol's face split into a smile, a delirious laugh tumbling from her lips. "You're ready."

Aya shot forward, faster than she'd ever moved before. Wind hissed in her ear. In seconds, she was across the room, grabbing Marisol by the back of her neck and slamming her to the floor.

"I *told* you I would make you pay," Aya snarled.

She released one hand and pressed it over Marisol's breast. A bolt of magic ripped from her palm, plunging into Marisol's heart, killing her instantly. Hot blood sprayed across her skin, splashing her lips. At once, the light in those kind eyes sputtered out. Blood pounded in her ears as she stared at what she'd done, feeling no guilt. Only that cold, hollow feeling carved her out, and left her teetering on the edge of a great abyss.

In the corner of her vision, Marisol's ghost materialized. A sad smile tugged at her mouth but it was her eyes that stopped Aya; the raw *agony* in those eyes, as though she were broken. It ought to have given her satisfaction, fed that crowing beast within, but as she jumped to her feet, she felt only tired and angry.

"You should leave."

Marisol's went to take a step forward, but as Aya flinched away, she stopped. Something flickered for a split second in those eyes.

Then Marisol was gone.

Aya, your friends... The spirit's voice stole through her mind, tearing Aya's focus from where Marisol had been standing.

"Tell me what to do." Aya dashed over to the bodies, dropping beside them.

Find the thread binding flesh to the soul. It will show you the way.

A glowing red thread sparked, materializing from Sabra's heart and twisting up and away. Aya followed the thread with her gaze.

Her heart froze in her chest. Barely a few feet away, Sabra's spirit watched her, eyes wide.

"Aya?" Sabra whispered.

She smiled, tenderly brushing her friend's pale blue cheeks. Tears glimmered in her eyes as she tried to fight back the tears. Blinking them away, she moved to Tobias and repeated the process. As color returned to his skin, he jolted upright with a gasp. Heavy breaths racked his chest as he looked at her.

"I—I was... Marisol... I was dead." He seized her arm. "You brought me back?"

She couldn't fight the smile that pulled at her mouth. "With a little help and right now, I could do with yours, if you're feeling up to it?"

CHAPTER 45

D EATH CAME WITH A cold breeze.

It slid over her skin and plunged through her skin like a thousand daggers. A shiver racked her body. Elaine slammed her eyes shut, imagining Aya's face, knowing that in a few moments, she would be reunited. All the agony she had endured would end.

All around her, the witches' whisperings fell silent. It was as though the word had gathered its breath, waiting for the moment to come.

The seconds ticked by. Each slower than the last. Her breaths steadied. What was Honoria waiting for? Some last stab of cruelty? She pried her eyes open, lifting them slowly. The witches weren't looking at her. Neither was Honoria. All their focus was back on the temple.

The shadows were a thousand spidery fingers reaching for a single point. Not to the temple, she realized, but to the three figures who had claimed the steps. One, a blue demon, with wreaths of smoke swirling about her. Another was a shining white wolf with glowing red eyes.

In the middle of them was an angel of death. Elaine drank in the sight of the leathery wings, the ribbons of glowing black energy swirling around those muscled arms, and eyes that glowed like burning coals.

Aya Sinclair had returned.

Once golden eyes burned like hellish black pools, void of any white or anything human at all. This was what she had read about. A necromancer unleashed.

Those dark eyes found her lingering for a moment. What passed in those mysterious depths, she didn't know, but she wasn't afraid anymore. Nor did death offer the welcome it had mere moments before.

At the bottom of her soul, a single flame sparked.

"Hello, Miss Sinclair." Honoria's voice cut like a knife, cold as death.

That chilling, predatory smile stretched across Aya's face. That monstrous gleam in those hellish black eyes sent shivers rippling right through Elaine's bones. For the first time, she realized she was truly seeing the monster that Aya kept leashed.

The silence crackled like a thunderstorm.

She expected Aya to speak, to make some witty remark to bait Honoria. Instead, Aya turned to Sabra, murmuring something. A feral smile curled those lips, and Elaine knew that death was coming. Not only for Honoria, but for all the witches who'd helped her.

The white wolf prowled forward, and as it dipped its head low, snarling softly, those hellish eyes found hers, and a sense of familiar warmth brushed her mind.

Are you okay? Tobias's gentle voice slipped into her thoughts.

She managed a nod when Aya moved, drawing her focus away. One foot in front of the other, that wicked smile deepening. Her heart slammed viciously against her ribs as she devoured every movement and met Aya's eyes, glowing with power.

Something inside of her kindled to life.

Even with the cold knife pressed at her throat, and the spell making her a prisoner to her own body, Elaine awakened. Heat warmed her veins, infusing her muscles. The fire flickered brighter, stretching up from the depths of her soul. Elaine caught a single look from Aya, lingering, cutting her to the bone.

Several feet away, Aya stopped and lifted her arms wide. She opened her mouth and called out to the shadows a single word that struck lightning through Elaine's soul.

"*Rise.*"

The ground trembled and groaned as if the very earth itself was stirring awake at Aya's command. Dust burst upward, eddying in the air, and swirled on breezes that surged in from the ancient woods. Yawning cracks split the earth open, and bone hands clawed out from the darkness.

The dead had been summoned. They emerged in tattered dresses and tunics, some in armor. Who they were, Elaine didn't know, only that they turned to the witches and advanced.

Too late, the panicking witches called forth their light magic as the first corpse launched at the nearest one, crashing through the shield they summoned, and driving her to the ground. A gurgled scream sounded off before it was choked into silence.

Shrieks and cries of terror ruptured the silence as all hell broke loose. Some turned to flee, others raised their hands to attack. The dead burst forward, taking off after the witches. There was a flash of movement catching Elaine's eye, and she glimpsed Sabra and Tobias as they flew past Aya. The pair descended upon the coven with vicious intent, vanishing into the ancient woods. Their agonized pleas rang out until silence reigned once more.

Elaine lifted her chin, meeting Aya's gaze. Her lover stood a few feet away, a single hand raised to Honoria.

"Get your hands off her."

The blade bit into Elaine's neck in response, a trickle of blood flowing freely down her skin. No fear chilled her. She was not alone. Not anymore. She was done running and hiding and being alone. This was home. With Aya and Sabra and Tobias, all in that wondrous house nestled in the woods, where she was free and happy.

She met Aya's gaze, the moment between them freezing the world in a single breath. Two souls linked. A witch and a necromancer.

"Do you trust me?" Aya asked.

She tried to form the words to reply, but none came, so she trusted in the look she conveyed in her eyes.

Yes.

Aya exploded forward. In one second, a figure loomed over her, and a hand shot out, driving into Honoria's chest with a deafening bang.

The pressure on Elaine vanished, the blade at her throat no more. All the power bound within her flared freely, erupting outwards. She surged to her feet, light flashing blindingly everywhere at once.

A primal scream filled the air.

It took her a second to realize it was *her*.

The sound choked off, and the light tapered away, revealing Aya before her, grinning. The darkness in her eyes was gone, revealing those glowing gold pools.

"You are *beautiful*," Aya murmured.

Elaine's chest shuddered. "I thought you died... and Sabra and Tobias..."

"I'm a necromancer. Death yields to me." Aya's gaze flickered behind her, narrowing, and the gold yielded to black once more. "Elaine, are you up to fighting? I can—"

She kissed Aya, short and fierce. "Let's end this."

Elaine turned to stand by Aya's side, calling on the light in her hands. If she was to defeat Honoria, then it was going to be through the same power.

Honoria staggered to her feet. The Grand Matron stretched out her hands, tipping her palms to the sky. Pillars of light roared from her, tearing up into the sky. Lightning cracked across the sky, splashing the ruins in white light. The thundering roar of power raged around her as if she had become a goddess of light. Honoria stretched a single hand to them, beckoning them with a cold, cruel smile. No hint of fear lit those chilling eyes.

"Come claim my life if you dare," Honoria taunted. "You cannot stop what has already begun."

Elaine took Aya's hand in her own, releasing a steady breath, resolved in what she had to do. "You keep her distracted. Her life is mine."

"As you wish, my love."

A thrill skittered through her belly at those words. Elaine pushed the flush of warmth back down. They'd address *that* statement later. After Honoria was dead and their lives weren't under threat.

Aya released her hand and burst forward. Elaine didn't waste any time as she summoned all the light to her hands, sprinting forward. Her feet pounded along the grass, kicking up stones and dust in her wake. Magic streamed from her hands. Up ahead, Aya collided with Honoria in a burst of shadow and light. With a tangle of blurring blows as they battled across the grass, Elaine powered forward.

Blood sang in her veins. She knew what she had to do.

"Aya in the air!" she screamed.

The instant Aya shot up into the sky, she slammed her palms into the ground. The earth split and rippled out. Bolts of light erupted from the ground, crashing into Honoria. The witch screamed, staggering back. Elaine raced forward and plowed into Honoria, throwing her palms into the witch's chest. Heat flooded down her arms, shooting to her palms. Honoria drove her hands into Elaine's side. Light flared. Searing pain ripped across her skin. Elaine screamed and held on, thrusting her powers against Honoria's chest.

Honoria's magic burst back, plunging into Elaine and sending her flying.

"*Elaine!*" Aya screamed.

She crashed onto the ground, sliding across the earth. Stones tore at her skin until she came to a stop. Clenching her teeth, she scrambled to her feet. Tipping one hand to the sky, she summoned Arcan's flames, and in the other, light flared, wrapping its way up her arm. Two magics danced through her veins.

Honoria stalked toward her. Aya dove for her, a hail of darkness crashing to earth, but Honoria spun at the last second. She grabbed Aya by the wing and hurled her across the field.

Elaine stormed toward her opponent in an explosion of light and bolts of magic, hurling everything she had. Unable to break through Elaine's onslaught, Honoria was forced to defend herself from behind her shield of magic.

A little bit closer...

As one of Honoria's bolts sailed past her face, she dropped low and threw her hands up. Blue fire shot up, creating a wall of light. Sweat dripped from her face.

Nearly there.

She thrust another wave of fire into Honoria's shield, forcing her to retreat.

There!

Honoria's back hit a stone wall. Her eyes opened wide in dismay. She had nowhere left to go, and all her witches had either dispersed or were already dead.

Elaine roared as she dug deep, ripping open the walls of her magic and forcing it forward. Fire and light-infused, woven together in a blazing wave that pressed on without mercy.

"*I am no sacrifice! I am Elaine fucking Tormelin!*"

Honoria's shield shattered. Magic collided in an explosion of pure energy and surged into the sky. As it struck the clouds, it flared outwards in a concussive wave, turning the sky to pure light. Elaine slammed her eyes shut as waves of pressure bore down on her, nearly driving her to the ground. The pulse of magic within her thundered.

And as quickly as it began, the light dimmed.

She pried her eyes open, breathing hard as she looked skywards. No trace of whatever had just happened remained. A trickle of unease rippled through her.

"Elaine?" It was Aya's voice that lured her to the world once more, compelling her to turn.

At once, the power flooded back into her body, sending her staggering. As she went to hit the ground, she tumbled into a warm embrace. Gentle arms, a familiar scent, the faint brush of a magic not her own but one she knew all the same. A soft breath tickled the shell of her ear.

"You're right," Aya chuckled.

"Huh?"

"You *are* Elaine fucking Tormelin."

An answering chuckle bubbled up from her belly, spilling from her lips. Her chest squeezed sharply, lancing daggers through her ribs. A wince pinched her face.

The sound of laughter reached her ears. She peered around to find the source. Sabra emerged first from the tree line, bloodied but otherwise okay. Tobias appeared a second later, his arms wrapped around Alexios. The pale vampire appeared gaunt and bruised, but he leaned into his mate's side, clinging on tightly.

It was Sabra who spoke first. "Did we win?"

Elaine opened her mouth but shut it. *Did they?* She didn't know. Honoria was dead, and though Aya hadn't said it, Marisol was as well. But as she recalled the light bursting into the sky at the Grand Matron's death, that unease wormed its way deep into her belly once more.

CHAPTER 46

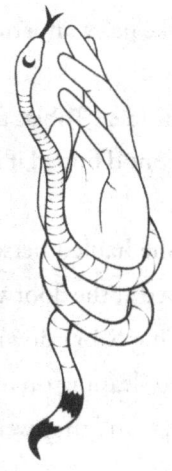

A YA CURLED UP ON the chair of the bedroom she shared with
Elaine, watching her lover sleep. Sunlight spilled in through
the window, warming the space. No bruises or scratches marred
Elaine's skin, and she was healthy.

No sooner had they returned to the house had Elaine fallen asleep.
Aya tried to follow but her mind was too busy; both old thoughts
and new battled within.

Even Sabra was not her usual self. She vanished into the woods for
hours at a time, checking the barrier religiously. For the moment,

it appeared as if nothing ill was happening...and still her friend continued looking.

It had been only a few days since the battle and Tobias drifted in and out of the home, spending much of his time with Alexios. All she knew was the pair were smoothing over the fallout of Honoria and Marisol's death, a situation that was still ongoing.

A knock at the door broke her wandering thoughts.

"Yes?"

Sabra ducked her head inside. "Tobias and Alexios are back."

Their reprieve was over. She'd hoped it might've been longer.

Oh well.

With great reluctance, she hauled herself from bed and padded out of the room. She lingered at the doorway, casting one more look upon Elaine before following Sabra downstairs. Tobias was seated by the cold fireplace, Alexios leaning on his chair. There was a little color in the vampire's cheeks, and they were fuller. His hair shone in the daylight.

"You look well, Alexios," she remarked as she dropped into the chair across from Tobias.

"As do you. How fairs Elaine?"

"She's still resting, but you didn't come here to discuss our health. What's the news?"

Tobias leaned back with a sigh. "For the moment, the remaining council members believe the information we've presented. Ryker has taken over as the dominant figure for the moment, and his desire to prove his son was a victim is working in our favor. They've also arrested Lilibet for her part in Honoria's plan, but..."

"*But?*"

"It's the matter of her scheme. They do believe she was attempting to bring down the barrier, as there have been some sightings of sections where the barrier has... opened up. Small cracks that seem to close by themselves. It's this idea of our home being a prisoner for some erased deity they're unsure of."

A rustling of footsteps followed as Sabra entered. "That explains why I haven't found any cracks. Buggers are closing before I get to them."

Alexios snorted softly. "If it appeases you, I suspect this issue is only going to escalate."

To Aya's surprise, Sabra offered no witty response as she sat down at the table. A deep frown marred her face, the troubles they were all feeling clear in her eyes. She reached across through their bond, nudging at her friend. Dark eyes flicked up, softening after a moment, as if to say, *I'll be okay, I'm just worried.*

"You mentioned Lilibet?" she murmured, dragging her gaze back to Alexios and Tobias. "Is she being held at the council cells?"

Sabra informed her of her friend's betrayal soon after they returned to the house. It came as no shock after what Aya found at the apothecary, confirming what she'd feared. It should've made the news of her arrest satisfying but Aya was tangled up in her own mind.

Alexios inclined his head. "She is, but they won't let you see her. Well, they're not permitting anyone to see her until her fate is decided. You, especially, are a complicated matter."

"*Me?*"

There was a pause stretching out to consume the room with a pregnant silence. It clawed at her skin and mind, making her itch for answers.

Tobias cleared his throat. "A few witches escaped the *army* you sent out and, well, they made it back to the temple. Suffice to say, the secret is out now. If everyone doesn't know already, they will. It's only a matter of time and, well, your new appearance would've raised questions, anyway."

Ah, yes, the wings now folded at her back.

She pressed her hand into her thigh to stop herself from touching them. "Guess I can't hide anymore."

Part of her once hoped when the secret was exposed a weight would be lifted. As it was in the room at that moment, she felt heavier and more uncertain than ever before.

"So, have you got any *good* news?" Sabra finally drawled.

Alexios and Tobias shared another look before the former spoke. "Whilst the council is *unsure* of what to do with you, your name—all of your names—have been cleared from Calix's murder. It might not be the win we're wanting right now...but it is what we have been given."

•••••••••

Aya curled at Elaine's side later that night, mulling over the news with a knife in her gut. Purgatory knew what she was, the barrier was starting to fail—just as Honoria promised that her plan wasn't over—and the council hadn't decided what the hell was to happen with them. It was a mess and normally she liked chaos, reveled in the carnage it brought, but she hungered for stability. To give Elaine the home she so desperately wanted, the very one Aya wanted to build with her.

She tightened her grip on Elaine, praying the night would never end. That she might hold her beloved and that the world would never dare to harm them again.

Elaine groaned, stirring awake. Her heart fluttered as those piercing eyes flickered open, finding her own.

"Aya?" Elaine mumbled hoarsely.

"Elaine, you're awake! Do you want me to grab Tobias? He ended up staying over. I mean, Alexios might grumble at me now—"

"Alexios?" Elaine's brows knitted together. "How long have I been out?"

"A few days." Aya recounted all that had happened. When she'd finished, she brushed the hair from Elaine's face, tucking it behind her ears. "Are you sure you're okay? You used up a lot of magic—"

"I killed Honoria," Elaine whispered.

"And how do you feel about that?"

Elaine's brow furrowed. "I don't know. I thought I'd feel...different. Maybe it'll hit later." She blinked when something flashed in her eyes. "You called me 'my love' in the fight."

Aya hadn't forgotten what she'd said but wanted to say those words again now Elaine was awake. She leaned in close, kissing her firmly, deepening it for a moment before she pulled away. Their eyes met, breaths tangling. The world froze.

"Because I love you."

A smile erupted on Elaine's face. She threw herself in Aya's arms and the pair tumbled back onto the bed. Aya's heart thundered as Elaine straddled her, staring down with a face framed by morning-lit tawny hair.

Laughter erupted from her chest, a smile splitting Elaine's cheeks.

Aya yanked Elaine in close, kissing her until they lost themselves in each other.

••••••••••

In the twilight hours, Aya prowled from the house. The darkness welcomed her, calling out in whispering tones and shifting shadows that danced across her skin. Soft leaf litter crunched underfoot and leaves rustled in a gentle breeze. It soothed something within her, if only for a moment, as she ventured deeper into the woods.

She hoped the time alone might clear her mind, allow her to decide what the next move was. Careful deliberation was in order for the uncertainty they found themselves in. Whilst she'd hoped with the death of Honoria might give them some respite, it appeared it was not to be.

When she emerged into a clearing, a figure awaited her. Aya stopped dead. Moonlight spilled through a gap in the clouds, washing over the very spirit she was so uncertain of.

"What do you want?" Aya asked, bone-tired and at her wits end.

The spirit glided forward. "Honoria's plan worked. The barrier is weakening and soon it will fall."

"Tell me something that I am not aware of."

The spirit released a shuddering breath before she spoke. "You must know, I didn't know of this. I swear it. It was only meant to be known if someone got close to freeing the goddess, a final cruel trick to make the person realize they could not complete their goal. Not without a terrible price."

Something inside of Aya snapped. "What is it?"

"If the barrier falls, everyone with a mark of Purgatory, will die."

EPILOGUE

In her prison, her eternal slumber continues.
But a new sound disturbs her prison, a song she has heard before. One
of death.
And slowly, she begins to awaken.

ACKNOWLEDGMENTS

A third book! What a journey this has been and it is crazy to think it has been over a year since I began my official career as an author. It has been a team effort, one full of tears and frustrations, triumphs and endless cups of tea. From multiple word docs, google docs, beta readings to zoom calls, whiteboard scribblings, we are here.

First and foremost, I must thank the endless support, love and patience my wonderful partner, Kyona, has given me. You never fail to make me laugh, drive me up the wall and gracefully handle all my chaos. I'm still very stunned that I found someone as amazing as you but grateful, adoring and happily in love all the same.

To my discord team, you guys will always get a shoutout. From your advice and support, to your aid in my battles with blurbs and the finicky side of self-publishing, you guys are incredible. Marjorie, you are one of my biggest rivals in our many discord sprinting sessions, and I adore every moment of it. To Sib, Wolfie, Heather, Lyric, Occa, Lyric and everyone else who in ways big and small, helped me to where I am today. I still can't get over how freaking awesome every single one of you are.

Kerry, where would I be without you? This is our third project together and your patience, wisdom and knowledge as my editor are invaluable. Every time I send you a manuscript with nerves and every time you wow me. I love our zoom calls, countless emails and twitter chats, and look forward to many more projects. It's going to be a busy 2023.

Now, this time I used a different cover artist. I was prowling a Facebook page for premades when I came across the cover used in this book. It was love at first sight so to speak. Zhandre Dex G (MC Damon), you are a wonder and I eagerly look forward to working with you in future.

To every single one of my tiktok and twitter followers, thank you so damn much. In such a short time, I have found myself in such a wonderfully supportive community.

Finally, but not least of all, to those who know me in real life. Your support and wonderful kindness are a delight. I cannot believe how lucky I am to have you all with me in this journey and am blown away.

I cannot wait to bring more stories to every single one of you and exciting things are coming.

C.M. Quinn

Also By

A Saga of Demons and Dragons
- **Book 1:** The Girl of Ash and Snow

- **Book 1:** The Queen of Blood and Fury

About Author

C.M. Quinn is an author from Perth, Australia, who has been writing since her early teens. She began writing on various online platforms in 2011 before making the leap to self-publishing in 2020. By the end of 2021, she published her first novel, The Girl of Ash and Snow, then followed it with the sequel in the following year. She is a queer author, with a deep love for fantasy and hopes to write more LGBTQIA+ stories in the future.